Acclaim for Robin Le

"In Love Without End, Robin Lee Hatcher once again takes us to Kings Meadow, Idaho in a sweeping love story that captures the heart and soul of romance between two people who have every reason not to fall in love. With an interesting back story interspersed among the contemporary chapters, and well-drawn, relatable secondary characters, Hatcher hits the mark with her warm and inviting love story."

— Martha Rogers, author of the series, *Winds Across the Prairie* and *The Journey Homeward*

"*Love Without End*, the first book in the new Kings Meadow Romance series, again intertwines two beautiful and heartfelt romances. One in the past and one in the future together make this a special read. I'm so glad Robin wrote a love story for Chet who suffered so much in *A Promise Kept* (January 2014). Kimberly, so wrong for him, becomes so right. Not your run of the mill cowboy romance—enriched with the deft writing and deep emotion."

— Lyn Cote, author of *Honor*, first in the Quaker Bride series

"No one writes about the joys and challenges of family life better than Robin Lee Hatcher and she's at the top of her game with *Love Without End*. This beautiful and deeply moving story will capture your heart as it captured mine."

— Margaret Brownley- *NY Times* bestselling author

"*Love Without End*, Book One in Robin Lee Hatcher's new Kings Meadow series, is a delight from start to finish. The author's skill at depicting the love and challenges of family has never been more evident as she deftly combines two love stories—past and present—to capture readers' hearts and lift their spirits."

— Marta Perry, author of *The Forgiven*, Keepers of the Promise, Book One

"I always expect excellence when I open a Robin Lee Hatcher novel. She never disappoints. The story here reminds me of a circle without end as Robin takes us through a modern day romance while looping one character through a WWII tale of love and loss and the resurrection of hope and purpose. *Love Without End* touched my heart and guided me to some wonderful truths of how God's love is a gift and a treasure."

— Donita K. Paul, bestselling author

"Some stories sweetly grab me from the first pages. *Love Without End* by Robin Lee Hatcher did just that. A slow dance of overcoming loss, daring to breath, and opening to love, the characters welcomed me to their world, and I didn't want to leave. A welcome escape into a world where healing happens through the lens of time and history. I highly recommend it!"

— Cara Putman, award-winning author of *Shadowed by Grace* and *Where Treetops Glisten*

"A beautiful, heart-touching story of God's amazing grace, and how He can restore and make new that which was lost."

— Francine Rivers, *New York Times* bestselling author, regarding *A Promise Kept*

"*Beloved* hits the mark. Hatcher's books have it all: characters full of personality, attention to detail that makes the history feel real and a gentle message of second chances. "

— *Romantic Times* 4½ star review for *Beloved*

"A wonderful, 19th-century-Idaho spin on the story of the prodigal son, *Beloved* has everything a great novel needs: genuine conflict, heartfelt emotion, characters you'll love rooting for, surprising twists and turns, and a breathless pace that will keep you reading late into the night. Above all, a powerful message of redemption rings through each chapter. You will love *Beloved*!"

— Liz Curtis Higgs, *New York Times* bestselling author of *Mine Is the Night*

"Hatcher is a consistent 'must read' author. Her books are always engaging, and *Betrayal* is no different . . . You'll feel a warm, satisfying glow after turning the final page of this touching novel."

— *Romantic Times*, TOP PICK! 4½ star

"Featuring an eye for detail and a strong female heroine, this wholesome romance marks a good start to this new inspirational historical series . . ."

— *Library Journal* starred review of *Belonging*

"Robin Lee Hatcher has created a memorable historic romance . . . she weaves in just enough historic fact and setting to transport the reader to the time and place without getting in the way of the story."

— *Idaho Senior Independent* review of *Belonging*

"Tender, evocative, and beautifully written, *Belonging* is a journey about love after loss, and about two hearts destined to become one—despite their stubbornness! *Belonging* is Robin Lee Hatcher at her best!"

— Tamera Alexander, best-selling author of *Within My Heart* and *The Inheritance*

Love Without End

Other Novels by Robin Lee Hatcher

A Promise Kept

WHERE THE HEART LIVES SERIES
Beloved
Betrayal
Belonging

Heart of Gold
A Matter of Character
Fit to Be Tied
A Vote of Confidence

Autumn's Angel,
a novel found in
A Bride for All Seasons

Love Without End

A Kings Meadow Romance

Robin Lee Hatcher

THOMAS NELSON
Since 1798

NASHVILLE   MEXICO CITY   RIO DE JANEIRO

Published in Nashville, Tennessee, by Thomas Nelson. Thomas Nelson is a registered trademark of HarperCollins Christian Publishing, Inc.

Thomas Nelson, Inc., titles may be purchased in bulk for educational, business, fund-raising, or sales promotional use. For information, please email SpecialMarkets@ ThomasNelson.com.

Scripture quotations from NEW AMERICAN STANDARD BIBLE®. © The lockman Foundation 1960, 1962, 1963, 1968, 1971, 1972, 1973, 1975, 1977, 1995. Used by permission.

Publisher's Note: This novel is a work of fiction. Names, characters, places, and incidents are either products of the author's imagination or used fictitiously. All characters are fictional, and any similarity to people living or dead is purely coincidental.

Library of Congress Cataloging-in-Publication Data

Hatcher, Robin Lee.
  Love without end / Robin Lee Hatcher.
    pages ; cm — (A King's Meadow novel ; 1)
  ISBN 978-1-4016-8767-0 (softcover)
1. Single parents—Fiction. 2. Man-woman relationships—Fiction. I. Hatcher, Robin Lee. II. Title.
PS3558.A73574L675 2014
813'.54—dc23   2014020470

Printed in the United States of America

14 15 16 17 18 RRD 5 4 3 2 1

To Ami McConnell & Traci DePree.
Thanks for making even editing a pleasure.

A Letter from the Author

DEAR FRIENDS

When I wrote about Kings Meadow in *A Promise Kept*, I had no intention of returning there for more stories. My calendar called for me to begin a new historical series. But Kings Meadow had gone deep into my heart, and I didn't want to let go yet. I was especially pleased that reviewers often mentioned the setting with great fondness, one even saying that they wanted to go live there. That's how I feel about it too. To be honest, I owed Chet Leonard a second chance at a happy ending after the grief I put him through in *A Promise Kept*.

Second chances. Don't you love them? I do. My life has been littered with mistakes and wrong thinking or wrong choices, and without the second chances God has given me, the results would be rather sad.

My mom and dad were thirty-four and forty-one when they met. Both had been married and divorced. Because of those failures in marriage, they had a better idea what they were looking for in a spouse. My dad proposed to my mom on their second date. He always said he would have proposed sooner if he hadn't been so shy.

Is it any wonder I'm a romantic? Love at first sight is in my DNA.

Something I discovered for myself is that the crazy physical feelings that come with falling in love—fast heartbeat, dry throat, dizzy head, roller coaster drops of the stomach—aren't only for the young. They are the same for the young at heart, no matter a person's physical age. Thankfully, *being* in love isn't quite so hard on a person as the *falling* in love. The settled comfort that comes with true commitment to a lifetime together is a blessing.

Now that Chet has found his HEA (Happily Ever After) with Kimberly, I hope you'll join me in Kings Meadow once again in the spring of 2015 for *Whenever You Come Around*. I'm busy giving grief to another couple who just might get a second chance of their own.

Happy Reading!

Robin Lee Hatcher
www.robinleehatcher.com

Anna

1944

HUNGER TWISTED ANNA MCKENNA'S BELLY AS SHE followed the deer track, leading the blood bay colt behind her. She didn't know where she was, and many days of walking hadn't lessened her fear that someone followed her. Every sound in the forest made her heart leap into her throat. Were they looking for her, the relatives who'd taken her in, claiming to want to give her a home? Would she starve to death before she found her way back to civilization? Would someone manage to take Shiloh's Star from her no matter how far she traveled?

"*Trust and listen,*" Mama's voice seemed to whisper in her ear. "*Trust and listen.*"

Thoughts of her mama caused tears to spring to her eyes. Thoughts of Daddy too. Both of them were gone now. Daddy killed in the war. Mama of pneumonia, the doctor had said, but Anna was pretty sure Mama died of a broken heart. The red colt had been a gift from her parents. Shiloh's Star was all she had left of them, and she wasn't going to let anybody take him from her. Not anybody. Including Cousin Luther.

Anna dashed away the tears with her fingertips, and as she did so, the pine trees parted and the path spilled onto a rocky plateau overlooking a beautiful emerald-colored valley. It was shaped like the boomerang she'd once seen in a general store. To her left, in the distance, she saw what looked to be a small town. Much closer and on the opposite end of the curve, she saw a house, barn, and outbuildings, cattle grazing in high grass.

God willing, she would get something to eat and maybe have one good night of sleep before she and the colt moved on.

One

CHET LEONARD WATCHED THE AUTOMATIC DOORS leading from the concourses of the Boise airport, hoping he would recognize Nana Anna when she came into view.

How much could she have changed in ten years? Perhaps a lot. The last time he'd seen her was about a decade ago when he and his family took a vacation to Disney World in Florida. They'd taken one day off from rides and games to spend an afternoon with Anna and her husband, Walter.

Anna McKenna wasn't any blood relation to the Leonards, but Chet considered her family all the same. And now, after the death of her husband, she was coming home to Idaho. Coming home to live once more on the Leonard ranch. A place she belonged.

He caught sight of a white-haired woman in a wheelchair. Was that her? If so, he might need to rethink where she would stay. The automatic doors opened and he took a step forward, then stopped. It wasn't Anna. He could see that now. Anna

McKenna was in her eighties, but aging didn't change a person's looks as much as that.

"Chet Leonard. Aren't you a sight for sore eyes."

His gaze moved a few steps beyond the woman in the wheelchair. A grin split his face. *This* was Nana Anna. Older, yes, from the last time he was with her, but he would know that smile and those merry blue-gray eyes anywhere. Not to mention that dark red hair—which these days came from a bottle.

A few quick strides carried him to her, and without any forethought, he lifted her feet off the floor as he gave her a tight hug. She laughed. He recognized that about her too. Setting her on her feet again and holding her at arm's length, he said, "You made it here fine, I see."

"Of course I did." She patted her collarbone. "And my, my. I swear you grew taller since I last saw you."

"I doubt it. I stopped growing years ago, Nana Anna."

Color bloomed in her cheeks. "Goodness gracious. It's good to be called that to my face again. I've missed it."

He held out his hand to take her small carry-on. "Let's go down to baggage claim. I assume you've got some bags checked."

"I do indeed."

Chet took Anna by the crook of her arm, and they walked toward the escalator.

"Can't believe how much this airport has changed," Anna said on the ride down.

He looked around. "Yeah. Guess it's a lot different from the last time you were here."

"I expect more than this airport's different. Time marches on."

Chet nodded.

They stepped off the escalator in companionable silence and followed other passengers toward the luggage carousels.

"Do you want to sit down while we wait?" he asked her.

"No, thank you. Been sitting too many hours as it is. Need some movement in my giddyup."

He grinned, remembering Anna as she'd been thirty years ago, before she married Walter Cunningham and moved to Florida. Already in her fifties—which had seemed ancient to Chet at the time—she'd been as active and hardworking as any man they had on the ranch. She could ride a horse all day, make a campfire, sleep on the ground, mend fences, and fix a mean breakfast.

"Chet?"

"Yes?"

"I know I said it over the phone, but I want you to know how sorry I am about all that's happened to you in the last few years. Rick and Marsha and all."

He nodded, words caught in his throat. He'd learned there was no escaping the sadness when it swept over him. He could go days without consciously thinking about the son who'd died in a car crash or the marriage that had ended despite his attempts to salvage it. But the memories and the heartache were there all the same, hidden in a deep corner of his heart.

Anna laid a wrinkled hand on his forearm. "One day at a time, Chet. That's all God asks of any of us. Just one day at a time."

Chet nodded again.

The warning light flashed and a loud beep sounded, then the conveyor belt went into motion. A short while later, bags appeared and plopped onto the oval-shaped carousel.

"What am I looking for?" Chet asked.

"Two purple bags with a bright red band around each one."

Black suitcases. Green duffel bags. Small and large boxes. One after another dropped into view. And then at last the awaited purple bags. The color was brighter than any other he'd seen so far. Appropriate for the colorful, much-beloved Nana Anna.

AT THE START OF THEIR DRIVE NORTH, ANNA expressed amazement at how much Boise had grown in the years she'd been away, but when they passed through Kings Meadow a little better than an hour later, she smiled and said, "This place hasn't changed all that much, has it?"

"You might be surprised. New library. New schools. New houses. We even have a couple of subdivisions. More changes than you'd think." He glanced at his passenger.

Anna's eyes were awash with tears, though her smile was broad. "It's good to come home, Chet. No place else ever felt quite right to me, no matter how much I loved Walter. Thanks for letting an old woman come back."

Chet felt a little choked up himself. Anna McKenna was the nearest thing to a grandmother—*great*-grandmother— his boys would ever know. Though she might not realize it, she was the one doing him a favor, not the other way around. Sam and Pete could use a woman in their lives again. Chet did his best, but he was a poor replacement for the mother who'd abandoned them.

It took another twenty minutes to reach the Leonard ranch, their land tucked between pine-covered mountains to the north, east, and west.

"Look at that," Anna whispered as the truck passed beneath the sign proclaiming: Leonard Ranch Quarter Horses. "Would you look at that? Prettiest sight I ever did see. And you've got several new outbuildings too."

By the time Chet's black Ford pulled up to the house, Sam and Pete were standing outside.

A soft gasp escaped Anna, and she covered her mouth with one hand. When she lowered it again, she said, "Look at those boys. They've grown so tall since you came to visit me and Walter in Florida. They look like you when you were their age. The photos you've e-mailed didn't do them justice."

"Yeah, they're Leonards to the core. No doubt about it. But I see more of my dad than me in Sam."

"And there's lots of Abe in Pete. I didn't know your grand-father when he was sixteen, of course, but I can still see it."

Chet chuckled. "Nothing wrong with your eyesight, is there, Anna?"

"Not a blessed thing. Eighty-four and almost perfect vision. 'Cept when I'm reading. Need glasses when I want to read fine print."

"So do I." Chet opened the door and hopped down from the cab. With quick strides, he rounded the front of the truck, opened the passenger door, and helped Anna descend. Then he took her by the arm and drew her toward the house. "Sam and Pete, do you remember Ms. McKenna?"

Sam stepped forward. "I remember. You showed us an alligator sunning himself near the road."

"Gracious. I'd forgotten that. But I'm not surprised a boy of seven would remember."

Sam leaned in and kissed her cheek. "Good to see you again, Ms. McKenna."

"I'd prefer to be Nana Anna to you boys. Or just Anna, if you're not comfortable with that."

"Sure."

"We're glad you're here . . . Nana Anna." Pete repeated the actions of his older brother.

Sam said, "I'll get your bags."

Chet watched his older son stride toward the pickup, then said, "Anna, you'll be staying in the main house with us until we can clear out the cottage. To be honest, it hasn't been a guesthouse since that first year after you moved away. We've used it for storage ever since you left. There's quite a collection of junk after three decades."

"That's fine with me. If you're sure I won't be in the way."

"Not possible. You're family. You belong with us." He gave her another grin. Then the sound of wheels on gravel drew his attention back to the long driveway. An older model blue sedan was approaching. "Excuse me, Anna. I'd best see who that is. Pete, you show Nana Anna into the house. I'll be along soon."

The blue car came to a halt near the barn. Chet was about halfway to it when the driver's door opened, and an attractive woman got out. Tall and lithe, she had long, curly dark-brown hair, the sides caught back with clips. She was a stranger. If they'd met before, he would remember her.

She saw his approach and lifted a hand to shade her eyes from the afternoon sun. "Mr. Leonard?"

"That's me, ma'am. How can I help you?"

Her eyes narrowed slightly, and she worried her lower lip with her teeth before answering, "It's about a horse."

"We've got plenty for sale. What are you—"

"No. No, I don't want to buy a horse. We . . . I mean, my daughter . . . she was given a horse."

Chet stifled a groan, pretty sure he knew what was coming.

"It's a wild horse. Well, not a wild horse like the mustangs you read about in the newspaper, but almost the same thing. Anyway, it needs gentled, and my daughter needs to learn how to work with it. My friend said you were the man to see. Chet Leonard, right?"

Maybe one of his buddies was playing a prank on him. "Who's your friend?"

"Janet Dunn."

Not a prank, then. Janet Dunn went to his church, and he knew her well. She wasn't the prankster type.

"I . . . we . . . my daughter and I are staying with Janet for . . . for a while."

She was a pretty thing. No doubt about it. But she also looked as skittish as a green-broke colt. The way her voice broke. The way her eyes couldn't stay on him more than a second or two at a time. "Listen, Miss . . . ?" He paused and waited for her to answer.

"Welch. Kimberly Welch."

"Miss Welch, I don't do that sort of thing anymore. Too much work around the ranch as it is."

"Please, Mr. Leonard. Please don't decide against it so quickly. Life has been hard in the last few years for my daughter. Her father died suddenly and . . . and we had to move from our home. We've had to move more than once in the last three years." She spoke rapidly, as if terrified he would interrupt to refuse again. "My daughter's lost so much. Her father. Her friends. Her school. I can't bear for her to lose one thing more. Tara's always wanted a horse, and now this gelding has been given to her by a friend of Janet's. Only I don't know the first thing about horses. I don't know if he is in good health or safe for her to be around or . . . or anything."

Against his better judgment, Chet asked, "How old is the horse, Ms. Welch?"

"He's three, I think."

"And why did you call him a wild horse?"

"As I understand it, he was born on a ranch over near the . . . what are they called? The Owyhee Mountains. He and the other horses on the ranch ran free over hundreds of acres. We were told this colt had no contact with humans for the first two years of his life. Then the man who bought him used punishment rather than patience and kindness to try to break him. I'm not sure how the horse went from that man to Janet's friend, but in the end, he was gifted to my daughter. And if Tara has to give him up now, it will break her heart. Please, Mr. Leonard. Don't make me have to break her heart all over again."

Good sense demanded he send Kimberly Welch packing. Good sense told him that he didn't have time to look at her gelding, let alone to train a horse that had been mistreated and a rider who knew little or nothing about horses.

But he always had been a sucker for a damsel in distress, and he couldn't say no to the pleading look in this woman's eyes. "All right. I'll have a look at him and talk to your daughter. Then I'll make my decision. No promises. Would tomorrow be okay?"

"Tomorrow would be fine. Thank you, Mr. Leonard. Thank you so very much."

Two

Halfway back to Janet's house, Kimberly pulled off to the side of the highway, pressed her forehead against the steering wheel, and wept. She wouldn't have been able to pinpoint one exact reason for her tears. It was a pent-up accumulation of life and hardships, loss and disappointments, and fear. Plenty of fear.

People always talked about addicts needing to hit bottom. Kimberly wasn't an addict, but she had definitely hit bottom. A person couldn't sink much lower than where she was right now. Once she'd been the stay-at-home wife of a prosperous businessman and the mother of a bright and popular daughter. Now she was a financially struggling widow, unable to find employment after too many years out of the job market, and mother to a hurting, sometimes sulky teenager whom Kimberly hardly recognized as the joyful child she'd raised.

Tears spent at last, Kimberly straightened, wiped her eyes with a tissue, then looked around at the valley that was surrounded on all sides by tall, tree-covered mountains. This valley was now home to her and Tara—thanks to Kimberly's best friend's generosity. Without Janet's help, they might be living out of their car on the streets of Seattle. The memory of their narrow escape from that end made her shudder. But even so, she wasn't as grateful as she should be.

"How did it come to this?" she whispered. The answer was, a hundred different ways. Little things, many of them, but when added together they became big and overwhelming.

Kimberly didn't want to be here, in Idaho, in Kings Meadow. The scenery that surrounded her was beautiful. She didn't argue with that. But it was also remote, and she hadn't grown used to the lack of sounds, both day and night. The prevailing silence made her feel even more lost, uncertain, abandoned. She missed her beautiful home in the exclusive neighborhood. She missed the theater and the opera. She missed Puget Sound and the Pacific Ocean. She missed dining out with friends in fine restaurants. She even missed the crowded freeways.

"I miss my life."

Perhaps if Tara weren't so temperamental, everything wouldn't feel this hopeless. Lately, her daughter seldom talked to Kimberly. It hurt all the more because they had been exceptionally close throughout Tara's childhood, and after Ellis died and their finances unraveled, mother and daughter had only had each other to cling to. They'd been inseparable. But since coming to Kings Meadow things had changed between them. Sometimes Kimberly felt as if Tara blamed her for Ellis's death.

She couldn't help wondering how much of this was

normal behavior for an almost-sixteen-year-old girl and how much was the result of the upheaval in their lives.

With a sigh, Kimberly started the engine and pulled back onto the deserted highway. The drive to Janet's house on the edge of Kings Meadow took another ten minutes or so. Long enough for Kimberly to feel more in control of her emotions. When she got to the house, she was relieved to see her friend's SUV in the driveway, meaning she was home from work. Kimberly steered her car to the side of the small garage and cut the engine. A glance toward a neighboring house, located halfway up a gentle slope, found her daughter, seated on the top rail of a corral, looking at the horse inside.

I never should have let her have it.

Kimberly got out of the car and stared a short while longer at her daughter. Tara didn't move, too mesmerized by her horse to have heard her mother's return. Kimberly sighed, then headed for the house. Janet was stirring something on the stove when Kimberly entered through the kitchen door.

"Hey, there." Janet set the spoon on a holder. "Did you go out to see Chet?"

Kimberly nodded. "Yes."

"And?"

"He agreed to come look at the horse and to meet Tara. But he says he doesn't do training anymore."

"Don't you worry. He'll do it."

"I forgot to ask what he charges. Once he knows I don't have a job or any money to spare . . ." She let her voice trail into silence.

Janet took up the spoon and stirred some more. "Don't

you worry. I've known Chet Leonard a long time. He's got a good heart. You'll see. We'll work something out. I know how important this is to you and Tara."

It would be nice to be as confident as her friend. About anything.

"Tara's up at the Lyles' corral," Janet added.

"I know. I saw her when I pulled in." Kimberly dropped her purse onto the small desk near the back entrance. "Can I help with dinner preparations?"

"Nope. Got it all under control."

"You never let me do enough around here."

Janet threw her a smile. "Not true. You're a big help."

"You should make up a chart of chores for me and Tara. We don't want to freeload. We're enough of a burden as it is."

"You aren't freeloading, and you aren't a burden. I asked you to come. Remember?"

"I remember. But it's still freeloading if I don't have a job or any money of my own." The words tasted bitter on her tongue. She supposed she should have grown used to poverty, used to needing help from others, but she hadn't. She hated it. Hated every bit of it.

"I wouldn't want your money even if you had some."

"And now there's that horse. It's got to have food too."

Janet set aside the spoon a second time before stepping toward Kimberly. "Stop it. You hear me?" She put a hand on each of Kimberly's shoulders. "Stop it right now. I have a healthy savings account and no debt. If I can't help out my best friend when she's in need, what good is any of it?"

"But—"

"No more arguments, Kimmie. This is your home. It's

Tara's home. For as long as you need or want it. And I think you did the right thing, accepting that horse. It'll be good for Tara. She's a lot like me when I was her age. A horse will be the best kind of medicine for what ails her."

The two women hugged. When they stepped apart, Kimberly said, "I've missed you so much. Have I told you that?"

"You have, but I don't tire of hearing it."

It was amazing, really, the depth and length of their friendship. Despite the differences in their personalities. Despite the many years they hadn't seen each other. Friends didn't come better than her.

Janet gave Kimberly a soft push toward the door. "Why don't you go tell Tara dinner's almost ready. She'll be anxious to know what Chet said."

"Okay. I'm on my way."

Kimberly took her time walking up the gentle hillside. After all, she didn't have much to tell her daughter. "Tara," she called as she drew close to the corral. "It's time to come in for supper."

Tara didn't budge, didn't even turn her head.

"Honey. Did you hear me?"

"I heard."

Kimberly stopped at the fence and looked through the rails at the brown and white pinto inside. "Have you decided on a name?"

"No."

"He ought to have a name."

"I'll get around to it. If I get to keep him." Tara cast a suspicious glance in her mother's direction. "What did that trainer guy say?"

"Mr. Leonard is going to come look at the horse and meet you before he decides."

"He won't do it, and then you'll make me give the horse away."

Given their financial situation, that's exactly what Kimberly should do. Poor people shouldn't own pets or livestock. It wasn't responsible. Besides, what if Kimberly finally found employment back in Seattle or in another city? What if there was no place to board a horse that they could afford or that was nearby? Any number of things could force her daughter to sell the horse or give it away. Life was full of difficulties. Full of things that were outside of a person's control.

"Tara, please. Let's not quarrel. I'm doing the best I can."

With a long-suffering sigh, her daughter swung her legs over the rail and hopped to the ground. "Whatever."

That single word was meant to be a lit match set to kindling. Tara was itching for a fight with her mother, but somehow Kimberly managed to hold her own temper, and the two of them walked in silence back to the house.

AFTER SUPPER, SAM AND PETE WASHED THE DISHES while Chet and Anna took a walk, stopping first to look inside the cottage. It embarrassed Chet to see how the family had stuffed the three-room house with boxes and castaways and anything no one had known what to do with at the time. The so-called guesthouse had been Anna's home for decades before she'd married Walter. It had to pain her that they'd let this happen to it.

But Anna simply laughed when she saw the stacks and

piles of endless clutter. "It's a good thing you have that spare bedroom in the main house, isn't it?"

"I'm sorry. We should have tried to do something before you got here, but there wasn't enough time."

"Don't worry your head about it. This looks like something I can do, a little at a time. I know a rancher always has more to accomplish than there are hours in the day."

Years ago, Chet had wondered why Anna didn't marry a rancher and stay in Idaho instead of marrying a businessman and moving so far away. She'd always been suited to this life. That had been clear to him even as a boy. When he'd asked her about it once, she'd answered that God liked to give her a surprise every now and then and that Walter had been the biggest surprise of all.

Which brought up another question he'd wondered now and again. "Care if I ask you something personal, Anna?"

"Don't mind if you ask. Whether or not I answer remains to be seen." She smiled, a twinkle of amusement in her eyes.

"Why didn't you change your name to Cunningham after you married?"

She was silent a few moments, her smile fading.

"I'm sorry. None of my business. I—"

"No." She touched his arm. "It's not something private. And you know, if my going by McKenna had bothered Walter, I would have taken his last name. But it didn't bother him, and changing my name wouldn't have made me love him any more or him love me any more. Besides, I'd been a McKenna for more than fifty years before we met, and the name fit me better than any other."

They left the cottage. Anna admired and commented

on the various outbuildings that were new to her, although a couple of those same outbuildings were far from new.

"Your Grandpa Abe would be mighty proud of what you and your father accomplished here," Anna said as they rounded the weather-beaten barn.

"Couldn't've done any of it, if not for you and Shiloh's Star. The Leonards owe you a lot, Anna. And not just for the horses."

She grinned. "I was paid back a hundred times over. Don't you think otherwise, my boy."

"Do you still ride?"

"Any chance I get, which hasn't been often enough in recent years. Got a horse suitable for an old lady like me?"

Chet suspected Anna could ride anything he might set her on, but he let the "old lady" comment pass and pointed toward a nearby paddock. "See that mare?"

She looked in the direction indicated, then gasped as she pressed both hands to her chest. "Good heavens," she whispered. "She looks just like him."

"Not surprised. She's a direct descendant of Shiloh's Star, and every one of her foals has been a champion of one kind or another. We're not breeding her anymore, but she's got plenty of life still in her. She'd be a good saddle horse for you. If you want her, she's yours."

"Oh, Chet." When she looked up at him, her eyes glittered with unshed tears. "What can I say? I'm overwhelmed. What's she called?"

"Shiloh's Princess."

Anna laughed softly.

"There is something I'd like from you in return."

Surprise pulled at her face.

Chet leaned his forearms on the top rail of the fence and looked at the horses grazing in lush spring grass. "The boys and I, we've got a good life here, and I'd say we're happy most of the time. But I'd be lying if I didn't say I worried about Sam and Pete. There's a fair share of hurt, deep down where it doesn't show much, because of the way their mom left, the way she cut herself off from them entirely."

Anna made a sound in her throat.

"I want them to have a better sense of family." He turned toward her. "I'd like you to tell my boys your stories about this ranch and my folks and grandparents. The kind you used to tell me. I want Sam and Pete to understand and appreciate their heritage. I want them to know all the Leonards through your eyes. They don't have anybody else who can tell them. Not like you can. They don't know everything the Leonards did through the years to keep this ranch and make it prosper, and when I try to tell them, they think I'm giving a lecture. As much as they love horses and ranching and this valley, I'm not sure they appreciate what it would mean if we lost this place."

"Lost it?" Anna's eyes widened. "Are you in danger of losing the ranch?"

"No." He shook his head. "But you know how it is. Land rich and cash poor. Times have been lean ever since the economic downturn. Seems I'm always robbing Peter to pay Paul, as they say. But we're surviving."

"I'm glad of that." She released a long breath. "Your dad used to say the same thing. Land rich and cash poor."

"I remember. Things haven't changed since then. We get

a little ahead and something happens. Horse needs vet care. Barn needs repair. Gotta have a new tractor or a new truck or a new furnace. Always something."

Anna placed a wrinkled hand on his forearm. "I'll do anything I can to help. Anything at all. I'm old but I'm not helpless."

He pulled her into the circle of his arms. "You know what, Nana Anna? God blessed the Leonards when He led you out of these mountains and into our barnyard." He kissed the hair on the top of her head. "Don't you ever doubt it."

Anna

1944

ANNA LED THE COLT INTO THE BARNYARD, STOPPING midway between the barn and the house. Chickens clucked in a nearby coop. A horse in the corral nickered a greeting at Shiloh's Star. Sheets hung on the clothesline flapped in a soft breeze. A dog rose from where it had been sleeping in the shade of a tree and trotted over to sniff at the newcomers. Anna was about to speak to the dog when the screen door on the house squeaked open and a man in bibbed coveralls and a blue shirt, sleeves rolled up to his elbows, stepped onto the porch.

Anna's heart began to pound. An all-too-familiar fear made her stomach twist. Had she made a mistake, letting herself and Shiloh's Star be seen by a stranger?

The man moved to the edge of the porch, hesitated, then came down the steps. "Howdy."

"Hello."

His gaze swept the barnyard as he walked toward her.

"Isn't anybody else with me," she said. "It's just me and my horse here. I was . . . I was wondering if there's . . . if there's any work I could do to earn a meal. We've been walking a long time, and I'm powerful hungry."

"Well, I—"

"Abe."

Anna looked toward the sound of a woman's voice. The man did the same.

A woman now stood at the edge of the porch, one hand shading her eyes from the sun. "Let the girl put the horse in the field and bring her inside."

The man called Abe looked at Anna once again. "My wife says for you to come inside. I reckon she means to feed you, whether we've got work for you or not." He motioned with his hand. "Let's turn your horse out to pasture."

He had a good face. A kind face. Clean-shaven but with the shadow of a beard showing. Dark blue eyes, the color of some glass bottles she'd seen in a store once. Friendly eyes. Not cold, the way some blue eyes could be. Some of her fear drained away as she led Shiloh's Star over to the pasture gate, which Abe opened before her.

"My name's Abe Leonard. My wife's name's Violet."

She removed the lead rope from the colt's halter. "I'm Anna. Anna McKenna."

"Pleased to meet you, Miss McKenna."

They left the pasture together, neither of them speaking again. When they reached the porch, Anna glanced over her shoulder for another glimpse of Shiloh's Star before they went into the house. The horse had his face buried in high grass.

In the kitchen, Violet Leonard stirred something that

smelled good in a large pot on the stove. "Abe," she said, "show our guest where to wash up."

"Yes'm." He stepped over to the stove and kissed the back of his wife's neck. "I'll do that."

Violet swatted at him with her free hand, although her smile said she wasn't the least bit annoyed. Just the opposite, in fact.

It made Anna think of her parents. Her mama and daddy had been playful like that, loving to tease each other, loving to smile, loving to laugh. But thinking of her parents made Anna's throat tighten and unshed tears burn her eyes. She hoped the Leonards wouldn't notice.

But Violet did notice. Her expression sobered. She put the ladle into Abe's hand and then hurried to where Anna stood. "What is it, child?" She didn't wait for an answer before wrapping Anna in her arms. "It's all right. It's all right. You go right on and cry if you need to."

It wasn't until the tears began to fall, her face pressed against Violet's shoulder, that Anna realized how long she'd been keeping the sorrow shut up inside her. Ever since her mama's funeral. She hadn't let herself cry since that day, although she'd wanted to plenty of times.

"She says her name's Anna," Abe said softly.

"It's all right, Anna. You have a good cry, and then we'll get you some of that soup to eat and you can tell us what you're doing here, all on your lonesome."

THAT NIGHT, HER STOMACH FULL FROM THE BEST dinner she'd eaten in ages, Anna stood near the slightly opened bedroom door, listening to the voices coming from downstairs.

"She's in trouble, Abe," Violet Leonard said. "She's just fourteen and scared. We have to let her stay."

Abe replied, "How do we know her folks are dead? Maybe she's got family looking for her."

"I can't explain why, but I believe her. She hasn't told us everything yet. And why would she? She doesn't know if she can trust us yet. But she's a good girl who's mighty afraid for some reason. She needs us. She needs our help."

"Vi, did you get a look at that colt? Finest piece of horse-flesh I've ever seen. Where'd a poor orphan girl come by a horse like that? What if she stole him? If we let her stay, we could get in trouble with the law ourselves."

I didn't steal him. I never stole anything in my life.

He added, "We ought to send for the sheriff and let him discover the truth."

Anna's heart skipped a beat or two. She held her breath. If the law got a hold of her, would they send her back to her cousin? Even if they knew how scared she was of him? Would they let him take Shiloh's Star?

"Abe . . . please don't call the sheriff. Please let her stay with us. I feel . . . I feel like God brought her here for a reason. I don't know why, but that's what I feel. Will you trust me in this?"

There was a lengthy silence. Anna forced herself to breathe again.

Finally, Abe answered, "All right, Vi. We'll do it your way. For now."

Anna eased the door shut, went to the bed, and lay

down. She was safe. For at least one night, her stomach was full and she was lying in a soft bed and she didn't have to be afraid.

In no time at all, sleep overtook her.

Three

ON SATURDAY MORNING, FOLLOWING A PHONE CALL from Chet Leonard, Kimberly and Tara went to the corral to wait for him. Janet tagged along. Not long after, they were joined by Susan and Ned Lyle. The Lyles were close friends of Chet Leonard, and Kimberly couldn't help hoping that was a good sign.

It was a quarter past eleven when a large black truck rolled into the driveway. A moment later, Chet hopped down from the cab, settling a battered brown hat over his dark hair as he did so. He looked around, saw the small group of folks near the corral, and started in their direction, moving with an easy gait.

Kimberly had never been attracted to cowboy types— although that might be because she rarely, if ever, met any—but she found this man good-looking in the extreme. He was tall and clean-shaven with black hair and dark blue eyes. He had a square jaw with the slightest of clefts. He didn't just look comfortable in his clothes: boots, jeans, plaid cotton shirt with a dark T-shirt visible behind the open collar. He looked comfortable in his own skin too.

According to all she'd heard from Janet and the Lyles, Chet Leonard was a salt-of-the-earth kind of fellow. If he was everything others claimed him to be, he was next to perfect. Only Kimberly didn't believe in perfect. Not perfect men. Not perfect people. Not perfect anything. Life had slapped her down too hard to go on believing in fairy tales or happily-ever-afters. The best she could hope for was to survive one day at a time.

Chet tugged at the brim of his hat. "Morning." His gaze encompassed everybody.

"Good morning," Kimberly replied.

"Hey, Chet," Janet said.

"Morning."

"Glad you came."

He nodded again. "Didn't expect a crowd."

Ned and Susan laughed in unison.

Chet's gaze shifted to Tara, standing beside her mother. Kimberly introduced them to each other.

Chet bent his hat brim a second time. "Pleased to meet you, Miss Welch. I hear you've got a horse for me to look at."

Tara nodded.

Chet stepped to the corral. Head and shoulders taller than the top rail, he rested his arms on it as he looked into the enclosure. Everyone else moved to stand by the corral too. The young horse inside began to move about, sensing he'd become the center of attention. The whites of his eyes showed as he tossed his head and snorted.

"Easy there," Chet said, almost too softly for Kimberly to hear.

But she did hear, and his voice calmed her along with the fidgety horse.

"How'd you come by him?" Chet glanced at Tara.

"Janet got him for me."

Chet looked over Kimberly's head to where her best friend stood. "Somebody gave the horse away?"

"Long story, but yeah, he was given to me for Tara. Nobody wanted to bother with him, I guess."

"But he isn't a mustang." The words were more statement than question.

"No," Janet answered, "he wasn't part of a wild horse roundup. He just never got any attention or training as a colt."

Chet looked at the horse again. "He's got pretty good conformation. Looks like he'll have powerful hindquarters when he's got his full growth." He returned his gaze to Tara, studying her with the same intense look he'd given the pinto. "Have you owned a horse before, young lady?"

"No, sir." She shook her head.

"Done any riding?"

"Not really."

"Owning a horse is a big responsibility. It might have been better to start with one that's already trained. One that's been ridden for a decade or so."

Tara turned her head toward her mother, accusation in her dark eyes. As if she believed Kimberly had made Chet Leonard say those words. "My mom wouldn't let me have a horse before, but I've wanted one since I was real little. I'm not giving him up. I'll take care of him. I'll do whatever it takes."

29

Chet didn't say anything more for a long while. Just looked from Tara to the horse in the corral and back again. Finally, he stepped away from the fence and turned toward Ned Lyle. "Did you bring the horse here?"

"Yes."

"How does he trailer?"

"Not bad. Little skittish at first but not bad. Especially when you consider his background."

"How about I pick him up after church tomorrow? I'll bring the trailer into town with me."

Ned nodded. "That'll do fine."

Chet turned again toward Tara. "You'll have to come out to the ranch and work with him most every day. Can you make that commitment?"

"Yes. If Mom can't bring me, I'll ride my bike."

"It's a bit far for that this early in the spring. Gets dark too early still. But you could catch a lift with the boys after school, then spend more time with him on the weekends until school lets out."

Tara didn't even blink. "Okay."

"You'll have to do whatever I say. No arguments. You don't keep your commitment, we'll end the training."

"I will. I promise."

Concern tightened Kimberly's chest. Chet Leonard hadn't said anything about what this would cost. If Kimberly had to disappoint Tara now, her daughter would never forgive her. "Mr. Leonard—"

"Call me Chet."

"Mr. Leonard." She stressed the word. "I don't have a job yet and we don't have—"

"We can talk about that later."

Was that pity she saw flicker in his eyes? She didn't want pity. She'd had to learn to swallow her pride, nearly choking on it more than once, but it still tasted like sawdust every time.

CHET HAD COME TO JANET'S HOUSE CONVINCED HE would tell Kimberly Welch and her daughter that he couldn't help them. And he should have done just that. He hadn't any spare time to train a horse and rider. He had too much of his own work to do. There was always more to be done on a ranch than there were hands to do it. Never enough daylight or money either.

Instinct told him what he hadn't given Kimberly a chance to say: She was flat broke. She didn't have the money to pay for lessons or training or boarding or anything else. Kimberly and Tara Welch hadn't come to Kings Meadow to visit Janet. They'd come because they needed a place to stay. He didn't know the reasons, but he knew in his gut that he was right.

Was Kimberly running from something or someone? Like Marsha had run from him?

The thought caused Chet to clench the steering wheel a little harder as he drove the ribbon of highway toward the ranch. Thoughts of his ex-wife never came without tension and regret. Time—and the good counsel of friends and mentors—had helped heal his broken heart, but he hadn't been able to stop himself from feeling like a failure. Try as he might, he'd let himself down. He'd let Marsha and his boys down. He'd let God down too.

It was a lousy way to feel.

Chet arrived at the ranch in time for the noon meal. His part-time ranch hands, Blake Buttons and Denny Haskins, joined the family in the dining room for lunch, as was routine for a Saturday. Anna was there, too, looking spry in a cotton shirt and Levi's and nowhere close to her real age. She fit right in with all the men at the table, the same way she had when Chet was a boy. Seeing her now improved his mood.

As serving dishes were passed around, Sam said, "So, Dad. Are you going to tell us what happened in town?"

"Horse looked sound. Girl seemed nice enough. I decided to work with them for a while. See how they both do."

Sam elbowed his brother. "Pay up."

Pete grumbled something unintelligible.

Sam explained, "I bet Pete ten bucks that you wouldn't be able to say no. You're a soft touch, Dad."

Everybody but Chet laughed. He tried to scowl at his son, but it was a half-baked attempt to look disgruntled. And all he accomplished was to make the others laugh harder. Before long, his laughter joined theirs. For the remainder of the meal, the conversation moved easily between ranch matters, school matters, and town matters, with a dash of good-natured teasing and more laughter added in.

"Blake and I are gonna go to the upper canyon and do some fence repairs," Denny said as he stood, his lunch dish clean of food. "Unless you need us to do something else."

"No. That'll be great. Thanks." Chet looked from his ranch hands to Anna. "What are your plans for the afternoon?"

"I thought I would start sorting through things in the guesthouse."

"Want one of the boys to help you?"

She shook her head. "Not necessary. Boys their ages would rather be outside on a beautiful spring Saturday instead of cooped up inside with me."

Chet sensed his sons holding their breaths to see what he would decide. They knew better than to try to wheedle their way out of something their dad wanted them to do. "All right then." His gaze shifted to the pair. "Got your chores done?"

"Yessir," they answered in unison.

"Then you can be excused."

Sam and Pete hopped up from their chairs and carried their dirty dishes into the kitchen. A short while later, they left the house through the back door.

"They're good boys," Anna said into the ensuing silence. "You've done a fine job raising them, Chet. You can be proud."

"I am proud." He paused on a sigh. "It was hard on them after Rick died. Harder still when their mom left. I tried to make sure they knew her going didn't have anything to do with them. Not sure they believed me, especially when she cut off all communication. I could handle her not wanting to talk to me. It was her marriage to me she was ending. But our sons?" He shook his head. "I'll never understand that. She just went off the deep end, and nothing I tried could bring her back."

"I'm sorry."

"You said they're good boys, and you're right. They are. And Marsha had plenty to do with that. She was a good mom." A lump formed in his throat, making it hard to continue.

"Where is Marsha now?"

Chet shrugged and forced himself to answer. "Got no idea. She was in Reno for a long time. That's where she got the divorce. But last time I tried to call her, the number'd been disconnected. Not a word from her in close to two years. Not even a phone call on the boys' birthdays or at Christmas."

"I'm sorry," Anna repeated. "You know, Chet. Some folks say God never gives us more than we can handle. I don't believe that's true. He doesn't give us more than *He* can handle. The battle belongs to the Lord. Let Him fight it for you."

Feeling a now-familiar surge of affection, he leaned over and kissed her cheek. When he drew back, she reached up and patted his face.

"Better get to it." He stood. "You call for help if you need any."

"Don't you worry about me. I'll be happy as a clam. Sortin' through memories is always fun, and there's decades worth of memories stored up in that old cottage." A grin crinkled the skin around her eyes. "But I don't know how you ever got to calling it a guesthouse. Barely room to turn around in there. Not that I'm complaining. Makes me feel needed."

"You don't need to sort through a lot of junk for us to need you, Anna."

"I know, but it's good to be busy all the same. Even at my age."

"Then I'll leave you to it." Chet took both her plate and his own into the kitchen before heading outside like the others, his Saturday half over but his work not yet half done.

Four

KIMBERLY HAD MANAGED TO GET OUT OF GOING TO church with Janet since arriving in Kings Meadow, but her best friend hadn't taken no for an answer that morning. And so there she was, in a pew near the back of the sanctuary, singing a familiar worship song, Janet on her left and Tara on her right.

When Ellis was alive, the Welch family had been active members of an upscale nondenominational church near their home, and for a time after Ellis's death, Kimberly and Tara had attended as faithfully as ever. But within months, the financial troubles had overwhelmed mother and daughter. The life insurance that should have been there wasn't; Ellis had allowed the policy to lapse as their debt spiraled out of control. The job—and then jobs—Kimberly had hoped for hadn't materialized. Her bank account had soon run dry. And finally their home and cars had been repossessed.

Sometimes Kimberly felt so much anger over what her

husband had allowed to happen to her that she thought she would kill him if he weren't already dead. And those feelings were always followed by a load of guilt. Ellis hadn't been a bad man or a bad husband. He'd simply made a number of very bad decisions in the years before his death. She was certain he'd believed he had plenty of time to turn things around. Who expected to drop dead when in the prime of life?

When the music ended, the worship leader—a girl of about twenty or so—said a brief prayer. Then there was a time of greeting. Janet introduced Kimberly to so many people, and she knew she would never be able to remember their names. It wasn't until the congregation took their seats again that she noticed Chet Leonard in a pew toward the front of the sanctuary.

Perfect. Just perfect. She'd forgotten this was his church too.

Kimberly had lain awake a good portion of the night, worrying that Chet might change his mind about Tara and her horse. She'd figured it would be better not to give him any opportunities to do that. The less he saw of her and her daughter, the better. At least for this first weekend.

Kimberly didn't pay a lot of attention to the sermon. She didn't mean for it to be that way. But her mind kept churning and churning. She used to come to church, eager to hear from God. Now she felt like an outsider. More alone than ever.

Am I a superficial Christian? A Christian in name only, not one in commitment?

Uncomfortable questions. She shifted in her seat and forced her thoughts back to Ellis. She would rather feel anger and guilt than explore her faith-life.

They'd had a happy marriage, she and Ellis. The only thing that had kept it from being perfect was her inability to conceive again after Tara was born. But maybe that had been for the best. It was hard enough keeping body and soul together with only her and Tara. What if there'd been more children to feed and shelter? It made her shudder thinking about it.

For how long had Ellis allowed her to spend beyond their income, never once letting on that they were in trouble? Years, probably. It made her feel so foolish. And she couldn't blame him alone. She wasn't stupid. She wasn't uneducated. She had a college degree, for pity's sake. If she'd been kept in ignorance, it had been her fault as well as Ellis's. She'd been content to let him make all decisions in regard to their finances and insurance and budget. If she'd shown the least bit of interest, would he have been honest with her?

She would never know the answer to that question. Ellis couldn't tell her. He'd been gone over three years, struck down by a heart attack at the age of forty. So young. Too young.

I'll be forty in a couple of years.

The thought made her want to shudder again. Look at her. Jobless. Homeless. And almost forty. Loser with a capital *L*.

IT TOOK CHET AND THE BOYS LONGER THAN USUAL to leave the church that morning. There were many people who wanted to speak to Anna on her first Sunday back in Kings Meadow after thirty years. The Leonards and Anna were invited to four different homes for dinner, but Chet had to decline them all. He had a horse to load in the trailer and drive back to the ranch. Proof positive that he needed his head examined.

He'd caught a glimpse of Kimberly Welch and her daughter with Janet Dunn when the service ended. Had they come to church with Janet before that morning? He didn't think so. He was positive he would have noticed Kimberly if she'd been there before. And she was gone by the time he and the boys and Anna made it down the center aisle. He supposed she wanted to get back to Janet's place to be ready for him.

Chet drove his truck to Susan and Ned's house, following a dirt road to the horse shed and corral. The Lyles were there with Kimberly, Tara, and Janet.

Anna said, "Looks like the Welcome Wagon came by."

"Looks like." He pulled around in a circle and backed the trailer toward the corral, leaving plenty of room in case the horse decided he didn't want to get in without a little persuasion. When Chet cut the engine, he asked Anna, "Want to stay in the truck? Shouldn't take long."

"Heavens, no. I don't want to miss this."

Chet glanced into the backseat. "Pete, help Nana Anna to the ground."

"Okay, Dad."

Chet got out of the cab and walked to the corral. "Afternoon." He nodded, taking in everyone with a sweeping gaze. "You're ready for us, I see." He looked at Tara. "Do you have a halter and rope?"

"Not that's mine. There's a halter that belongs to Mr. Lyle."

Chet glanced behind him. His sons and Anna stood not

too far away. He performed quick introductions, then said, "Sam, get a halter and rope out of the trailer, please."

"Sure thing, Dad."

When Sam returned, he and Chet walked to the corral gate and went inside the enclosure. The pinto crow-hopped away from them, tossing his head, snorting his distrust.

"Easy, boy," Chet said.

Behind him, he heard Pete ask, "What's his name?" and Tara answer, "Doesn't have one yet."

There was something about the way the girl said the words that tugged at Chet's heart. Maybe because he was used to the banter of teenage boys. Girls of that age were a puzzle to him. Whatever the cause of his sympathy, he wondered if it might cloud his better judgment in the days to come.

Chet cleared his throat and refocused his attention on the horse that had begun to settle down. That was a good sign. A little bit of patience, lots of human attention, and the gelding might turn out to be a decent horse for Tara.

"Hey there, fella. Let's get this halter on."

The pinto snorted as he spun away, putting as much distance between him and Chet as the corral allowed. While Sam moved in one direction, Chet circled around in another, talking all the while to the horse. The words themselves weren't important. Only the tone he used.

The pinto eyed Chet, clearly not ready to be friends with him. But the horse had seen Sam on his other side, arms outstretched. Instinct had informed the animal of the futility of trying to escape. He bobbed his head again, snorting. The skin on his withers shuddered, as if the humans were pesky flies he wanted to be rid of.

Chet moved carefully, drawing the halter over the pinto's muzzle. It surprised him that the horse didn't do more to prevent the completion of the task. Perhaps there was a little bit of trust in him after all.

With the halter on and the buckle fastened, Chet led the gelding toward the gate. Sam opened it before him. The pinto held his head high, offering only slight resistance. Then they got within three or four yards of the trailer. That was when he pulled back hard, jerking Chet to a standstill.

He faced the horse, staring into his dark eyes while stroking him. "You're gonna have to go in, boy. You might as well make up your mind now. We can do it the easy way or the hard way."

The horse showed the whites of his eyes as he jerked his head upward again. But Chet was ready for it this time and didn't give too much ground.

"Sam. Pete. Let's get a rope around his rump, and we'll give him a little encouragement."

He and his boys had done this sort of thing many a time. They moved in a comfortable rhythm, unhurried, confident, watchful. The first touch of the rope against the pinto's buttock caused the horse to step toward Chet and the trailer. When the rope touched him again, he kicked out with his right leg. Not that it did any good.

Little by little, they inched the gelding forward. Chet kept talking in a calm voice and hoped they wouldn't have a real fight on their hands when he asked the horse to take that first step up into the trailer. While it wouldn't have been a crisis—he'd dealt with much flightier horses than this one—he didn't want to have to prove who was boss in front of

Kimberly Welch. He could tell she wasn't any too sure about this horse as it was.

God must have been smiling on Chet, because when the time came, the pinto stepped into the trailer as if it was his favorite thing to do. "Show-off," he said softly as he tied the lead rope.

Sam was waiting to close the trailer gate when Chet stepped out. "That wasn't so bad," his son said.

"Nope. It went okay, all things considered." He glanced toward the small audience of folks. "Pete, help Anna back into the truck."

"Sure thing, Dad."

Chet turned toward Tara. "You can ride to the ranch with us if you want."

"Yes. Thanks."

His gaze moved past the girl to her mother. "Is that all right with you? She can eat dinner with us, and then we'll start laying some ground rules. She ought to be ready to leave by four o'clock or so."

"Mr. Leonard?" Kimberly stepped close and lowered her voice. "We really must discuss how much this training will cost."

"Let's see how the next week goes. I'll have a better idea by then what's needed and how long it'll take."

Uncertainty flashed in her eyes. "I *hate* being in debt to anyone. I've already got more of it than I can pay back in my lifetime."

"We'll work something out. Don't worry about it."

As Chet turned toward truck and trailer, Susan Lyle spoke up. "Chet, are you sure you and your family won't join us for Sunday dinner? We'd love to have you, and you know I want to get to know Anna. You've spoken of her so fondly for so long."

"Thanks, but we've got a roast in the oven. It'll be done to a crisp if we don't get back to it soon."

Anna and Pete were already in the truck by this time. After hesitating a moment to look at her mother, Tara hurried to the pickup and slid into the center of the backseat. Sam climbed in beside her and closed the door.

"I'll be out to the ranch at four," Kimberly said.

Something in her tone drew Chet around one more time. "This is going to be a good thing for Tara, Mrs. Welch." He didn't know why he'd felt compelled to say that, but when he saw the tears well in her eyes, he knew she'd needed to hear it.

Thank you, she mouthed.

He tugged on the brim of his hat one final time before getting into the cab of the truck and starting for the ranch.

Anna

1944

FOR ANNA'S FIRST TWO MONTHS ON THE LEONARD ranch, wariness was her constant companion. She had the proper papers to prove Shiloh's Star belonged to her, so Abe's doubts in that regard were quickly quashed. But worry that her cousin Luther would find her was driven away less easily. It wasn't like him to give up. Had she hidden her escape route so well he *couldn't* find her? She had a hard time believing it. She'd been lost, wandering without direction, and too desperate to keep moving to try to hide her tracks.

As the days passed, one by one, she began to believe her cousin wouldn't find her. And then she began to believe she and Shiloh's Star had found a safe haven. A new home and even a new family. Not that anyone could completely fill Daddy's and Mama's shoes.

Nights were the worst times. Bad dreams were all too frequent. Dreams of a soldier standing on their front porch with the news about her father. Dreams of her mother lying

43

so pale on the bed, her breath rattling in her chest. Dreams of Anna's vile cousin, Luther Poole—a second cousin twice removed, she liked to remind herself—lurking in the hallway, a living, breathing threat. A man who liked to touch, who liked to strike.

But even the nightmares began to fade with the passing of weeks.

Because the ranch was a good piece from the town of Kings Meadow, Violet Leonard—once a schoolteacher—offered to tutor Anna instead of sending her to school by horseback five days a week, especially since winters could be harsh in the mountains. Anna was grateful. She loved to learn, had always been a good student, but the less she was seen outside of the ranch, the better.

In the crisp days of autumn, when Anna wasn't working on her school lessons, she spent a good deal of time outdoors, helping with the chickens and cows, mending fences, and working with Shiloh's Star.

"You know your way around a horse," Abe commented one hazy October afternoon. "Where'd you learn so much so young?"

In a steady rhythm, Anna ran a brush, followed by her free hand, over Star's back and rump. "My father. Only thing Daddy loved more than horses was Mama and me." She smiled even though her heart ached at the memory. "That's what Mama always said to him. And he always said he loved us more, but he understood horses better than any female."

Abe chuckled. He had a nice laugh.

"Before he went to war, Daddy bought Shiloh's Star and promised that when he came back, we were going to raise champions by him one day. That was his dream. He worked hard to make it happen. Now it's up to me."

"Where'd your horse come from?"

"Texas. His bloodlines trace right back to Shiloh himself."

Abe leaned his forearms on the top rail of the corral. "Afraid that doesn't mean anything to me."

Anna turned to look at him, her eyes wide. How could anyone not know that name? She'd heard about the famous stud since she was a toddler. "Shiloh's one of the foundation sires of the Quarter Horse breed."

"Sorry. Never been around fancy horses. You know, with pedigrees and such. The ones we've got on the ranch are here to ride and to pull. They work hard, like everybody else on the place. Doesn't matter if they're thoroughbreds or mustangs."

"Maybe you oughta think about raising Quarter Horses. All it would take to get started is a couple of good brood mares, and Star could do the rest."

Abe's gaze shifted beyond the corral, looking over the land where cattle grazed. "My grandpa came to this valley back in 1864. The gold rush was raging up in the Boise Basin. All of those miners needed food, and they liked their beef when they could afford it. So he raised cattle to sell to them. Before I was born, my pa managed to triple the size of the original ranch. People knew they could come to the Leonards and get a fair price for beef on the hoof." He rubbed a hand over his face, as if to wipe away a bad memory. "The Depression was hard on us. I was fourteen—your age—when the crash happened, but I was old enough to notice how the years that followed turned my pa into an old man. Then Grandpa George, his father, died, and not long after, my mother passed too. Pa just gave up. Gave out, more like it." Abe fell silent for a while, then continued. "By the time he passed away, I was already managing the ranch, married to Vi, and making sure we could hold onto the place. We'd weathered the Depression without losing it or selling off chunks of it. Even in hard times, folks want to eat beef. I reckon the same can't be said for horses."

In the months Anna had lived with the Leonards, those were the most words she heard Abe say at any given time. He was a tall, quiet sort, even around his wife. A wife he loved, sure and true. The way Daddy had loved Mama.

Anna swallowed the lump in her throat and went back to brushing Shiloh's Star. Another time she would talk to Abe again about raising horses. She wasn't going to give up on her father's dream, a dream that was now her own, and she couldn't help believing God had brought her to Kings Meadow to see that dream fulfilled.

Somehow she would make Abe Leonard believe it too.

Five

CHET WATCHED AS KIMBERLY WELCH'S SEDAN DROVE away from the house and barnyard, her daughter in the passenger seat. All things considered, the afternoon had gone much better than anticipated. Tara was a willing student and quick to obey what he said. Of course, it remained to be seen if that was temporary. Eager today. Not so much tomorrow.

With a shake of his head, he walked toward the house. Anna sat on the porch, enjoying the pleasant spring day, a glass of iced tea in one hand. Chet climbed the steps to the porch and sat in the chair next to her, his gaze on the horses in the nearest pasture.

"How did it go?" she asked.

"Good." He nodded. "Pretty good."

"She seems like a nice girl."

"She is. I just hope I don't regret bringing her and her horse out here."

"What do you mean?"

"Mrs. Welch doesn't have a job, and she's worried how she'll pay me for the boarding of the horse and her daughter's lessons." Chet shrugged. "Not like it will make or break me whether or not she pays me anything, but it seems to bother her. I'm not sure how to handle it."

"Do you mind an old woman butting into your business? I might have an idea."

He turned his head toward her. "Wouldn't be butting in. Not from you, Anna. Anything you've got to say, I want to hear."

Smiling, she reached out to touch his cheek with her fingertips.

"What's your idea?"

"I wasn't much younger than Tara when I first came to this ranch. And your grandfather put me right to work. He made me feel like I was a part of the family. That what I did made a difference. Like I belonged here. That girl"—Anna looked down the driveway—"she doesn't feel she belongs anywhere right now."

"Did she tell you that?"

"Heavens, no. But, you get to be my age, you pick up on things that others are too busy to notice. Little clues here and there."

Chet wondered if he would ever learn to read people that well.

"I think you should hire Tara to do some work around here. Let her pay for the training and her lessons herself. Don't let that fall on her mother's narrow shoulders. If Tara wants this, she should work for it. It will be good for the girl, and it will relieve her mother's anxiety over how to reimburse you at the same time."

Chet grinned. "You sound like Grandpa Abe."

"I should. Learned old-fashioned common sense from the Leonards."

"Tara Welch is a city girl. She might be more bother than help around the barnyard and livestock."

"Let's start with her helping me go through things in the guesthouse. There's lots of organizing and winnowing out that has to be done, and some of it could use a younger and stronger back than mine."

Chet felt instant concern. "You haven't overdone, have you?"

"In three days?" She harrumphed, her glance indignant. "I'm not *that* fragile, Chet. There's still some oomph left in me."

Her comment made him smile again.

"It's settled then. Tara will help me organize and clean out the guesthouse as payment for boarding and lessons. There are so many decades of keepsakes and boxes of papers and who knows what all—it'll take us weeks to go through it all."

"I'm sure you're right." Chet laughed softly.

Anna sighed as she leaned back in the chair, then fell into silence as she sipped her tea.

"I'd better call her mother and tell her what's been decided." Chet stood. "Make sure it meets with her approval."

"Yes, you should do that. It'll take some worry out of Mrs. Welch's pretty eyes."

Chet hesitated a moment. Anna was right. Kimberly

Welch *did* have pretty eyes. Unique eyes. A lighter shade of green than he'd seen before. Or maybe they only seemed lighter because of her dark brown lashes and eyebrows.

Not that any of that mattered to Chet.

"Mom, if I took a driver's ed class, I could get my license. Then I could drive out to the Leonard ranch by myself if you didn't want to take me or if it would be too late for me to ride my bike home again."

Kimberly looked up from the food on her dinner plate. "You aren't sixteen yet."

"In Idaho, kids can sign up for driver's ed when they're only fourteen and a half. That's what one of the girls at school told me."

Kimberly turned from her daughter to Janet. "Is that true?"

"Yes. Idaho's a rural state. Farmers want their kids to drive tractors or be able to take the truck to the nearest town to pick up supplies. Plenty of folks in these mountains have been driving anything and everything since they were fourteen."

Kimberly shook her head in disbelief.

"Please, Mom."

"Sweetheart, even if you took a class and got licensed, I don't think I could afford insurance for you. Not until I get a job."

Tara dropped her fork onto her plate and pushed back her chair. "It isn't fair. That's always your answer. We don't have the money. I *hate* this!" She darted from the kitchen.

Kimberly fought the tears that flooded her eyes, determined they wouldn't fall.

"Teenagers are like that sometimes," Janet said softly. "It isn't personal. Not really."

"I know." She drew a deep breath. "What Tara doesn't seem to know is how much I hate having to say no to her."

Janet patted Kimberly's shoulder. "Hang in there, girl-friend. It'll get better."

Would it get better? It didn't seem that way.

The telephone rang, and Janet got up to answer it. A moment later, she said, "It's for you, Kimmie. Chet Leonard."

Her stomach flip-flopped at the sound of his name. If he'd changed his mind—and why else would he be calling?—Tara would blame her for that too. With great reluctance, she walked to where Janet stood holding out the receiver. She took the phone and put it to her ear. "Hello?"

"Mrs. Welch?"

"Yes."

"Chet Leonard."

She could hardly hear him over the hammering of her heart.

"About your daughter and her horse."

"Yes?" The word came out a breathless whisper.

"I know you're concerned how to pay for the boarding and lessons, but I think we have a solution. Instead of you paying cash, we thought Tara could work for us here on the ranch."

There came those tears again. Nothing Tara could do on the ranch would come anywhere close to covering his fees. She was certain of that. His generosity touched her, as did his sensitivity toward her situation. He'd managed to let her keep a little of her pride.

"It would mean she'd have to spend more hours out here. Not just when she's working with the horse."

"What . . . what would she be doing?"

"It'll probably change over time. But to start, she'd be helping Anna sort through boxes and such in our old guesthouse. She can help feed the horses and shovel out stalls too."

"Mr. Leonard—"

"How about you call me Chet and I'll call you Kimberly?"

"Sure. Okay. Chet, how often would you need Tara to come out to work?" The price of gas flashed in her head, followed immediately by the small balance in her checkbook.

"Saturdays and a couple other days during the week until school lets out. More often during the summer."

She released a soft sigh. "It sounds very generous." Too generous, perhaps, but an offer she couldn't refuse.

"Great. Then let's plan for her to start next Saturday morning. She can help Ms. McKenna for a few hours, and then Tara and I will do some work with her horse."

"All right. Thank you, Mr. L—Chet."

He was silent a moment before saying, "You're welcome, Kimberly."

Six

Thanks to Janet, Kimberly received a call shortly after eight o'clock on Monday morning with the offer of a temporary position at an insurance agency. The regular receptionist/secretary/girl Friday had taken a bad fall while hiking over the weekend, breaking several bones in her right leg and ankle, and was awaiting surgery in a Boise hospital. Kimberly would be needed to fill in for at least four to six weeks. Perhaps longer.

To Kimberly, four to six weeks' worth of wages sounded wonderful after such a long stretch without any income. She wasn't the fastest of typists, but she was accurate and organized, and she had a nice—if slightly dated—wardrobe for work attire.

By ten o'clock that morning, Kimberly was at the office learning the ropes. Her employer, Christopher Russell, was an affable bear of a man. He was at least six feet four and must have tipped the scales at two hundred and seventy-five pounds.

He not only dwarfed Kimberly, he made the office space seem too small as well. Nonetheless, she liked him at once.

She returned home shortly after five that evening, tired but surprisingly satisfied. Another surprise awaited her in the kitchen. Tara was helping Janet with dinner preparations—and she seemed happy about it. Hope blossomed in Kimberly's heart. Maybe they were over the worst of their trials. Maybe this was the beginning of a new era for the two of them. Maybe Kimberly wouldn't have to disappoint her daughter again. Or at least not on a daily basis.

"How was school?" Kimberly asked when they sat down to eat. It was a question she asked of Tara most weekdays.

Instead of the usual shrug and a grunt, Tara answered, "Pete Leonard's in my English class. I thought he looked familiar when I saw him yesterday. Anyway, Pete said I can start riding with him and his brother this week if I want. That way you won't have to drive out there so often."

Kimberly had a job now, temporary as it was. She could afford to do a little more driving. But that was no reason to refuse Tara's request.

"Please, Mom. I'll ride my bike if I have to when you're working or when I can't catch a lift with Pete and Sam. But riding with them will give me more time with my horse and to do whatever Ms. McKenna or Mr. Leonard need me to do."

"All right, honey." She smiled and nodded. "But you'll have to confirm with Mr. Leonard that it's still all right for you to ride with his sons. And you also need to ask what afternoons he wants you to come. Your lessons have to be on his schedule, not yours."

"I'll call him right now." Tara started to rise.

"Sit down and finish eating. He's probably having dinner, too, and you don't want to interrupt him." She glanced at the clock on the wall. "Wait about an hour."

Tara picked up her fork even though it was obvious she wasn't the least bit interested in the food on her plate. Not any longer.

Kimberly envied her daughter, to have something in her life that she was this excited over. It was hard to remember the last time Kimberly had felt the same way. Troubles had piled so high in recent years that they'd obscured more pleasant memories. Would she ever get them back? She hoped so.

DINNER IN THE LEONARD HOME WAS A FAMILY TIME, strictly adhered to. Other meals might be eaten on the fly—the boys grabbing something quick from the microwave or toaster oven before they raced out the door for school, Chet doing much the same before beginning his morning chores—but for the evening meal, everybody sat down together. Chet asked Sam and Pete questions about their day, about their friends, about their schoolwork, and his sons were expected to answer in more than a half-dozen words.

Tonight, Pete didn't have to wait for any questions.

"Guess what, Dad? Tara Welch is in my English class. I never even noticed her before. She's been there three or four weeks already, and I never even noticed." He shook his head. "Must be something wrong with my eyes."

Sam punched his brother in the shoulder. "You're an idiot."

Chet hid his smile. Up to now, his youngest son hadn't shown interest in girls, preferring to spend his free time with horses and playing video games. Sam, on the other hand, had a date most Friday nights, although the options for "going out" were severely limited in Kings Meadow.

Then again, maybe he shouldn't have been amused. Tara Welch was going to spend a lot of time on the Leonard ranch. Would Pete's new awareness of this pretty newcomer to Kings Meadow prove to be a problem? Chet hoped not. He wasn't keen on that kind of complication. Every boy had to get his heart broken at some point, but there'd been enough heartache for the entire Leonard family in recent years. Chet would just as soon Pete postpone the kind that came with a crush on the wrong girl.

The wrong girl. What made him think that? He didn't know Tara well enough to make that kind of judgment call. The few hours he'd spent with her on Sunday she'd been polite and pleasant. However, she was a city girl, despite her interest in horses. She knew nothing of their way of life. Ranching was bred into the Leonards as surely as the color of their hair and eyes.

"Dad?"

Yanked to the present by Sam's voice, Chet blinked. "Sorry. My mind wandered."

"Pete and I want to go down to Boise for a youth rodeo."

"When?"

"Saturday after next. We'd need to use the four-horse trailer. Couple of friends want to tag along."

"Sure. It's okay with me. Just be sure your chores are done that morning before you take off."

Sam feigned an innocent expression. "Don't we always?"

Chet laughed. "No, come to think of it, you *don't* always."

"Nana Anna," Pete said, turning toward her, "would you like to come along and watch us?"

"Gracious. It's been ages since I was at a rodeo." Her eyes sparked with interest. "What events do you enter?"

"Team and calf roping," Sam answered.

"Tempting. Very tempting. But I'd best say no. A bit too far from home and a bit too long of a day, I imagine. Maybe there'll be another time I can go?"

"Sure thing. You just say the word. You're always welcome."

Chet didn't try to hide his smile this time. He took great pleasure in hearing Pete invite Anna to one of their activities without any prompting from his dad. Not that Chet was surprised. He'd known the boys would take Anna to heart.

When dinner was finished, Sam and Pete cleared the table and washed the dishes while Chet and Anna went into the living room. As soon as they were both settled, Anna said, "I hope I didn't hurt Pete's feelings. I would love to go, but the sound of a long drive there and back and sitting on bleachers for an entire day wasn't very appealing. Not to my old bones."

"He understood. Don't worry about it. You only got here four days ago. You're entitled to do as you please."

Anna released a sigh. "That's good." She paused a moment, then added, "I believe I'll make an early night of it, if it's all the same to you." She got to her feet.

Chet stood too, but Anna waved him to sit down again.

"Nothing's wrong, so don't ask. I'm going to lie down with a good book." With that, she headed for her bedroom.

Rather than sitting again, Chet returned to the kitchen. "Nana Anna went to bed," he said to the boys. "I'm going for a short walk."

Sunset was a good hour away, but the air was a lot cooler now than it had been in the afternoon. Chet shrugged his shoulders, tempted to return to the house for a jacket. But instead, he quickened his stride as he walked to the barn. Once inside, he checked the three horses in the stalls. The first was a gelding who'd tangled with some barbed wire. The horse's wounds needed doctoring a few times a day. The other two were mares who would drop foals in the next week or two.

Satisfied all was well, Chet moved out the doorway at the opposite end of the barn and went to the nearest paddock where his favorite stud grazed. When Chet leaned his arms on the top rail, the stallion raised his head to stare, looking ready to challenge an intruder. King Billy was a ten-year-old bay who'd already sired many champions, including Sam's current roping horse.

"Hey, Billy," Chet said.

The horse tossed his head before trotting over to the fence, no doubt in hopes some sort of treat awaited him. All King Billy got was a friendly pat on the neck. After a few moments, he snorted his disgust and trotted back to the center of the pasture, leaving his backside toward his master.

Chet laughed, and his gaze rose to the smattering of white clouds overhead while words of thanksgiving played in his heart. Thanks for this ranch, this home, this valley. Thanks for his folks and grandparents and Nana Anna, too, who had made it possible for him to live on the same land and raise his sons here. Thanks for all of that and much, much more.

He stood there for a long while, drinking in the mountains and the sky and the grazing land, enjoying the crisp, clean, pine-scented air. Maybe some folks took the beauty of this area for granted. He wasn't one of them.

"Dad?"

He turned to see Pete exit through the barn door.

"Tara called. I hollered for you but you didn't answer."

"Didn't hear you. Did she say what she needed?"

"She wants to take you up on your offer for her to ride home with us after school a couple times a week. Her mom'll pick her up after she gets off work. Tara asked what days would be best for her to come. I told her any day but Wednesday since you've got your men's group that night. Hope that was the right thing to say."

Chet nodded. "Sure. It's fine."

And it was fine. Only he'd made the offer for the ride-along before Pete had taken notice of the girl. All Chet could do now was hope his youngest son's attention wouldn't become something more serious before these training sessions were over.

Anna

1944

CHRISTMAS DAWNED TO A BLANKET OF NEW SNOW on the ground and temperatures that frosted the windows.

When Anna first awoke, she snuggled down beneath the blankets on her bed and tried not to think about her daddy and mama. This would be her first Christmas without both her parents, and she missed them so much it was a physical ache in her chest. Memories of Christmases before Daddy went off to war, before he was killed and Mama took sick, flitted through her mind, and she cried. Silent tears. Guilty tears. After all, she had a new home with good people who cared for her.

A soft rap sounded at her door, followed by Violet's voice. "Anna, are you awake?"

"Yes." She swiped away the lingering tears as she sat up. "I'm awake."

The door opened and Violet stuck her head in. "Merry Christmas, Anna. I've made pancakes. Put on your robe and come down to eat. There are presents to open when we've finished breakfast."

Guilt hit Anna again. She didn't have anything to give to the Leonards. Why hadn't she thought of presents before this moment? How could she be selfish and thoughtless when they'd been so kind?

Violet smiled. "Hurry now. I'm a kid in a candy store on Christmas morning."

Anna reached for her robe. A short while later, slippers on her feet and robe cinched around her waist, she went down the stairs and entered the kitchen. Violet was there ahead of her, turning bacon on the griddle. A stack of pancakes waited on a plate nearby.

"Good morning again." Violet glanced toward the back entrance. "Abe went to check on something in the barn. Could you call for him to come and eat?"

"Okay."

She walked to the door and opened it. But she didn't have to shout anything. Abe was standing in the snow, just beyond the steps, holding the lead rope to a palomino mare.

"So, Anna," he said, "what do you think of her?"

"She's beautiful. Did you buy her? Is she yours?"

"Yep. She's ours. She's sort of your Christmas gift to me and Vi."

Anna shook her head. "My what? I didn't—"

"I got to thinkin' about what you said, a couple months back. About raising Quarter Horses. Goldie here is the start. Golden Girl, her papers say. As long as Shiloh's Star is willing to do his part, she oughta throw some nice colts." His eyes twinkled in the early morning light. "What do you think, Anna? Can we do this?"

There was that stupid lump in her throat again. "I think it's wonderful. Yes! Yes, we can do this."

"Abe," Violet said from close behind Anna, "put the horse back in the barn and come inside. Breakfast's getting cold, and there are some packages under the tree to be opened."

"Yes'm. On my way."

"Anna?"

She turned to face Violet.

"You okay, honey?"

She nodded—lumpy throat, threatening tears, and all. Mama had told her to keep trusting the Lord, even when trouble came. Things would work out. And so it seemed they had.

Seven

ANNA SURVEYED THE COLLECTION OF BOXES AND odd household rejects that filled the living room of the cottage. Beyond a closed door, there was more of the same in the bedroom.

Today, she and Tara would get to work on clearing the clutter, although she was in no hurry to get the job done. She liked being part of the hustle and bustle of the family in the main house. The two teenage boys always on their way somewhere or returning from somewhere. The ranch hands eating lunch in the kitchen. Chet sitting at his desk, reading glasses perched on his nose as he studied the account records or a horse journal or sitting in his easy chair in the evening, visiting with Anna over a cup of decaf.

Still, this small house had been Anna's home once upon a time, and everyone expected her to want to live in it again. Even she'd expected it. Abe and Violet had built the cottage especially for her. She'd moved into it on her twenty-first birthday and hadn't left it until she'd married Walter thirty-three years later. And though she'd never told her husband, a piece of her heart had grieved for this little house, for this ranch, for this place all the years she was away.

A poignant smile curved her mouth as she remembered how hard it had been to say good-bye to the Leonard family all those years ago. If she hadn't loved and adored her new husband to distraction, she never would have had the courage to venture so far away. Florida had been more than just another state. It had been another world. A flat, flat world. Glory, how she'd missed these mountains.

The creak of the screen door alerted her to Tara's arrival. Anna turned around to see the girl and her mother in the doorway.

"Good morning," Kimberly Welch said, stepping in behind her daughter. "I hope we haven't kept you waiting too long. It's entirely my fault. I got a late start."

Anna waved her hand in dismissal. "Didn't mind waiting. I have nowhere to be."

Kimberly looked around the room. "There *is* a lot to go through. Isn't there?"

Quite the understatement.

"Indeed," Anna answered.

Kimberly lowered her voice, saying to her daughter, "Don't let Ms. McKenna do any heavy lifting."

Anna almost announced that her hearing was excellent and she was stronger than she looked. But better not.

"Call me if you need me to come sooner," Kimberly continued. "Otherwise, I'll be here at three."

"It won't be sooner, Mom. I'm gonna get to ride today, when we're done here."

"You're going to ride your horse?" Tara's mother sounded alarmed.

"No. He's not ready for that. I'm gonna ride one of Mr. Leonard's saddle horses."

"Isn't it awfully soon for that? You've barely started your—"

"*Mom!*"

Anna turned away, pretending not to notice the sudden tension between the pair. Through the years, friends had talked about mothers and their teenage daughters, about the push and pull that happened between them. Anna didn't pretend to understand it much. She'd spent most of her life around men and boys. There never had been much that was girlish about Anna McKenna. Except for her red hair, which she'd worn long in her younger days. She'd been more than a little vain about it—and keenly aware of the effect it had on men when she'd let it flow loose down her back.

Foolish old woman, she scolded herself. *Those days are long gone.* It had been eons since any man had made note of her. Except perhaps to offer an arm to help her across the street.

"Ms. McKenna?"

She turned again. Tara's mother had left the guesthouse, and the girl was now standing a short distance away, looking at her questioningly.

"Where do we start?" Tara asked.

"How about with that stack of boxes over there?" Anna pointed. "That should keep us busy until lunchtime."

CHET CAME OUT OF THE BARN IN TIME TO SEE Kimberly Welch walking to her car. When she noticed him, he waved and started in her direction. She waited by the driver's side door.

"Morning," he said, stopping on the other side of the automobile.

"Good morning."

"Heard you got a job this week."

"Yes."

"Chris Russell's a good man." Chet removed his hat and raked his fingers through his hair. "You'll like working for him."

Cannot kern text to avoid orphan. Please edit text to correct.

"Mr. Russell is very nice, but the job is only temporary."

"It's a start."

"Yes," she said softly. "A start. Hopefully one that will lead to something better." She drew in a deep breath, her slender shoulders rising and falling. "How is Tara doing?"

"All right. She's eager to learn. Does what she's told. This is her first day to help Anna." He glanced toward the guesthouse.

"You're lucky she wasn't here at six this morning. She was so eager to get started. Too bad she isn't as excited about cleaning her own room or doing her homework."

Chet grinned as he met her gaze once again. "Kids."

After a moment, she returned the smile. "Kids."

He wondered, suddenly, what had happened to Mr. Welch. Where was he now? Had he walked out on Kimberly, the way Marsha had walked out on him? Or was Kimberly the one who did the walking? Not that it was any of his business.

"I'll be back to pick Tara up around three." She opened the car door. "Have her call me if she needs to leave earlier than that."

"Will do."

After he watched her drive away, Chet went to where his horse was tied. He stepped into the saddle and rode out to check some fences. But the pretty Mrs. Welch wasn't soon forgotten.

ANNA AND TARA HAD BEEN SORTING THROUGH BOXES for over two hours by the time they came across a metal box filled with tax receipts. Fragile slips of paper with handwritten information filling the lines. The oldest one was dated all the way back to the twenties when George Leonard—Abe's father—raised cattle on the land.

"My, oh my," Anna said. "Isn't this something?"

"What is it?" Tara peered over Anna's shoulder.

"A tax receipt for this ranch. See that name there? George Leonard. He was Chet's great grandfather. And it was George's father, John, who came to this valley during the gold rush in the 1860s and started this ranch."

"You mean the Leonards have lived on this same ranch for over a hundred years?" Tara asked, eyes wide with surprise.

"Hundred and fifty years, more like." Anna nodded. "Six generations of them, counting Sam and Pete."

"Never heard of anybody staying in one place so long. Have you always lived here too? Are you Mr. Leonard's grandma?"

"I spent most of my life here, but no. I'm no relation by blood. I was an orphan when I came to this ranch during

World War II. Just about your age. A bit younger. Chet's grandparents took me in and made me a part of their family. Sometimes I still can't believe the many ways God blessed me, bringing me to this valley when I was so scared and alone."

"Wow. Wish the Leonards would take me in. I'd give anything to live on a horse ranch like this one."

Anna smiled at the girl, feeling a kinship with her. "They ran mostly cattle back then, but it's been all horses for a lot of years now."

The screen door creaked and Pete stepped through the opening. "Hey, Na—" He broke off, then continued, "Anna, Tara. Dad says for you two to come eat. Lunch is about ready to go on the table."

"Good heavens." Anna looked at her wristwatch. "I had no idea it was that time already. Did you, Tara?"

"No. But I am kinda hungry."

Anna pushed herself up from the chair. "Come to think of it, so am I."

Pete held the screen door open and waited for both Anna and Tara to pass. Then he let it swing closed. Anna didn't look behind her, but she knew when Pete fell into step with Tara.

"How's it going in there?" he asked.

Tara answered, "Okay."

"You need any more help? I could lend a hand if you wanted."

Pete has a crush, Anna thought with a smile.

If Tara noticed, too, her voice didn't reveal it. "Nah. We're doing all right." She was silent a moment before adding, "Your dad's going to let me ride today. Maybe right after lunch."

Anna felt sorry for Pete. It would be difficult for him to compete with a horse for Tara's attention. At least that was how it had been for Anna when she was fifteen.

It promised to be an interesting spring and summer.

Eight

FOR THE THIRD YEAR IN A ROW, NED AND SUSAN
Lyle invited Chet and his family to share Easter dinner with
them. For the third year in a row, Chet accepted. Holidays
were still hard for him. They stirred up too many memories
of when his family was whole and happy. He credited Ned,
his closest friend, with helping him through the darkest times
and deepest hurts, first when Rick was killed in that accident,
and later when Marsha walked out on him and their two sons.
Without Ned's compassion and wisdom, Chet didn't know
what would have happened to him.

He wasn't surprised to find others had been invited to
the Lyles' dinner. Susan was well-known in this valley for
her hospitality and delicious Sunday dinners. This year, the
other guests were Kimberly and Tara Welch, Janet Dunn,
and the new—new by comparison to most residents, anyway—Methodist pastor, Reverend Tom Butler.

Even in April, Easter was often cold, sometimes still snowy, in this mountain valley. But not this year. The sun spread a blanket of golden warmth over Kings Meadow. While the women visited in the kitchen and finished the last of the dinner preparations, the teens disappeared into the family room to play games on the Wii, and the men went outside onto the deck to enjoy the fine weather. They each settled into a brightly painted Adirondack chair and sat in companionable silence for a long while.

It was Ned who spoke first. "Tom, tell Chet about yourself. Chet, did you know Tom came to Kings Meadow from Africa?"

"Africa?" Chet echoed.

"Yes, I served in a church there for three years. In Kenya."

"Must have been quite the experience."

"Oh, it was. But I have to admit, it's good to be back in the States again, and I'm delighted to be serving the church here in Kings Meadow."

Chet was about to ask some questions about Kenya when the sliding door to the deck opened and the men were summoned to the table. They arrived only moments before Sam, Pete, and Tara emerged from the family room. A delicious feast awaited them. After Ned said the blessing, hosts and guests dined on plum-glazed ham, scalloped potatoes, asparagus amandine, a salad made with tossed greens, strawberries, pears, and crumbled blue cheese, and homemade dinner rolls.

Although his earlier attempt to ask the Methodist minister questions about his years in Africa had been interrupted, such was not the case during dinner. Tom Butler didn't seem to mind either. Not at first anyway. He shared several fascinating stories while the food on his plate grew cold.

Taking pity on the reverend, Susan told Tom that Kimberly and her daughter were new to Kings Meadow. "But they didn't come from as far away as Kenya," she added.

"Where are you from?" the reverend asked, looking at Kimberly.

"Washington. Near Seattle. I . . . we . . . I want to return there, when I can find the right job. I . . . miss the city."

Chet glanced up from his plate. It didn't surprise him, hearing her say that. He'd suspected as much.

Tom Butler turned his gaze toward Tara. "And what about you? Do you miss the city?"

"No, I like it here better. So would Mom if she'd give it a chance."

"Tara," Kimberly warned in a low voice.

"Well, you would, Mom. There's lots here to like. You oughta come look at the stuff in the guesthouse I'm helping Ms. McKenna clean out. You'd go crazy over some of it." Tara looked around the table. "When we lived in Washington, Mom used to go antiquing all the time. My dad said where he saw junk, Mom saw potential." She focused her eyes on Chet, excitement lighting her expression. "Mr. Leonard, I'll bet there's stuff in that house my mom could fix up and sell online. You'd make a bundle."

"A bundle, huh?" He cocked an eyebrow in Kimberly's direction.

She flushed but didn't answer.

Once again, Susan played the experienced hostess, this

time turning toward Anna. "I'll bet you have some stories to tell about Chet when he was a boy."

Anna's eyes twinkled with mischief. "A few."

"We're dying to hear some of them," Susan said with a laugh.

Chet frowned at Susan, pretending a displeasure he didn't feel. "And here I thought we were friends."

KIMBERLY COULDN'T REMEMBER A TIME WHEN SHE'D felt as included as these people made her feel. She didn't know why. She and Ellis had had good friends. Many good friends. They'd attended and they'd hosted dinners very much like this one through the years. And yet today felt different.

Perhaps it was seeing Tara's smile and hearing the laughter in her voice. She'd let her daughter down so often since Ellis died. But for now, things were looking up. Kimberly was employed. They weren't homeless. Tara even owned a horse, as impossible as that seemed.

She heard several gasps, and her attention was drawn back to Anna McKenna.

"And there Chet sat on the back of that green-broke horse, pleased as punch, holding onto his mane, while I nearly had a heart attack," the older woman finished.

"How old did you say he was?" Susan asked.

"Only four, but he already had a way with horses. That gelding he got on didn't so much as twitch until after I got Chet off and out of that corral."

Her thoughts wandering, Kimberly had missed most of Anna's story. But she'd caught enough to understand the danger Chet had been in. Did he have more common sense than that today? Would he make sure her daughter didn't do anything foolish around the horses?

"Do you ride, Kimberly?" Anna asked.

She shook her head. "No. Not really. When Janet and I were girls, she got a pony and we rode double. I was the one in back, hanging onto Janet for dear life. I can't say I cared for the experience much."

"You should take a few lessons along with Tara. It would take your fear away."

The very idea made Kimberly shiver with dread. "I'm sure Mr. Leonard doesn't need another student taking up more of his time." Against her will her gaze slid to Chet.

His expression was inscrutable.

"Well, if he's too busy," Anna continued, "I could give you lessons. My time's not so valuable."

Kimberly's eyes widened as she turned toward the older woman again. "You still ride?"

"At my age, you mean? Of course I do. I even have my own horse again, thanks to Chet."

"I didn't mean to insult you," Kimberly said quickly.

"You didn't insult me, dear. Not in the least. Plenty of folks besides you would be surprised to find someone my age riding a horse. But I'll keep doing it as long as I'm able. Nothing so grand as sitting astride a horse, riding through these mountains on a soft summer day."

The woman's words almost made Kimberly want to experience it. Almost.

Chet spoke up. "If you're interested, Kimberly, I think we could accommodate you without much trouble."

Was that the first time Chet Leonard had called her by her given name? If he'd done it before, she hadn't noticed. But noticing it now made her feel quite strange—and just a little delicious.

Nine

On the first Saturday in May, Tara squatted next to her pinto, slowly applying polo wrap around the horse's left front leg. Pete stood at the pinto's head, holding the lunge line.

Chet observed from outside the round pen. He was pleased with the girl's progress. Hard to believe she had little actual experience with horses prior to her move to Kings Meadow. She appeared as comfortable as Pete was. And what she didn't know, she didn't hesitate to ask about. He liked that trait. It showed good character and wisdom.

"I've decided on a name," Tara said to Pete as she glanced up at him.

"About time. What's it gonna be?"

"Wind Dancer." She stood and patted the horse's neck. "I think it fits him. Don't you?"

Chet smiled to himself. It had taken him awhile to realize Tara hadn't wanted to name the pinto as long as there was any chance her mother might change her mind and sell him or give him away. If Tara was naming him now, she must feel more confident about the long term.

Pete said, "Yeah. It's a good name. I like it."

Chet figured his youngest son would have thought Green Goo a good name if that was what Tara had decided on.

"Thanks." She moved to the horse's right front leg, squatted down, and began to wrap it too.

The young horse was coming along almost as well as his mistress. Better than Chet had anticipated when he'd agreed to take on his training.

Finished wrapping the right leg, Tara stood and looked over the horse's back toward Chet. "How did I do, Mr. Leonard?"

"Good." He nodded. "Now let's see if you and Wind Dancer remember what to do next."

"You heard his name. What do you think?"

"Pete's right. It's a good name. But it doesn't really matter what we think. It only matters if you like it."

"I like it." Tara moved to take the lunge line.

Pete hesitated a moment before handing it to her. Afterward, he shoved his thumbs into the back pockets of his jeans, as if not knowing what to do with his hands. A few more moments and he seemed to realize Tara was waiting for him to clear out of the round pen. His face flushed a bit as he turned away and strode toward the gate, but Chet was pretty sure the girl hadn't noticed. Tara's eyes were back on her horse. Wind Dancer was all that mattered to her.

"All right. Let's go." Chet leaned his forearms on the top rail.

Tara let out some of the line and pointed the small training whip behind Wind Dancer's rump to urge him to move out. "Walk on."

Chet didn't say much over the next twenty minutes or so as he watched Tara put the horse through his paces. She lunged him counterclockwise at a walk, a trot, a slow canter, a trot again, and finally a walk to a halt. Then she turned him in a clockwise direction and repeated the exercise. She remembered to keep her voice calm but firm and didn't fumble the commands. She remembered how to hold the lunge line and pointed with the whip only when necessary. Wind Dancer responded as if the two of them had been working together for months instead of a few weeks.

When the horse was stopped once again, Chet said, "Okay, Tara. That's good. Give him a rub down."

"Sure thing, Mr. Leonard."

He opened the gate, and Tara led the pinto out of the pen and toward the barn. Pete fell in beside her. Not that Tara needed anyone's help. By this time, she knew exactly what to do and where she would find whatever she needed.

Chet turned and started toward the house, then stopped when he saw the now familiar car coming toward him. Kimberly Welch was a little on the early side today. He waited for her to stop the car and get out.

"Afternoon." He touched the brim of his hat.

"Hello." Her gaze went to the side of the barn where Tara was tying her horse at the rail. "How did it go today?"

Here was something else Chet had figured out. Kimberly was nervous around horses. She didn't dislike them, and she wasn't all-out terrified of them. At least not obviously so. But she wasn't eager to be near them either, and that made her worry about her daughter more than most.

"Good," he answered. "Tara's a good student. So's the horse."

Kimberly's eyes returned to him. "Ms. McKenna asked me to look at some things in the guesthouse. She wants to know if any are worth selling instead of giving away."

"She did?" He remembered Tara saying her mother was some sort of expert with antiques, but Easter was the only time he'd heard it mentioned. He hadn't known Anna pursued the topic with her. "Well, come with me then."

They walked together toward the house, Chet shortening his stride to match hers.

He'd learned a few other things about the Welches, thanks to the hours he'd spent with Tara. He'd learned the girl's father had passed away three years ago, and apparently the man had left their finances in a mess. Their house had been foreclosed. Cars repossessed. Kimberly had tried to find work, but her fine arts theater degree hadn't helped on that front. She'd been a stay-at-home wife and mom since college, so she had no work history to make her desirable to employers. Her inability to find employment was what had finally brought them to Kings Meadow to stay with Janet. According to Tara, Kimberly would leave in a heartbeat if she found a job in the city. The latter he hadn't needed Tara to tell him. He'd already figured it out for himself. Well, good luck to her. He couldn't imagine himself living anywhere else, but he'd discovered it was useless to try to make anyone want to stay. His ex-wife had taught him that.

Anna stepped through the back doorway of the main

house as Chet and Kimberly drew near. "Hello, Kimberly. Thank you for coming."

"How could I refuse?" She smiled. "Tara is always telling me about something new you've found. She's piqued my curiosity."

Anna looked at Chet. "Want to join us? We're on a treasure hunt."

"No thanks. I'm pretty sure I'd be in the way."

"Suit yourself." Anna hooked arms with Kimberly. "But you don't know what you're missing."

The two women set off for the guesthouse.

Chet had been surprised at first at the amount of time it was taking Anna to sort, keep, toss out. But then he'd realized she was in no hurry to occupy her old home. She would rather stay in the main house than have privacy in her own place. He'd thought it odd since she'd loved the cottage back before she got married. But it also pleased him, knowing she preferred to stay in the midst of his family.

While Anna might not be in any hurry to live in the cottage—if that ever happened, which he now doubted—she seemed to enjoy sorting through the collection of boxes and cast-offs, deciding what should stay and what must go. He also suspected the time she spent with Tara was valuable to the girl. And now Kimberly had been added to the mix. Perhaps time with Anna would be valuable to her too.

For some reason, that thought made him feel good.

KIMBERLY'S HEART GAVE A LITTLE SKIP WHEN SHE saw the items that Anna and Tara had set aside. Things not deemed to have any chance of reuse had been taken to the county's refuse collection site by Sam and Pete. Things that Anna knew must stay in the Leonard family had begun taking up residence in one corner of the bedroom. The things still in question had been placed in a back corner of the living room.

The latter was where Kimberly stood now.

"See anything of value there?" Anna asked behind her.

Kimberly hardly knew where to begin as her gaze trailed over a washstand, a tarnished silver tea set and tray, a pair of Victorian table lamps, a large copper washtub, and a shoe box full of jewelry. And those were only the items easily seen.

"Should we keep any of it?" Anna asked again.

"I would. That washstand, for one. It must be at least a hundred years old. If it was sanded and stained, it would make a beautiful addition to any home. Especially if there's an old porcelain washbowl and pitcher to go with it."

"You're right about its age. It belonged to Violet Leonard's mother. Violet brought it with her when she married Chet's grandfather."

Kimberly looked at Anna. "You really know the history of this place, don't you?"

"Yes. That's true."

"But you were away for a long time. Didn't you say thirty years or something like that? I would think you'd have forgotten some of it."

"Funny thing about getting older, Kimberly. The things that happened the longest ago, the people you knew when you were young, that's what you remember best most of the time. Yesterday can get hazy. Forty or fifty or sixty years can be clear as a bell."

Kimberly felt an unexpected ache for the grandmothers she'd never known. It would be wonderful if she could ask questions about her own family. But it was just her and Tara now, and their history had shallow roots, a tree that could be ripped up by the wind.

"Are you all right, my dear?" Anna laid a hand on Kimberly's shoulder.

"Yes. I'm fine." She took a step deeper into the corner, preferring to think about antiques rather than be reminded of the people and things that weren't part of her life.

Anna

1945

THE WAR IN EUROPE WAS OVER!

Abe, a very pregnant Violet, and Anna piled into the Model T and motored into town to join the VE-Day celebrations. The bells in the Methodist church tower pealed across the valley. There was music and singing and dancing in the streets and liquor consumed by more than a few residents of Kings Meadow. People laughed. People cried. Those who had lost someone in the war cried the most.

At least that was true for Anna who felt afresh the reality that her daddy would never come home from Europe.

After an hour or so, she wandered away from the crowds until she found a place where she could be alone to remember her daddy. With the passing of each month, it had become harder and harder to remember the details of his face without the help of the photograph of her parents that she carried with her. The memory of his voice had become little more than a whisper.

But one thing hadn't changed. Whenever she was with Shiloh's Star, she sensed her daddy's presence. It gave her courage when she felt like sliding back into fear. It helped her hold onto the dream that had been his first and was now hers to see to fruition.

"Next year, Daddy," she said aloud, her eyes squeezed shut. "Next year there oughta be a colt or a filly out of Golden Girl by Shiloh's Star. He doesn't say it, but I think Abe's as excited as I am." She paused, willing her words to reach her father. Could those who'd gone on to heaven hear the folks left on earth? She wanted it to be so. "They're good to me, the Leonards. Real good. Tell Mama I'm doing fine and behaving, like she taught me I should."

With her forearm, she wiped away the last of her tears and opened her eyes again in time to see Violet walking across the field toward her. Waddling might be a better description of the way she moved through the tall, pale-green grasses of spring, one hand resting on her swollen abdomen, the other pressed against the small of her back. And she still had six weeks to go before the baby was due. How much bigger would she get?

"Anna? Are you all right, hon?"

Anna nodded.

Violet stopped beneath the tree where Anna sat and awkwardly lowered herself to the ground next to her. "We got worried when we couldn't find you."

"Sorry. I was . . . I was—" Her throat closed up, cutting off her words.

"You were thinking about your father," Violet finished for her.

Anna nodded.

"I don't blame you. If I'd lost somebody close to me in this awful war, this day'd make me feel the same way. Over at last but such a huge price was paid. And still not done in the Pacific." She put her arm around Anna and drew her close. "It's all right, you know, to ask God why things happen the way they do. I used to think I had to pretend that I was all right with everything the way it was, that if it was God's will for something to happen in my life, then I ought to be happy about it. But that was just pretending. God doesn't need me to pretend, and He isn't afraid of my questions. You go right on and pour out your feelings to Him. Don't hold back. He'll listen, and then He'll comfort. You see if He doesn't."

Ten

KIMBERLY STIFLED A YAWN AS SHE OPENED THE bottom drawer of the desk and took out her purse.

"Headed home?" Chris Russell asked from inside his office.

She moved to stand in his doorway. "Yes. Did you need something before I go?"

"Yes, I do." He leaned back in his chair. "I know when you started we thought it would be for six weeks, tops. But are you willing to stay on for another four? I talked to Madeline, and the doctor says she won't be able to put any weight on her foot for at least that much longer and thinks it best that she not return to work."

Kimberly forced herself not to smile. After all, Madeline was having a difficult time. But four more weeks of drawing a paycheck would be a blessing, and she would be grateful for every one of them. "I'm happy to stay on as long as you need me, Chris."

"Good. I appreciate the work you've been doing. You caught on fast."

"Thanks." She took a half step back, then turned. "See you in the morning."

There was a definite spring in her step as she left the office and walked toward the grocery store. She was tempted to splurge on some big, juicy steaks for dinner, but Tara would appreciate tacos or pizza more, and either of those would cost a good deal less than prime cuts of beef.

Wistfully she remembered the times when she'd prepared a romantic dinner for her and Ellis. Candlelight. A little red wine. Her best crystal and china. Soft music from the iPod speakers. Steaks grilled to perfection. Ambience and presentation had been important to her.

In her memory, she saw the way Ellis looked at her when they'd enjoyed one of their special evenings at home. Eyes filled with love. Ellis had had such expressive eyes. One time, maybe six months before he died, he'd surprised her at the end of the meal with a gorgeous diamond necklace. It hadn't been her birthday or their anniversary. He'd bought it because he loved her, he'd said.

How would she have reacted if she'd known how deep in debt they were?

The pleasant memories spoiled by reality, Kimberly pushed open the swinging glass door and entered The Merc. She pulled a shopping basket from the stack near the entrance and started down an aisle, looking for the items on her list. It didn't take long. Choices were not abundant in this small-town grocery store. Nothing like the superstores where she'd done her shopping for most of her adult life.

She paid for her purchases at the checkout, then gathered a brown paper sack in each arm. At the exit, she turned her back to the glass door and pushed it open with her backside. As she turned again, she nearly collided with an incoming customer.

"Whoa there."

She recognized Chet Leonard's voice even before she lifted her gaze to his face, shaded as always by his brown cowboy hat.

"Here. Let me help you with those." He took one bag from her, then the other. "Where's your car?"

She shook her head. "I walked to work this morning. It's not very far to Janet's. Not on a day like this."

"It is fine out."

Kimberly began to feel awkward, standing there in front of The Merc, Chet holding her shopping bags. How was she supposed to take them back from him?

"I'll carry these for you," he said in answer to her unspoken question.

"Oh, you needn't do that. They aren't heavy. Really. I . . . it's—"

"Come on. I'll bet you've got the fixings for supper in these sacks. Better get you home so you all don't starve." He swiveled on his heel, then gave her a glance that said he was waiting for her.

What else could she do? She moved to his side and they set off toward Janet's home.

After a brief silence, Chet said, "Tell Tara that we've got two new foals as of yesterday."

"They both came? She'll be disappointed she didn't get

to be there to see at least one of them born. She told me all about the mares when she got home Saturday."

"Yeah, she seems eager to learn everything about horses and ranching."

"Maybe it's for the best she wasn't there. She might be a little young to watch a live birth."

Chet looked at her, eyebrows raised. "You're kidding, right? She's almost sixteen."

She supposed he was right. Tara wasn't a little child.

"Sorry," he said. "None of my business. But when you live on a ranch, the natural order of things is something you learn early on. Tara's more ready than you think she is."

"I know. I can be overprotective sometimes."

"I guess you've got a right to be, after all that's happened to the two of you."

She winced, realizing how much he must know about her personal affairs. "I take it Tara's told you about her father and how bad things got after he died."

"Yeah. She told me a little."

A little? She knew Tara better than that.

"Look, Kimberly. I wasn't trying to pry. I promise."

She released a humorless laugh. "I know you weren't. Tara doesn't filter her thoughts much. Not when she's comfortable with someone." She looked at Chet again. "She feels at ease around you. She feels at ease with everybody at the ranch."

"That's good to hear." He smiled, kindness in his eyes. "I wasn't sure how she and I would get along at first. I'm used to dealing with boys. Never have spent a lot of time with girls." He paused on a sigh. "Maybe that's why I'm divorced. Maybe I still don't understand girls."

His last comment raised a number of questions in Kimberly's mind. She knew far less about him than he knew about her. At least when it came to his failed marriage and ex-wife. Perhaps she might learn more if she asked a question or two. But something in his expression stopped her. Something told her talking about it still caused him pain.

She understood only too well.

IT HAD BEEN A STRANGE IMPULSE, TAKING KIMBERLY'S sacks of groceries and then offering to escort her home. Chet wasn't sure why he'd done it. For the same reason he'd agreed to work with Tara and her horse, he supposed. Couldn't help himself. Chet to the rescue. It was a character trait he wished he could change. Not everybody needed or wanted to be rescued, not even when they looked or sounded like they did. Marsha hadn't. That was for certain. His ex-wife had wanted to lead her own life and make her own decisions, far away from him. Without having to report to anyone.

Report to anyone.

Those words had stung. They still did.

He'd thought they had a partnership. He'd thought they were each one-half of a whole. He'd thought they were able to tell each other anything and everything. He'd thought they were married for life.

Which just went to prove his point. He'd thought wrong. Again.

"Chet."

Kimberly stopped walking, and Chet was pulled back to the present.

She held out her arms. "I can take those now. We're here. You needn't come any farther."

See, Kimberly Welch didn't want to be rescued either. He thought he was doing the polite thing, and she thought he was intruding on her personal space. Couldn't be more clear about it. He passed the two sacks into her waiting arms.

"Thanks for your help." She took a step back from him.

He wondered if she meant it. "Glad to do it." Now he wondered if he meant it.

"I'll tell Tara about the foals. She'll be eager to see them tomorrow."

He nodded and gave his hat brim a tug, then turned and headed back toward the center of town, ready to get home, whatever had brought him to the grocery store in the first place forgotten.

KIMBERLY RAPPED ON THE DOOR TO TARA'S ROOM, then opened it when she didn't answer. Her daughter was lying on her stomach on the bed, holding a book out in front of her with both hands as she read.

"Homework?" Kimberly asked.

Tara shook her head as she turned the cover of the book so her mother could see it.

Of course. A book about horses. What else?

Kimberly entered the room and sat on the edge of the bed. "I saw Mr. Leonard a little bit ago. He said to tell you the two new foals were born."

"They were? Both of them?" Tara sat up. "Wish I'd been there."

"You'll see them tomorrow."

"This book has pictures of a foal being delivered." She flipped quickly through the pages, stopping when she found what she wanted. "It says a foal will normally stand within the first hour and can trot and canter that very first day. Cool, huh?"

"Very cool."

"Kinda makes me wish Wind Dancer was a mare so we could have a colt one day."

Kimberly reached out and pushed Tara's dark hair back from her face. "You'd best be happy with the one horse you've got." Silently she added, *We couldn't even afford him if not for Chet Leonard's generosity.*

The thought brought his image back to mind, and her heart did a small, unexpected flutter. He was so old-school polite around her. The code of a cowboy, perhaps. And truth be told, she was beginning to find that code rather attractive.

Eleven

SAM'S VOICE RANG ACROSS THE BARNYARD. "HEY, DAD!"

Chet turned his attention from Tara and the sorrel mare she was saddling. "What?"

"You're wanted on the phone."

"Who is it?"

"He didn't say. Just says it's important he talk to you."

"I'll be right there." He looked at Tara. "You wait for me to get back before you mount up."

The girl made a soft sound of impatience, but didn't voice her objection.

Chet took off for the house. Once inside, he bumped his hat back on his forehead with his knuckles and picked up the handset of the kitchen telephone. "Hello."

"Mr. Leonard? Scott Webb here."

Scott Webb. A trainer from over in Payette, a town near the Idaho-Oregon border. A man looking to buy several new horses from the Leonards. "Afternoon, Mr. Webb."

"I'm afraid I have some bad news. I won't be able to make it up to see your horses tomorrow."

"Not a problem." Even as he spoke, he felt a premonition that it might be a problem. "When will you be able to come?"

"Doesn't look like I'll be buying any new stock this year. My wife's got some health issues and has taken an unexpected turn for the worse. The medical expenses will have to be paid before I can consider any new horses. That could be awhile."

Chet sank onto a tall kitchen stool, disappointment sharp in his chest. "I'm sorry to hear your wife's ill. Hope she makes a quick recovery."

"Thanks. And I'm real sorry about not getting those horses."

"It's all right. Appreciate the call. And you come when you're able. Might not have the same horses you were looking at, but there are always others."

After they both said good-bye, Chet punched the Off button and put the handset in its charger. He rubbed his forehead with his fingertips, as if trying to erase the sudden worry. He'd counted on that sale to improve his cash flow. He could usually tell, even over the phone, when someone was just looking and when they were ready to buy. The website he'd had designed by Allison Kavanagh made him even more accurate in his assessments, because folks came to the Leonard ranch already knowing what horse or horses they wanted to see. And Scott Webb had been ready to buy some prime stock.

But no one could know the future. Illness or tragedy could strike anybody at any time. As much as he felt the loss to his bottom line, Chet wasn't devoid of empathy for whatever the Webbs were facing.

He started toward his office on the lower level of the house, then remembered Tara was waiting for him to continue her riding lesson. Not exactly what he wanted to do at the moment, but out the door he went. First thing he saw was Pete sitting on the corral fence, talking to Tara. He wasn't surprised to see him there. The boy's crush on the girl had been growing more and more obvious by the day. Anybody could see it—except Tara herself, that was. All she seemed to notice were the horses. Chet preferred it to stay that way.

"Sorry about the interruption," he said when he reached the corral. "Have you got the mare ready to go?"

"Yes," Tara answered.

Chet went into the corral and checked the cinch and saddle. "Good job."

"Hey, Dad." Pete hopped down from the fence. "Care if I saddle up and come with you?"

"Suppose not. We aren't doing much today. Just getting Tara beyond the paddocks for a change. Thought we'd head up by the creek."

"Great. I'll be ready in no time." Pete left the corral and disappeared moments later into the barn.

The boy was as good as his word, and soon they were all mounted on horses and riding away from the barnyard.

TARA WAS NOWHERE IN SIGHT WHEN KIMBERLY arrived at the Leonard ranch a little before 5:30 on Tuesday evening. Usually, the girl was brushing her horse when Kimberly got there. But not today.

She parked the car in the usual spot, then walked to the

barn and looked inside. "Hello?" she called into the darker recesses.

Nobody answered.

She turned around. Chet's black pickup truck was there. So was the truck his sons used and two more besides. She was trying to decide where to look next for her daughter—at the main house or in the guest cottage?—when two men rode into view through a copse of trees beyond some outbuildings. She didn't recognize them. When they noticed her, they slowed their mounts from a trot to a walk. Kimberly took a couple of steps back as the horses got closer, nerves erupting in her belly.

"Howdy," the one with the dark hair said. "You must be Tara's mother."

"Yes."

"Blake Buttons, ma'am. Pleased to meet you."

She offered a quick smile, wanting to move farther away from the large, sweaty animals but not wanting to be rude to their riders. "Hello."

"Me and Denny saw Tara ridin' with Chet and Pete about an hour or so ago. Up above the north pastures there. I reckon they're on their way back by now, but I wouldn't expect 'em any too soon."

The blond-haired cowboy—Denny, she assumed—slipped from the saddle. "Might as well make yourself comfortable, ma'am." He jerked his head toward the house. "Ms. McKenna's inside. She's sure to like your company."

"Thank you. I'll go see her."

But before she could move, she saw Anna walking in their direction. The elderly woman wore jeans, boots, and a bright green western shirt. Her dyed red hair was worn in a ponytail. She looked and moved like someone thirty years her junior.

"You must be early," Anna said.

"A little."

"While you wait, let me show you our new additions."

The ranch hands touched their hat brims, bid her a good day, and led their horses away.

"Come with me." Anna took Kimberly by the arm, a gesture of friendship rather than an older person needing help. "The foals were born on Sunday a couple of hours apart. One of them is the spitting image of Shiloh's Star when he was a colt. The other is going to be a blue dun."

Kimberly didn't bother to say she had no clue what any of that meant.

They moved through one end of the barn and out the other. The mares and foals were in two nearby paddocks. The babies, now about forty-eight hours old, moved around on their gangly legs with surprising agility, although they didn't go too far afield from their mothers.

"Aren't they the prettiest creatures God ever made?"

The wonder and excitement in the elderly woman's voice was so much like Tara's that Kimberly had to smile. "Tara must have been beside herself when she saw them."

"She surely was."

"When she isn't here at the ranch, she's reading books from the library about horses. I wish she was as eager to learn history or geometry or English lit."

"Are you learning about horses along with her?"

"A little. But I might as well ask a dumb question. What's a blue dun?"

Anna laughed. "Abe always said there was no such thing as a dumb question, and I agree. Basically the blue comes from a black horse with cream-colored genetics. It gives the horse a grayish coat with darker gray markings. And a dun has a dorsal stripe, which runs from withers to croup." She pointed. "See it there?"

Kimberly nodded.

"Maybe you'll think twice about those riding lessons we offered to give you. The offer still stands."

"I'll pass, Anna. Thanks anyway."

There was a merry twinkle in Anna McKenna's eyes. "But be warned. I intend to conspire with your daughter to change your mind."

Kimberly didn't doubt for a moment that they would try. But there was no way on earth she would ever agree to it. No matter what.

Anna

1945

MUFFLED MOANS AWAKENED ANNA BEFORE DAWN ON the Fourth of July. Barefoot, she went to the bedroom at the opposite end of the hall and tapped on the door. "Abe?"

The door jerked open a few moments later. Perspiration beaded Abe's forehead, and his eyes were filled with concern.

"Is it Violet?" Anna asked, although she knew the answer. "What can I do to help?"

"We need Minnie York to come right away. I don't think this baby's going to take long, no matter what they told us to expect. Can you ride over to the York farm and get her? The telephone isn't working. I tried about an hour ago."

"I'll get dressed and go right now." Anna spun away and ran to her room. She dressed in a hurry and tied her hair back with a ribbon without bothering to run a brush through the tangled curls. Then she was down the stairs, out the door, and into the barn where she saddled Shiloh's Star and rode away from the yard as dawn became a pale promise in the east.

According to what Violet had told Anna a few weeks before, Minnie York had delivered most of the babies in Kings Meadow for the last twenty years. Certainly the experienced midwife had delivered more babies than the young physician, David Chapman, who'd opened his practice in the valley this past spring. Luckily for Anna, the York farm butted up against the Leonards' east pastureland. It didn't take Shiloh's Star long to carry her there.

Almost as if she'd been anticipating Anna's arrival, Minnie York opened the door with her leather bag already in hand. "Is it time?"

"Yes. Hurry. Abe says the baby's coming fast."

"What does he know? All he's delivered is calves and pigs." She closed the door behind her and strode toward her automobile. "If you get there first, tell Abe and Violet I'm on my way and to stay calm."

Anna turned Shiloh's Star around, and they began the race toward home again. The young horse gave her everything he had, his long strides eating up the ground beneath them. By the time they galloped into the Leonard barnyard, the sky overhead had turned from pewter to blue. Anna tied the reins around the hitching post and ran into the house.

Upstairs, the door to the bedroom was open. Violet's groans filled the hallway. Looking scared to death, Abe stood beside the bed, holding his wife's hand.

"Abe, Mrs. York's on her way."

He glanced toward the door. "Did you tell her to hurry?"

"I did. She was getting in her car when I started back. She should be right behind me."

As if to prove Anna told the truth, an engine backfired below the bedroom window.

"Go see if she needs any help," Abe ordered, his gaze returning to his wife.

Anna was quick to obey, but the most the midwife wanted from her were clean linens and hot water. After that, Anna had to be satisfied with sitting in the kitchen, listening as Violet strained to bring her baby into the world.

Twelve

ON FRIDAY AFTERNOON, ANGRY VOICES DREW CHET out of the house in time to see Pete take a swing at his brother and miss. Sam was quick to retaliate. He connected with Pete's nose, knocking him to the ground. The younger boy was back on his feet in seconds, this time using his head as a battering ram, flying straight into Sam's midsection. Sam was thrown backward. He slammed into the side of the truck that had carried the two boys home from school not long before.

"Sam! Pete!" Chet ran to put himself in between them. "Stop it!"

He didn't succeed in pulling the brothers apart until one of the hired hands, Blake Buttons, showed up to assist him. Chet got ahold of Pete. Blake dragged Sam in the opposite direction.

Chet turned his youngest son around to face him. The boy had a bloody nose, and his right eye was starting to swell. "What's going on?"

"Ask him." Pete spat the words as he jerked his head toward his brother.

"You're acting like a baby," Sam returned as he fingered his split lower lip.

With a cry of rage, Pete tried to pull free from his father's grasp.

Chet held on tight. "I want to know what's going on between you two, and I want to know *now!*"

Sam was the first to answer. "He's mad, 'cause I asked Tara Welch to go with me to the prom next week and she said yes."

"You know I like her. You know it. You coulda asked somebody else. Any girl but Tara."

"So what if you like her? You aren't her boyfriend, and you couldn't take her to the prom anyway. You're a sophomore. Why shouldn't I ask her?"

"You wouldn't have asked her if it wasn't for me."

"Ah, grow up."

This time, Pete managed to jerk away from his father's grasp, but he didn't try to go for his brother again. Instead he stormed off toward the barn.

Blake appeared to be hiding a smile as he relaxed his grip on Sam's arms. He sent a questioning gaze toward his boss. Chet nodded, silently telling him he could go. Without comment, Blake returned to whatever he'd been doing before the fight broke out.

Chet focused his attention on his eldest son. "Is that true? Did you ask Tara out just to hurt your brother?"

"*No.* I thought I was doing her a favor. She's new at school and doesn't seem to have many friends yet." He touched his lip again, then checked his fingertips for blood, his brows knitted together in a deep frown. "I figured she'd *want* to go to the prom. And like I said, it isn't like she's Pete's girlfriend. They aren't going out or anything. He's never told her he likes her. He's too chicken for that."

Chet had worried Pete might get his heart broken by Tara, this being his first serious crush, but he hadn't figured on Sam being the reason. The brothers had squabbled before for many different reasons, but he'd never known them to go at it with fists—and certainly never over a girl. "You need to make it right with your brother, Sam."

"How? Do I tell Tara I can't take her to the prom 'cause Pete's jealous?"

"No, that wouldn't be fair to her. Not if she already accepted."

"She did."

Chet rubbed his chin, hoping for an idea. Nothing came to him. "I don't know how you'll make it up to him," he answered at last. "But you'd better find a way."

"I'll do what I can. Just don't expect a miracle." Sam grabbed his backpack off the ground and walked toward the house, slipping past Anna who had come outside sometime during the commotion. Chet followed a few moments later.

"What was that about?" Anna asked when he reached her.

"A girl."

Anna looked toward the barn. "Tara?"

"Yeah."

"Oh, dear."

Her words added an extra weight to his shoulders. "Yeah."

When Kimberly walked through the back door into Janet's kitchen, Tara was waiting for her. The girl's eyes were brilliant with excitement.

"Mom, I got asked to the prom. It's next weekend. I've gotta have a dress." The words tumbled out of her with nary a breath. "Can we go find a dress tomorrow? Please, Mom. Please."

"The prom?" Her daughter hadn't mentioned a prom before now. Tara had never shown any interest in school dances or fancy dresses. It had always been horses, horses, horses. "Who invited you?"

"Sam Leonard."

Kimberly relaxed slightly as she set her purse on the small table near the door. Sam seemed a nice boy, and he came from a good family. That offered some relief. But a prom dress was another matter entirely. How could they afford one?

Janet appeared in the kitchen doorway. "Mind if I butt in? Couldn't help but overhear."

Kimberly shook her head, then nodded, desperate for any help that might be offered.

"There's a secondhand store in Boise that specializes in formal gowns for teens at reasonable prices. The dresses are as good as new but at a fraction of the price you'd pay in the department or specialty stores. Why don't you two drive down tomorrow and see what you can find? Make a day of it."

Money for gas. Money for a dress. Could she manage it? Of course she could. She'd have to manage it. A girl's first prom was an important milestone, and Tara deserved to go to it. She'd done without so much since her father passed away.

Kimberly forced away any remaining negative thoughts,

the kind that came to her all too easily. "All right." She smiled. "Let's do it. A girls' day out. Just you and me. It'll be fun."

"I'll have to call Ms. McKenna and tell her I can't be there tomorrow."

"Oh, dear. I'd forgotten that." Kimberly frowned in thought. "Maybe I could volunteer to go with you on Sunday afternoon or one evening next week so that Ms. McKenna has double the help. We don't want Mr. Leonard to feel as if you're taking advantage of him or shirking your duties." Even as the words left her mouth, intuition told her Chet Leonard wouldn't feel that way. He would understand. Still, she added, "Your horse eats, whether you help around the ranch or not."

"Sure. That'd be great if you could come help. I'll call now."

Kimberly watched as her daughter picked up the phone and punched in the number, but she didn't wait for someone to answer on the other end. She wanted out of her work clothes and into her favorite pair of jeans.

Janet followed her to the bedroom door. "Tara's super excited."

"I didn't think anything but a horse could get her so worked up."

"Sam's a nice kid."

"He seems like it." She stepped behind the open closet door and began to change clothes. "But I'm not sure I'm ready for Tara to fall for him or any boy. Inevitably what follows a first crush is the first heartbreak."

"We all have to go through that, Kimmie. It's how we learn as we grow up."

She tugged on her jeans. "I know. But I still wish I could

protect her from it for a while. These last years have been hard ones. I'd like to see her happy for a good long spell."

"Despite all that's happened to the two of you, Tara's got her head on straight. You've done a good job raising her."

Kimberly looked around the closet door. "Do you really think so?"

"I really think so." Janet smiled at her before turning away. "I'm going to grill hamburgers for supper."

"I'll be out in a sec to help." Kimberly pulled on a T-shirt, then glanced in the mirror above the dresser. "You need to learn not to worry," she told her reflection. *If only I could.*

THAT EVENING, DINNER IN THE LEONARD HOME WAS AN uncomfortable affair, anger an almost physical presence in the room. Neither of the boys said more than a dozen words the entire meal. Tired of the tension, Chet excused Pete and Sam from doing the dishes. Easier to wash up himself, he decided, than let his sons' foul moods give him an ulcer.

When he'd finished cleaning up in the kitchen, he headed for his office, intending to accomplish some much-needed bookkeeping. Instead he sat at his desk and stared toward the window, unseeing.

If Marsha were here, he wondered, would she know how to handle this rift between brothers? Or would she feel as helpless as he felt now?

Chet would have given a lot to have had a brother when he was a kid. He'd had a great childhood, but sometimes he'd been lonely. He'd decided early on that, when he married, he wanted a big family. No only child for this Leonard. Four generations of that was enough. He'd wanted a bunch of kids to fill the bedrooms of this old ranch house as they'd never been filled before.

He thought back to the births of each of his three sons, remembering the joy he felt the first time he'd held them in his arms. Happiness had seemed a promise for the rest of their days. But that kind of thinking had been naïve. Nobody got to be happy forever. Not on this earth. Trials came to the just and unjust, like the rain. He'd heard it said that happiness and joy were two different things. Happiness because of circumstances—and ever so fleeting. Joy because of trusting God, despite the circumstances. Was that true? He wasn't sure.

He stood and walked to the window. Sunset was a ways off, but the lowering sun had painted the barnyard with the muted shades of evening. He always liked this time of day on the ranch. Everything moved slower. Nothing was pressing. Chet closed his eyes and leaned a shoulder against the window case. As he released a deep breath, he let the concern for his battling sons go on a silent prayer.

That you may know the way by which you shall go, for you have not passed this way before.

He'd read that passage from the book of Joshua during his morning devotions, and as the words returned to him, he felt some of the worry drain away. This was new ground for them as a family, but they'd passed through a lot of new ground over the years. And somehow they'd always managed to find their way through it. With God's help, they would do so once again.

Thirteen

KIMBERLY AND TARA LEFT KINGS MEADOW AT NINE o'clock on Saturday morning. It was one of those perfect days in May when the sky was crystal blue and the earth splashed with varying shades of green. Green was not a color Kimberly thought of first when she thought of Idaho. Not after spending her life in the Seattle area where the average annual rainfall was over three times more than here.

The highway followed the Payette River, which ran high on its banks and roiled and frothed over boulders and trapped logs, but Kimberly couldn't enjoy more than the occasional glance in the river's direction. The winding road required her full attention.

Once they were out of the mountains and headed into Boise, Tara read aloud Janet's detailed directions to the recommended shop. Fifteen minutes later, the car turned into the parking lot beside Déjà Vu Couture. Nerves tumbled in Kimberly's stomach.

Please let there be a dress that Tara likes that I can afford.

With the prayer repeating in her head, she opened the car door and got out.

The secondhand clothing store was in a converted brick house in an older section of the city. If not for the store's name and advertising, no one would have known the beautiful gowns inside had been worn before.

Before her husband died, Kimberly hadn't entered thrift shops for any purpose other than to drop off items they no longer wanted or needed. She'd done her shopping in upscale department stores and specialty shops. When she'd seen something she liked, she'd bought it, scarcely noticing the price tag. It shamed her now to remember it. She'd been careless with their resources. She'd forgotten—if she ever knew it at all—that Christians were stewards, not the owners, of whatever God entrusted to their keeping. It had been a difficult lesson to learn—or relearn—and she often wondered if she hadn't been a spendthrift when Ellis was alive would things have turned out differently after he passed?

Tara made a beeline to the round racks holding dresses in her size. Kimberly followed at a more sedate pace.

A clerk soon joined them. "May I help you find something?"

Tara looked up from the dresses. "I'm going to the prom next week and need a dress."

"I thought all the Boise and Meridian proms had been held already."

"We live in Kings Meadow," Kimberly answered.

"Oh. Of course." The woman eyed Tara. "We should have a good number of dresses that would look wonderful on you. Do you prefer long or short?"

Tara glanced at her mother.

Kimberly answered, "Whichever you like, honey."

"Short, I think."

"Well then, you're in the right spot." The clerk patted the top of the round rack. "But if you change your mind, the floor-length gowns are over there." She waved her hand in the direction of the racks holding long dresses that lined the far wall. "Call if you need assistance. The dressing rooms are in the back." Again she motioned.

"Thanks." Tara started to look through the gowns before her.

Kimberly stood back and waited for her daughter to pick the ones she liked best, hoping they wouldn't have any arguments. Like many mothers and daughters, she and Tara often disagreed on style choices, especially when it came to tops that exposed too much skin or cleavage. Kimberly refused to budge on that one. Not that they'd done much clothes shopping recently. Not even in secondhand shops.

The first dress that caught her daughter's eyes was champagne colored with a rhinestone-embellished waist. Unfortunately, it was a strapless gown and a little mature for Tara. But Kimberly held her tongue, willing to wait until her daughter tried on all her finds.

The next one was a sleeveless black dress with various sized gold sequins scattered over the fabric. It had a sheer neckline and a keyhole opening in the back. Modest, yet appropriately flirty for an almost-sixteen-year-old girl. That was a relief.

Tara released a soft gasp. "Mom, look at this one."

Her daughter drew a turquoise dress from the rack and held it against her torso. The gown had a wide strap over one shoulder, and the bodice—which covered all that Kimberly wanted covered—glistened with silver sequins. The top-layered skirt was scattered with beadwork. The underskirt had a playful ruffled hemline. It was perfect.

"How much?" Kimberly asked, afraid to know the answer.

Tara checked the tag. "Thirty-five dollars."

Kimberly was able to breathe again. It was an amazing bargain. The dress must have cost at least two hundred dollars when it was new. "Try it on, honey."

Tara didn't hesitate for a moment. She hurried through the racks toward the dressing room, leaving her first two choices behind, along with her mother.

Kimberly smiled as she followed after Tara, her gaze scanning the store. In addition to gowns, there were shelves of shoes off to her right and trays of jewelry in a glass case near the register.

The woman who'd helped them earlier looked up from some papers on the counter and said, "I guess your daughter found something she liked?"

Kimberly nodded. "If it fits, it will be perfect."

And it *was* perfect. When Tara stepped out of the dressing room a short while later and spun in a slow circle before the mirrors, tears welled in Kimberly's eyes. Where had this stunning young woman come from?

"It's beautiful, Tara," she managed to say past the lump in her throat. "*You're* beautiful."

"Can I get it?"

Kimberly nodded, thankful that she didn't have to say no. God bless Janet for telling them about this store. And thank God for her temporary job.

"What about accessories?" the sales clerk asked as Tara disappeared back into the dressing room.

"Perhaps some shoes. Nothing else." To herself she decided they would stop at Fred Meyer to get Tara a strapless bra before heading back to Kings Meadow, right after they enjoyed a nice, relaxing mother-daughter lunch.

Kimberly sent up another quick prayer of thanks for the ever-increasing hope she was starting to feel in her heart.

Anna

1945

ANNA FELL IN LOVE WITH ABE AND VIOLET'S BABY boy the instant she laid eyes on him.

Richard George Leonard—named for his maternal and paternal grandfathers—bellowed at the top of his lungs, his eyes squeezed shut, his face bright red and blotchy. Although the midwife declared him one of the biggest babies she'd delivered over the years, he still looked small to Anna, especially when Violet passed him into her arms.

Anna touched her fingers to the inky black hair on his head. It was as soft as down. She couldn't help but draw him closer so she could kiss the top of his head.

"Hello, Richie," she whispered. "You are such a lucky baby. You've got a wonderful mommy and daddy. They're going to love you and take care of you and watch you grow into a man. And I'm going to help them."

As if he understood, the baby stopped crying. After a couple of hiccups, he went to sleep.

"Well, look at you, Anna," Abe said. "Aren't you the perfect big sister. Look at how he trusts you already."

She wouldn't have thought anything could make her feel any happier, but being called Richie's big sister did. God had given her a home and a family to care for her. He'd given her hope for the fulfillment of her daddy's dream for Shiloh's Star, and now He'd given her something she'd always wanted—a little brother.

Anna passed the baby back to his mother, fighting hard not to let tears spill from her eyes.

Someday, she hoped she would fall in love with a man like Abe Leonard. And when she did, she hoped they would have a dozen babies just as perfect as Richie Leonard.

Fourteen

On Sunday, two days after the brothers' fist-fight, Sam and Pete still weren't speaking to each other. Chet was fed up with both boys, but he didn't know what to do to improve matters. It didn't help that Kimberly and Tara Welch were going to work with Anna in the cottage that afternoon. Chet wouldn't have minded a longer cooling-off period before Tara came to the ranch again. He didn't need another fight on his hands because of the girl.

Okay, that wasn't fair. None of this was Tara's fault. At least not from anything he'd observed. If she liked Pete, it had more to do with their shared interest in horses than anything else. As for Sam, Chet hadn't seen Tara spend much time with him at all when she was at the Leonard ranch. Perhaps it was different at school.

"They just need a little time," Anna had said yesterday. "Let the boys work it out themselves."

Easier said than done.

Sam and Pete had always been close. Just ten months separated their birthdays. Sam's was on the first of June, Pete's the first of April. Almost like having twins, Marsha used to say of them, and that was pretty close to the truth. Although their appearances were different, they thought, spoke, and acted much the same.

Their dinner that Sunday was another silent affair, the same as every family meal over the previous two days. Anna and Chet tried to get some kind of conversation going, but neither of the boys did anything but shoot daggers at each other with their eyes. Tension sucked most of the air out of the room. It was a relief for everyone when the meal was over. After the dishes were washed and dried, Sam disappeared up the stairs to his room to do homework. Pete went out to practice roping the life-size steer dummy set up in the field on the back side of the house.

Anna patted Chet's shoulder after the screen door swung closed. "It will be all right. You'll see."

"I've never seen them like this."

"They'll get over it." She smiled briefly. "Now, I'm going outside to wait for Kimberly and Tara. They should be here any minute."

Chet couldn't decide whether he should make himself scarce or not. Despite acknowledging the fight between brothers wasn't Tara's fault, he still wanted to blame the girl, and he didn't care much for that less-than-charitable inclination. Better not let others see it, he figured. He opted to go into his office and close the door.

Chet tried not to work on Sundays—not counting taking care of the needs of the livestock, of course. Animals didn't know a Sunday from a Monday. They still needed food and water. Sometimes one of them needed doctoring. If a foal came in the middle of the night, Chet had to be there. It was all part of being a rancher, one he willingly accepted. But bookkeeping work on a Sunday was another matter. Still, it would keep him occupied for an hour or two and out of sight of the Welches, and that was what he wanted.

He sat at his desk and fired up his computer. His electronics were getting a bit long in the tooth, something that happened mighty quickly these days. Seemed a person walked out of the computer store with the latest and greatest in his arms, and by the time he got it home, the next newest thing was being touted on the Internet and in television advertisements.

He leaned back in his chair and released a soft groan as he closed his eyes. Another year and a summer and he would have a son in college. Two years and both of them would be off to college. He'd been putting a little away in their education funds since before they were born, but it wouldn't be enough to cover four years each. Not even if they remained in Idaho for their schooling.

He opened his eyes again and reached for the mouse, but the crunch of tires on gravel followed by the closing of car doors drew him up from his chair and to the window. Kimberly and Tara walked toward the house, side by side. Both of them wore their long, dark hair in ponytails. With it pulled back like that, Kimberly looked more like Tara's sister than her mother.

It bothered him that he noticed that. He wasn't attracted to Kimberly. And even if he was, he wouldn't act on it.

Kimberly Welch didn't plan to stay in Kings Meadow, which meant she was all wrong for him. Best he remember it.

ABOUT TWO HOURS AFTER THEIR ARRIVAL AT THE ranch, Kimberly pulled a dusty sheet away from a piece of furniture in the center of the bedroom, revealing a wooden cradle. The craftsmanship was simple yet exquisite. An obvious heirloom.

"Oh my word," Anna said softly from the doorway. "I haven't seen that since Chet was a baby."

"This wasn't purchased in a store."

"You're right. It wasn't. Chet's grandfather Abe made it. I watched him make it." Anna came to stand beside Kimberly, then reached out to give the small bed a push, setting it in motion. "I rocked Richie in this cradle often. Until he outgrew it. That seems like only yesterday." Her voice softened. "I rocked Chet in it too."

Tara asked, "Did Sam and Pete use it when they were babies?" She turned away from the box she'd been sorting through.

"I don't know," Anna answered. "I was living in Florida by that time. But I'm sure they and their older brother must have."

Tara's eyes widened. "What older brother? I didn't know there was another one. Where is he?"

"Rick was killed in a car accident. Not quite three years ago." Anna covered her mouth with her fingertips, as if trying to stop the sad words. "So tragic. For the whole family."

Kimberly's chest hurt, thinking about what Chet must

have gone through, losing a son like that. It was hard enough losing a spouse unexpectedly. But a child wasn't supposed to die before his parent. It had to cause a special kind of grief.

"Did I have a cradle, Mom? Did you keep some of my baby stuff?"

Strange, how those words—so matter-of-factly asked—could sting. There had been things handed down in Kimberly's family and in Ellis's family that she would have loved to pass on to her daughter. She had saved Tara's christening gown and her first pair of little shoes, among other items. Perhaps none had been as sentimental as this handmade cradle, but meaningful all the same. But they were gone now, casualties of a collapsing life. Keepsakes require a place to store things. Having a home foreclosed took away more than a place to live. She didn't care for that reminder.

If only . . .

Sadness overwhelmed her. A feeling she'd come to despise. A feeling she didn't want Tara or Anna to see.

"I think I need some fresh air. I'll be back in a little while."

Her words trailing behind her, she hurried outside. She didn't have a destination in mind. She just kept walking. Her feet carried her away from the barnyard, home, guesthouse, and outbuildings, following a dirt track with open fields on one side all the way to where the mountains rose up, covered in trees, and a wire fence broken up by wooden posts along the other side. It wasn't a road, exactly, but wagons, tractors, and trucks had carved their passing into the earth over the years.

The air smelled clean, and she breathed it in deeply. From the first day she and Tara arrived in Kings Meadow,

Kimberly had been aware of how fresh everything smelled. Even in town, but especially out here on the Leonard ranch. Sad thoughts seemed to be blown away by the gentle breeze. She inhaled as peace settled, allowing her pace to slow now that the walk had served its purpose.

"You're going to be all right," she said to herself, her eyes fastened on the uneven ground before her. "God is faithful. Things are looking up. Life is getting better. Keep putting one foot in front of another. Keep moving forward. Tara is healthy and she's happy again. You're healthy and you have a home with your best friend for as long as you need it, and you have a job, even if it is temporary. Don't think of all you've lost. Be thankful for what you have."

It was a familiar pep talk. Sometimes it worked. Sometimes it didn't.

The sound of hooves striking the hard ground caused her to look up. Chet rode toward her on a big golden-colored horse, his face shadowed by the brim of his ever-present cowboy hat. But she knew when he saw her because he reined in, drawing the horse from a canter to a walk. Kimberly stopped and awaited his arrival.

"Afternoon." He dismounted. "Did you walk all this way alone?"

Kimberly glanced behind her, surprised at how far she'd come. At least a mile, she guessed. Perhaps even a mile and a half. She couldn't see any of the buildings of the ranch complex because of a swell in the land.

"Nothing clears the cobwebs like getting outside on a day like this," Chet added.

She met his gaze again. He and his horse had come a little

closer. She felt a flutter of nerves. Because of the size of the horse? Or because of the man? The latter question disturbed her much more than the former.

A tiny smile played at the corners of his mouth. "If you're headed back, I'll walk with you . . . if you don't mind the company."

"No, I don't mind." What else could she say? It would be rude to say she didn't want him to walk with her. And she did need to return to the cottage. Anna and Tara would surely be wondering where she went after the abrupt way she'd left.

She turned and began walking. A tall man with a long, easy stride, Chet fell into step beside her. Although she didn't glance his way, she was keenly aware of his muscled biceps beneath the short sleeves of his close-fitting T-shirt.

Oh, this was not good. This wasn't good at all. She hadn't been aware of men in any kind of physical way since Ellis. And the last man in the world she wanted to notice, even in passing, was a cowboy.

Fifteen

"MAY I ASK YOU SOMETHING, MR. LEONARD?"

Chet grinned as he looked at her. "I thought we were done with the formality. I'm Chet to everybody I know, except kids and teens."

"All right. May I ask you something . . . Chet?"

"Sure."

"How do you feel about Sam taking Tara to the prom?"

He didn't know what he'd expected her to ask, but that wasn't it. For a moment or two, he couldn't put together a reply.

She stopped walking. "You're against it."

He'd taken one extra step and had to turn to face her. "No. I don't have any objection to Tara as a date for Sam, if that's what you mean."

"Are you sure?"

"I'm sure. But I'm afraid it's caused some hard feelings between brothers."

She raised her eyebrows, waiting for him to go on.

"Pete's got a crush on your daughter."

"Oh, dear. I didn't know."

"Maybe I should ask you the same question. How do *you* feel about Sam taking Tara to the prom?"

She gave him a somewhat shaky smile. "Nervous. She's never been on a date before, let alone gone to prom." She slid her fingers into the back pockets of her calf-length black pants. "I worry about Tara. Maybe more than I should. All she's cared about is horses since she was little more than a toddler. I used to hate that, her constant asking for a horse of her own, her disinterest in pretty, girly things." Her smile faded, sadness filling her expressive eyes. "But now I . . . I just don't want her to get a broken heart. They take so long to mend, you know."

Sympathy welled inside of him. *Who broke your heart, Kimberly?* He swallowed, not sure he wanted to know the answer even if he had the nerve to ask the question. "Yeah, I know."

They resumed walking.

"Sam's a good kid," he said after several minutes of silence. "He'll treat Tara with respect. I promise you that."

"I believe you. He impresses me as a nice boy. Both of your sons do. But will it complicate things . . . with you as her trainer if . . . if this goes beyond one dance?"

"No. Tara and I will be okay." Strange, how important it felt to Chet that Kimberly trust him with her daughter. It shouldn't matter that much, but all of a sudden it did.

Silence enveloped them for another short while before Kimberly said, "It isn't easy. Being a single parent."

"No. It isn't easy." Chet sent a sideways glance toward

her. "But life has a way of handing us the unexpected, and we just do the best we can. Making lemonade out of lemons, like the old saying goes."

She released a soft laugh. "Lemonade has become my least favorite beverage. But it will get better once Tara and I are able to go back."

"Back?"

"To Seattle. I much prefer living in the city, and there are so many more opportunities there."

It wasn't like this was news to him. She'd said something similar on Easter. But it hadn't mattered to him then. Now it did, crazy as it seemed. "You plan on going anytime soon?"

"As soon as I can find a job that will support us."

Chet didn't care much for the way her words made him feel. Abandoned. Rejected. Left behind. Familiar feelings. Time to change the subject. "How are things going in the cleanup of the cottage?"

"It's been an interesting few hours. Before I left to take a walk, we uncovered the cradle your grandfather made before your dad was born. Anna said it was your cradle too."

"Yeah, it was." Welcome memories flitted through his head. "Haven't seen that cradle in a month of Sundays. Well, not in almost sixteen years anyway. Pete was the last to use it, and he outgrew it fast."

"It's a beautiful example of furniture made by a true craftsman." She stopped walking once again and gave him a pointed look. "It's not right to hide it under a sheet. It should be displayed somehow."

He had no choice but to stop and answer her. "Tara said you have an eye for antiques."

"I appreciate them. That's all. I'm not a trained expert. But I used to love decorating our home with antiques." She swept some loose strands of hair away from her forehead. "A cradle like the one in your guesthouse doesn't have to be relegated to a bedroom. It could hold silk flowers in a corner of your living room. Maybe drape it with some sheer fabric. You could—"

Kimberly's suggestions made him laugh.

"Did I say something funny?" She frowned up at him.

"No. I'm sorry. I wasn't laughing at you. Not really. But I don't think decorating is in the Leonard men's DNA."

Her frown eased, replaced slowly by a soft smile.

Mercy, was Kimberly Welch ever pretty when she smiled. Why did he have to notice it now, when he knew her plans were to go back to Seattle as soon as she was able? But knowing that didn't seem to matter. His mouth went dry and his heart began to thump as he continued to stare at her, unmoving. What was he? Sixteen again? That was how he felt. Tongue-tied and discombobulated. He had to look like an idiot to her.

"Hey, Mom." Tara's voice came to Chet's rescue.

He broke his gaze away from Kimberly, looking toward the barnyard. Tara waved at them.

Kimberly called, "Coming, honey."

They fell into step once again, their pace a bit faster than it had been before.

Tara hurried forward to meet them. The first thing she did was pat Chet's horse's neck. "How you doing, boy?" Then she looked at her mother. "Wait until she sees what we uncovered after you left. An oil painting of Ms. McKenna when she was about my age. Mom, she looked like a movie star back then. I'm not kidding. You won't believe it."

Kimberly put an arm around Tara's shoulders. "I guess we'd best get inside so I can see it." She glanced at Chet. "Want to see it too?"

There went that odd thump in his chest again. "I'd better put my horse up. I'll see the portrait later."

A coward's retreat, but the wisest course of action to take. So he took it.

KIMBERLY PAUSED AT THE FRONT DOOR TO THE COT-tage, letting her daughter enter before her. She hesitated long enough to look over her shoulder and watch Chet walk toward the barn.

What was it about the way he looked in those clothes— jeans and boots, T-shirt and hat? What was it about the picture of him leading that horse by the reins that made her feel so peculiar on the inside? What was it that had passed between them a few moments ago? What was it—

"Mom? You coming?"

"Yes." She gave her head a shake. "Yes, I'm coming."

The portrait in question had been brought into the living room and leaned against the old upright piano, where light from the window could fall upon it. When she saw it, she stopped still and stared.

When they first met, Kimberly had thought Anna McKenna attractive for a woman her age. If there were beauty pageants for women in their eighties, Anna would surely win. Still, Kimberly hadn't realized what a real beauty

Anna had been in her youth. Unless the portrait painter had lied with his brush, Anna could have been a sister—perhaps a twin—of the actress Maureen O'Hara in her earliest films. The color of her hair. The arch of her brows. The shape of her mouth. The flawless pale complexion.

In the painting, Anna stood near a fence made of lodge pole pine. Beyond the rails stood a bay horse, his coat the exact same dark shade of red as Anna's hair. The girl smiled as she looked toward the artist, and something about the look in her eyes made Kimberly think of a girl in love, perhaps for the very first time. Who had been the object of that love? The artist? One of the hired hands? A boy at school?

"Hard to believe I ever was that young." Anna stepped to Kimberly's side. "I still feel that way sometimes on the inside, but the outside hasn't looked like that in decades."

"Who painted it?"

"His name was Miles Stanley. He came to Kings Meadow with an army buddy of his. Gracious. What was his friend's name?" Anna's eyes narrowed as she searched her memory. "Oh, yes. Frank Jansen. Frank's father owned the hardware store in Kings Meadow. Jobs were hard to come by right after the war, so the boys were both glad to get employment in the hardware store. I don't suppose Mr. Jansen actually needed two clerks working for him. It wasn't a big store. He hired Miles more out of gratitude, I'm sure. Miles saved Frank's life in some battle outside of Paris, though I've forgotten the details now."

"He had this kind of talent, and he was working in a hardware store?" Kimberly asked.

Anna stepped away from Kimberly's side and approached the portrait. With a tender gesture, she reached out and touched the horse on the canvas. "Van Gogh only sold one painting in his lifetime. Did you know that? The other nine hundred some-odd paintings by the master became famous after his death."

"I didn't know that."

Anna smiled over her shoulder as she moved to one side of the painting, opening it to Kimberly's view again. "I wouldn't have known it either if Miles hadn't told me."

"How old were you in this portrait?"

"Seventeen. Almost eighteen."

Kimberly took a couple of steps closer to the painting, studying the way the artist had used his oils to create shadow and light, to bring life to the girl and her horse. She had no talent for painting herself, but she had a good eye for the talent of others. This young man had had talent in abundance.

"Miles painted this not long before he left Kings Meadow," Anna said softly. "He was pursuing an opportunity in California. One that would allow him to paint more, to grow as an artist."

"I'm surprised I've never heard of him."

"Many artists with talent remain in obscurity. Miles was one of them."

"You were in love with him, weren't you?"

Anna nodded, her eyes turned misty.

Kimberly felt her throat thicken in empathy. She suspected this was a tragic love story and that it would be better not to ask the older woman for details. The sadness she'd felt earlier came rushing back. Her own love story hadn't had a happy ending either. Did she believe it could happen for anyone? For her? She wasn't sure she wanted to know the answer.

Anna

1946

IT WAS A COLD JANUARY DAY WHEN ANNA MET FRANK Jansen and Miles Stanley for the first time. She had come to town with Abe in the sleigh to pick up supplies. Their last stop was Jansen's Hardware Store.

Home from Europe and freshly mustered out of the army, Frank and Miles had close-cropped haircuts and the look of men who'd seen things they would rather forget. Especially Miles. Something about his expression as Mr. Jansen made the introductions tugged at Anna's heart. She'd never felt anything like it before.

"You look good," Abe said as he gave Frank's hand a hearty shake. "Glad to have you back. We lost too many young men."

"Yes, sir. We did."

Abe turned to Miles and repeated the handshake. "Welcome to Kings Meadow, young man."

"Thank you, sir."

After living with the Leonards for more than a year and a half, Anna knew Abe had a sore spot when it came to the war. A leg injury as a boy had left him with a permanent limp, and when he'd tried to sign up to fight right after Pearl Harbor, he'd been turned down. Not that he hadn't been able to do a hard day's work around the ranch—both then and now—but that hadn't mattered to the army physicians. They still wouldn't take Abe into their ranks.

Mr. Jansen said, "We're planning a potluck at the church come Saturday to welcome the boys home. Hope you and your family will be there."

"Wouldn't miss it," Abe answered. "Long as the weather holds."

"How's that baby of yours?"

"Crawling so fast Vi can hardly keep track of him." Abe beamed with pride. "Richie's gonna be a handful when he learns to walk."

Frank and Miles excused themselves and returned to their duties. Anna stopped listening to the two older men as she watched Miles walk to the front of the store where he'd been washing the large window when Abe and Anna arrived. He picked up a rag and continued.

Miles hadn't really noticed Anna. She was sure of that. Why would he? She wasn't yet sixteen, and he was a man who'd fought in a war and had seen things in Europe that she couldn't even imagine. He was in his early twenties, she guessed. Not *that* many years older than she, but enough he could still think of her as a child.

From somewhere within, she found the courage to try to change that. She followed the same aisle to the front of the store and leaned her back against the wall. "Do you like it here, Mr. Stanley?"

"Sure do." He glanced at her as his arm continued to make circles on the glass with the rag. "What's your name again?"

She felt her cheeks grow warm. "Anna."

"Hi, Anna." He smiled at her. "It's nice to meet you."

Pleasure warmed her more deeply than any fire could have. "Do you plan to stay in Kings Meadow?"

"Not sure. For a while. Maybe a year or two. Jobs aren't easy to come by right now with all the soldiers coming home again." His attention returned to the window washing. "I guess I'll stay until the Jansens are sick of having me around."

Anna tried to think of something else to say, but nothing seemed right. And Miles was so intent on that silly window that he didn't seem inclined to come up with something on his own. As the seconds dragged past, she began to feel fool-ish. She mumbled a good-bye, but he either didn't hear her or didn't want to be bothered with her any longer.

It won't always be like this, Miles Stanley. I'll make you notice me yet, no matter how long it takes.

Sixteen

When Sam walked down the stairs the following Saturday, dressed in his new suit, Chet remembered the night Rick had taken a girl to the school prom. Marsha had insisted on snapping dozens of photos before Rick left the ranch. Chet didn't make the same kind of fuss over Sam as Marsha had over Rick, but he did make sure to take a few pictures with his digital camera.

"When you pick up Tara, tell Mrs. Welch that I'd like to get copies of any photos she takes."

"Sure, Dad. I'll tell her."

Anna retrieved the corsage from the refrigerator and handed it to Sam. "You look very handsome, young man. I hope you and Tara have a wonderful evening."

"Thanks." He leaned down and kissed Anna's cheek. "We will."

Chet cleared his throat. "Be careful. I know you won't

drink or do drugs, but other kids might not behave the same. So watch out on the roads. Keep your mind on your driving."

The look Sam gave Chet said he'd heard that warning from his father many times. Too many times. But that didn't matter to Chet. He couldn't lose another son to the winding Idaho roads.

Anna took Chet by the arm and drew him with her onto the porch, so they could wave as Sam drove away from the house. After the pickup was out of sight, she said, "Maybe you should try talking to Pete again."

"I doubt it'll do any good."

"Try anyway. He's around back."

"Practicing his roping again?"

Anna nodded.

Chet drew a deep breath and let it out slowly. "I'll give it another go." He went down the steps and rounded the house in time to see Pete release the lariat. It settled with ease over the dummy steer's head. "Nice one," Chet called to him.

Pete acted as if he hadn't heard his dad as he went to free the rope.

Sometimes parenting was for the birds.

Chet forced himself forward, all the while trying to remember what his father had said to him when he got out of line. But nothing helpful came to mind.

Pete returned to the worn spot in the grass where he liked to stand to toss the lasso. "Is he gone?"

It seemed a dumb question. Pete couldn't have missed seeing the pickup driving down the lane to the highway. Chet answered anyway. "Yes."

"I hope he gets a flat tire," the boy mumbled, the words probably not meant for his dad's ears.

But Chet heard them. "Not a nice sentiment."

"I don't care." Pete adjusted the lariat in his hand.

"Pete . . ."

"I don't, Dad."

"Son." Chet placed a hand on the boy's shoulder, stopping him from tossing the rope again. "Look at me."

Reluctantly, Pete obeyed. An angry scowl knitted his brows, and defiance sparked in his eyes.

"You can't go on feeding your resentment the way you have been. It isn't good for you or for the family. I like Tara. She's a nice girl. But you'll like quite a few girls before you graduate from college. For whatever reason, they'll come and they'll go in your life until you meet the one you'll want to marry." He paused for effect. "But Sam's the only brother you've got. He loves you and you love him."

"It isn't fair, Dad."

"Nobody said life is fair."

Pete lowered his gaze to the ground. "Why not?"

"Because the world is a broken place, Pete, full of broken people. None of us are perfect. Even the nicest people we know, even the most upstanding Christians, are going to hurt others. That's just how it is." He squeezed the boy's shoulder. "Sam was trying to be thoughtful to Tara, not get in your way."

"That's what he says."

"I believe him."

"Yeah, you would."

Irritation sparked, and Chet decided to leave well enough

alone before he said something he shouldn't. He'd tried again to make Pete see reason. That was all he could do.

KIMBERLY DIDN'T LIKE TO GET ALL MUSHY AND weepy in front of others. However, as a woman who cried over certain commercials during the Christmas season and wept during romantic movies, it seemed a foregone conclusion that she would, at the very least, tear up as her daughter prepared to leave on her very first date.

Sam Leonard was almost as tall as his father and easily as handsome. He wore a cowboy hat and a western tie with his suit, and somehow, both looked just right. He even brought Tara a corsage. Kimberly had wondered if boys in the Idaho mountains would do that.

"Okay, you two. Before you go, I need to take some pictures. Stand in front of the fireplace, please."

Tara looked like a fairy princess in her turquoise dress, all sparkling and shimmering. Tomorrow, no doubt, she would be back into jeans and boots, but tonight she was one hundred percent frilly female. A real girly girl. Kimberly snapped as many photos as the couple could tolerate, then bid them a good night and watched as they went to the truck where Sam opened the passenger door and helped Tara up to the seat.

"Remember our first prom?" Janet asked from nearby.

"Mmm. I sure do." Almost as if it were yesterday, she envisioned the dress and the hair and the limo that four of the boys had chipped in on for the evening. She remembered—

"My night was a disaster," Janet interrupted her musing.

Kimberly turned from the door. "It was? I didn't know that."

"That's because I never told you. You were all gaga over your date. He was all you could talk about the next morning. Him and how perfect everything had been." With a shake of her head, Janet walked from the kitchen into the living room.

Kimberly followed. "How could I not have known? You were right there in the limo with me." Although it had happened two decades before, she felt a twinge of shame over her failure to notice. What kind of best friend did that?

Janet sat in a chair and picked up her crochet hook and yarn, setting them in her lap. "You know what, Kimmie? I wouldn't be that age again for a million bucks."

"Me neither."

"But it would be nice to fall in love again."

Kimberly sank onto the sofa. "Again? Who were you in love with?" She really was a lousy best friend if she didn't know Janet had been in love. "When was it? Back in high school? Do I know him?"

"No." Janet shook her head. "I met Dan after I moved to Kings Meadow. He was a super nice guy, but it didn't work out. We wanted different things. Too different, it turned out. So I broke it off, and not long after, he took a job in Arizona."

"You never said a word," Kimberly said softly.

A smile briefly curved Janet's lips. "It was a long time ago."

Kimberly didn't like the glimpse she'd caught of herself. Janet had been and still was her dearest friend. The only friend who had opened her home to a mother and daughter in desperate straits. But how often through the years had Kimberly been there to help Janet? Not enough if Janet hadn't felt free to tell her about a failed love affair.

"What about you, Kimmie? Would you like to get married again?"

"No."

Janet cocked an eyebrow in response to Kimberly's swift answer.

"Well . . ." She shrugged. "Maybe someday. Not anytime soon." Unbidden and unwelcome, the image of her stepfather came to mind. "Not until Tara's out on her own."

Kimberly had been thirteen when her mother married for the second time, and the turbulence in their home over the following years had been in the extreme. Kimberly and her stepfather, Paul, had fought frequently, and more often than not, her mother had sided with her husband. Kimberly would never risk doing the same to Tara. Not ever.

Janet seemed to read Kimberly's thoughts. "You wouldn't make the mistake your mom made. You've got better sense than that." The crochet hook and yarn began to fly between her fingers. "Don't let what happened with your stepdad keep you from finding happiness again."

Another image came to mind. This one a tall cowboy with a slow and slightly crooked smile. A strange feeling shimmered in her stomach.

No. Absurd. If ever she looked for love again, it most assuredly would not be in a place like Kings Meadow!

KIMBERLY WAS OUT OF BED THE INSTANT SHE HEARD the closing of the truck's doors. She slipped her arms into her robe and tied the belt around her waist. By the time she stepped out of the bedroom, she heard voices and knew that Tara stood in the kitchen doorway, bidding her date good night. Waiting was hard, but somehow she managed to hold her ground until she knew Sam was gone. Then she hurried out of the hallway. Tara had brushed the curtains aside and was looking out the window, presumably watching Sam drive away.

"Hi, honey. Did you have a good time?"

Tara turned around. She wasn't smiling but neither did she look unhappy. "It was okay. I'm not a very good dancer. Sam was real nice the whole time, and he made sure I met all his friends."

"But?"

"I don't know." Her daughter shrugged. "It's like I think I should really like him. You know, like a boyfriend. I thought when he asked me out that's what I would feel when we were at the prom. Only I didn't. Is that messed up?"

Kimberly offered a small smile. "No, it isn't messed up."

"Sam feels the same way, I think. I mean, he was real nice and all, but it wasn't like he wanted to kiss me or anything."

Thank goodness for that. "Some boys are just meant to be friends, not boyfriends. It's okay to feel that way. For both of you."

"Sorta like you're just friends with Mr. Leonard?"

Odd, the way she felt as she answered, "Yes, sort of like that."

Tara yawned. "I'm going to bed."

"Good idea." She put her arm around her daughter's shoulders, and the two of them walked down the short hallway. In the bedroom, after helping Tara unhook the back of her gown, she kissed the girl's forehead. "Good night, honey. Sweet dreams."

"You, too, Mom." Tara yawned again.

Laughing softly, Kimberly returned to her own room and closed the door. The relief she felt made her almost giddy. Relief that Tara's first date and first prom hadn't been a disappointment. Relief that Tara wanted to be friends with Sam and not something more. Relief that Chet Leonard wouldn't have cause to worry.

Sorta like you're just friends with Mr. Leonard?

The giddiness left her, replaced by that odd sensation she felt whenever Chet entered her thoughts. All too often of late.

She removed her robe, turned out the light, and got into bed. Closing her eyes, she willed away all thoughts of Chet, of his dark good looks, of the way he walked, of the sound of his voice, of his smile.

She had to stop this. They weren't meant to be anything but friends. If even that. She was moving back to Seattle the first chance she got.

141

Seventeen

By the following Saturday, tensions had eased between the Leonard brothers. Today, Pete had volunteered to ride with Tara up to the Gold Digger's line shack. Chet thought that was a good sign.

Tara continued to use one of their calmest geldings for any lesson that carried her away from the ranch complex, but it wouldn't be long until her pinto was ready for her to take beyond the enclosed paddocks. Training sessions continued to go well. Not only that. When Tara was at the ranch, she did whatever was assigned to her without complaint. And that girl could pitch manure and straw from a stall as well as any hand he'd ever employed.

The thought made Chet smile as he watched Pete and Tara ride north. He noted Tara's posture in the saddle, the way she kept her heels down in the stirrups, and that, too, made him smile. *Good job, kiddo.*

He turned, his gaze sweeping past Kimberly Welch's car,

then returning to it. Kimberly was inside the guest house with Anna. This was the second weekend she'd come to help the older woman sort and organize. He suspected that, to the two of them, what they were doing was more fun than work. It was tempting to set aside his own chores to see what they were up to. What treasures would they uncover today? What stories would Anna tell at the supper table because of a jogged memory?

Still smiling to himself, he headed for the large metal building beyond the barn that served as a workshop and, in the worst part of winter, a garage. Awaiting him inside was the old John Deere tractor, the one his father had purchased in 1965, two years before Chet was born. The tractor wasn't used for any heavy-duty work these days. Chet kept it more for sentimental reasons. He'd learned to drive steering this old piece of equipment around the fields.

At the workbench, he switched on the CD player. Josh Turner's deep voice came through the speakers, singing "Long Black Train." One of Chet's favorites. He turned up the volume. Then he grabbed a wrench and a rag and went to work on the tractor. When "Me and God" started to play close to fifteen minutes later, Chet sang along, feeling a spark of joy, knowing that he and God were a team, as the lyrics said. Something he needed to keep in mind more often.

When the tune ended, in the brief silence before the next track began, he heard a soft clearing of a throat. He pulled his head back from the tractor engine to see Kimberly in the wide doorway.

She smiled slightly when their gazes met. "Sorry to intrude."

"No problem." Chet set the wrench aside and strode to the workbench to pause the CD. When he turned again, he found Kimberly had closed the distance between them.

"Who was that?" she asked.

"On the CD?"

She nodded.

"Josh Turner."

"Loved his voice. Yours too."

He liked the way the compliment made him feel. Kind of warm on the inside. Then, just as quickly, it bothered him that he'd liked it. "Thanks."

"I never listened to country music until we moved in with Janet." Kimberly looked around the interior of the metal building. "She doesn't listen to anything else, so I'm starting to learn who some of the artists are. I like it more than I thought I would." Her gaze returned to him once more.

Chet couldn't help but ask, "What's your favorite kind of music?"

"Classic rock." She shrugged. "Songs my mom loved in her youth. We used to rock out together in the car when I was little."

The notion made Chet smile again as he pulled the rag from his back pocket and wiped a spot of grease from his hands.

"Anna sent me to get you. She says it's time for some of the boxes to go into the attic." Returning his smile, Kimberly pretended to flex her right bicep. "I told her I could do it, but she insisted I come get you."

"She's right. Don't need either of you getting hurt trying to lift heavy boxes."

"I'm stronger than I look."

I bet you are, Mrs. Welch. He gave his hands another wipe, then dropped the rag onto the workbench. "Well, let's get 'er done."

They headed out of the metal shed.

When they were halfway to the cottage, Kimberly said, "I don't see Tara anywhere."

"She finished working with Wind Dancer, so she and Pete went for a ride. Don't worry. I told Pete to keep track of the time. They'll be back before you need to leave."

"No hurry. Janet's in Boise for the weekend, so nobody's expecting us to be home at a certain time. Nothing more exciting awaiting us than a bowl of hot air popcorn and a DVD."

An invitation burst from his mouth before he could reconsider it: "Why don't the two of you stay and have supper?"

She glanced at him. "Are you sure? It seems you're always putting yourself out for us."

"I'm sure." And he was. More sure than he'd been of anything in quite a while.

KIMBERLY WAS ABOUT TO PASS THE LAST OF THE boxes up to Chet, who stood on a stepladder beneath the attic's trapdoor, when Sam raced into the guesthouse with a shout.

"Fire! Dad, the barn's on fire!"

Kimberly's arms tightened around the box, her breath caught in her throat.

"Anna, call the Fire Department." Chet leapt off the ladder and ran out of the house right behind Sam.

What should she do? Stay with Anna? Go with Chet and Sam?

Anna must have seen her uncertainty. "Go with them. I'm fine. I'll make the phone calls. Don't worry about me."

When Kimberly got outside, she saw black smoke billowing skyward from the right side of the barn. Before she got close, two horses ran out of the barn doorway, their iron shoes clattering on the hard ground of the barnyard, one of them neighing in fright. Kimberly felt like making the same kind of shrieking sound when she saw them, though the horses came nowhere near her.

Chet and Sam came out of the barn a few moments after the horses. "Hose down the other buildings," Chet shouted to his son. "Make sure the roof of the house is soaked."

"What can I do?" Kimberly called as she hurried toward him.

He spun on his heel to look at her. His eyes told her how serious it was.

"How can I help?" she repeated.

"Turn the horses out of those paddocks. Get them away from the barn. Can you do that?" He motioned with his arm.

"Yes. I can do it," she said it with a confidence she didn't feel.

Heart thundering in her chest, she circled around the barn and slipped through the rails of the nearest paddock. The horses in the paddocks raced the fence lines, alarmed by the scent of smoke. Fear they would trample her made it hard for Kimberly to think what she should do first.

A rope. She should have a rope with her. Turning around, she spied a lead rope fastened to a halter hanging from a nearby post. She grabbed them and hurried to the gate on the north side of the paddock. The latch resisted her fumbling attempts to open it at first.

"Don't do this to me. Open up."

The latch slipped free, as if at her command, and she swung the gate wide. Then she turned toward the wild-eyed mare and foal, still running from one corner of the enclosure to another.

"O God, help me," she whispered.

Kimberly circled away from the gate, angling toward the far side of the paddock. During one of Tara's lessons, Kimberly had seen her daughter hold out her arms and talk aloud when attempting to put a halter on a horse in this same paddock. It couldn't hurt to try the same thing. Up went her arms.

"You need to go out that gate. Go on, lady. Take your colt and go."

The mare tossed her head and bolted for freedom, her foal following hard on her heels.

"Well. That wasn't so bad."

Her pulse slowed a bit as she turned toward the adjoining paddock. There were three horses in that enclosure. All big. All frightened by the fire and smoke. All running along the fence, wanting to get away from the danger. Her pulse sped back up again.

The adjoining gate was directly opposite the one she'd opened minutes before. She walked to it, resolute. Determined to accomplish the job that needed to be done and not give in to her fear. Again her fingers felt ungainly as she tried to release the latch so she could open the gate, but it wasn't quite as difficult as before.

Gate open, she moved into the second paddock. "All right, boys. Let's get out of here while we can. Shall we?" She opened her arms wide a second time.

One of the horses kicked out with his hind legs at another. Then the lead horse spun about and reared up. The other matched him, standing on hind legs and lashing out with his front hooves. The sounds the horses made sent terror streaking up Kimberly's spine, but it was the sight of the third horse galloping straight toward her that caused her to turn and run. She didn't even notice at first that the animal had sped past her and was out of the paddock.

Instinct demanded she follow the horse through the opening and keep running. Keep running until she was far, far away from anything with four legs. Especially anything *big* with four legs. But before she got to the gate, Anna appeared. At the sight of the older woman, Kimberly burst into tears. An instant later, she stumbled over uneven ground and fell onto her hands and knees.

"Kimberly." Anna was at her side in no time. "Are you hurt?"

"No." The answer came out more croak than word.

"Here. Let me help you up."

Kimberly swiped at the tears on her cheeks before getting to her feet. "I'm all right. Thanks, Anna. I just . . . I just got frightened."

"Of course you were frightened. Now you wait right over there." Anna picked up the halter and lead rope from where Kimberly had dropped them. She swung the end of the rope in a circle as she moved toward the remaining two horses. "Let's go." She made a clicking sound with her tongue.

And just like that, the horses obeyed, running side by side like the best of friends. Out of the paddock, through the next, and out into the pastureland beyond.

Kimberly forced herself to take a deep breath and blow it out hard. Once, then again and again. It seemed foolish to her now, allowing fear to overwhelm her.

Walking toward Kimberly, Anna looked as if she were about to say something. But the siren of the Kings Meadow VFD reached their ears first. The two women turned to see the fire truck rumbling up the drive, several pickup trucks full of volunteers following in its wake. Only then did Kimberly realize how much worse the fire had grown in the time she'd been trying to move the horses from the paddocks.

Wordlessly, Anna and Kimberly put their arms around each other. They watched as the firefighters and neighbors tried to save as much of the barn and the rest of the outbuildings as possible.

CHET FELT AS IF HE'D FOUGHT THE FIRE FOR twenty-four hours, but in truth, it hadn't taken long for the barn and all that was in it to be destroyed. At least none of the nearby outbuildings had been lost—and no horses either. He was grateful for that mercy.

As the firefighters began to mop up, Chet turned toward the house. Kimberly and Anna were on the porch with Pete and Tara. Chet had no idea when the two teenagers had returned from their ride, but it was good to know they were home and safe. He had enough to worry about.

The barn was a complete loss. It would have to be rebuilt

without delay. He couldn't run an operation like this one without a sizable barn. Feed had been lost too. And tack. Lots of tack. Where would the money come from to replace all of that? Insurance would cover a lot but not all. Not enough. Insurance never covered enough. He would have to take out a bank loan, and that didn't sit well with him. Chet preferred to heed the Proverb that warned, "the borrower becomes the lender's slave." But what choice would he have now?

Feeling the weight of it all press down on his shoulders, he walked toward the house and climbed the steps to the porch.

Anna reached out to touch his forearm. "Chet, I'm so sorry."

Sorrow mingled with weariness in her eyes, and for the first time since her return to the ranch, Chet thought she looked her age. He patted her hand, at a loss for words.

"How did it start, Dad?"

Chet looked at his younger son and shook his head. "I don't know."

Sam came up the steps then. His face was streaked with soot, his hair gray with ash, his expression grim. Like Chet's own expression, he imagined. Sam glanced back to where the barn had stood. "The chief says they'll be here until they're sure there's no more chance it could flare up again."

Kimberly said, "If you'd like, Tara and I could fix sandwiches for everybody. Get something for the men to drink. They must be hungry and thirsty by now."

"That's a good idea, dear," Anna added. "I'll help too."

The threesome went into the house, leaving Chet alone with his sons.

"It's bad, isn't it, Dad?" Sam said. "Money-wise, I mean."

"Bad enough."

"You can use my college fund if you want."

Chet laid his hand on Sam's shoulder. "Not a chance. You're only a year away from graduation. You're going to need that money . . . and a scholarship."

"Doubt that's going to happen."

"You'd better *make* it happen."

It was something Chet had said often to Sam, especially over the last couple of years. Not that it did a lot of good. Sam was a smart kid, but he wasn't an enthusiastic student. He never had seen much value in the extra effort it would take to get straight A's. He was as content with a B or a C. Pete, on the other hand, loved to learn, loved to excel at whatever he tried his hand. He enjoyed a mental challenge.

"Dad?" Sam's voice pulled Chet's wandering thoughts back to the present. "What do you need Pete and me to do now?"

Chet rubbed a hand over his face before answering. "Better find the horses we turned out of the barn when the fire started. Don't want them getting onto the highway." He glanced west. "Last I saw them, they were running that direction."

Both of the boys nodded without comment, then went down the steps. Chet watched them walk to the two horses Pete and Tara had ridden earlier. Sam adjusted the stirrups, swung into the saddle, and the brothers rode away from the barnyard.

Drawing a deep breath, Chet headed back toward the remains of the barn and the mop-up efforts.

Anna

1947

It was a Sunday afternoon. One of those soft spring days, late in May, when warmth painted the valley and surrounding mountains in a golden haze. Calves and colts frolicked in the fields not far from their mothers. Kittens meowed and squeaked inside the barn, and puppies played with Richie—who would be two years old come July—in the small fenced yard on the side of the house.

As for Anna, her attention was fully captured by Miles Stanley as he stood with Abe near one of the corrals. Why was he here? Had he come to buy a horse? Or maybe he hoped to find work on the ranch this summer. Abe had mentioned not long ago that he needed some extra help around the place. Wouldn't it be something if Miles became the new hired hand? Her heart thrilled at the mere thought of it.

"Go join them." Violet reached to pick up her son, who giggled and tried to run beyond her grasp. "Invite Miles in for some coffee and cake when they're through with whatever they're discussing. I'm going to put Richie down for his nap."

Anna's stomach twisted into a knot of nerves. It had been more than a year since Miles had come to live and work in Kings Meadow, and he still didn't seem to know she was alive. Oh, he was polite and courteous but nothing more. If he thought anything of her, it was that she was still a child. Why couldn't he see how much more grown-up she was than when they'd first met? She was seventeen, a young woman, and she loved him with a woman's heart.

She smoothed her hands over the new dress Violet had made for her. It was the latest style, inspired by a designer named Dior. She was thankful she hadn't changed out of it after church. She'd meant to. She'd planned to go for a ride after the family had eaten their dinner and the dishes had been washed. But then Miles had arrived, and every other thought had fled her mind.

Drawing a deep breath, she walked across the barnyard to where the two men stood. Abe noticed her first. "Anna, come over here. I was telling Miles about the horses we've added this spring."

Her cheeks flushed as Miles turned toward her. "Hello—" Should she call him Miles or Mr. Stanley? "—Miles."

He smiled. It was a glorious smile. Did he have any idea the effect it had on her? "Good to see you again, Anna. Been awhile."

Ages and ages. Even in such a small town, they managed to miss seeing each other. "Violet wants you to come inside for some coffee and cake when you're through out here." She wanted to groan. She sounded like a child delivering a message from her mother. But she wasn't a child. How could she make Miles see that?

"Sounds good." Another smile. "Abe showed me your stallion. He's really something."

Horses. She was comfortable talking about horses. "Did you come to buy one of Star's foals?"

"No." He shook his head. "No place to keep a horse, even if I had the money. Which I don't."

Anna didn't know what to say next. Did he want her to leave? If he didn't say something soon, she—

"Would you let me paint Shiloh's Star?" he asked.

"Paint?"

Abe said, "Miles is an artist in his spare time. Haven't you seen the painting he did for Emma Carter? I thought everybody in town had seen it by now."

Anna shook her head.

"We'll have to make certain you do. That's why Miles is here today. I've asked him to paint a family portrait. But don't tell Vi just yet. I want to surprise her."

Still looking at Anna, Miles said, "It means I'll be spending quite a bit of time out here. Hope I won't be a bother."

A bother? Never. Abe had just given Anna an even better present than he planned to give Violet.

Eighteen

THE DESTRUCTION OF THE LEONARDS' BARN WAS the main topic of conversation the following morning before the service at Meadow Fellowship. Chet, Anna, and the boys weren't present, no doubt because they were still cleaning up what the fire and firemen had left behind. Kimberly heard several men mention driving out to the Leonard ranch that afternoon to offer whatever help they could. She decided she and Tara would do the same.

She'd had a difficult time sleeping the previous night. She'd kept seeing the look on Chet's face before she and Tara left the ranch. Discouragement had been etched in the corners of his mouth, in the creases of his forehead. She wanted to do *something* to help ease his worries. He'd been kind to her and her daughter. Much more generous with his time and resources than he'd needed to be with a couple of newcomers to the area.

When the church service came to an end, Kimberly

couldn't remember anything the pastor had shared in his sermon. It made her feel a bit guilty as she shook his hand on the way out of the sanctuary.

Once they were in the car, Kimberly drove to the grocery store to purchase fried chicken. A large bucket of it. If Chet had a bunch of volunteers show up, he would need plenty to feed them. She also bought large containers of potato salad and coleslaw and three dozen rolls. It cost more than she could afford to spend, but she didn't care. It wasn't like she had a lot of overhead expenses, thanks to her best friend's generosity, as well as Chet's.

Neither Kimberly nor Tara needed to go home to change clothes. Jeans and boots were the norm on Sunday mornings. One of the pluses of attending a church in a community like Kings Meadow. So after a second stop, this time at the gas station, they headed up the highway to the Leonard ranch.

The Welches were not the first to arrive. A mix of pickup trucks and automobiles was parked in the field on the left side of the lane leading to the house. Kimberly pulled into the first open space. When they walked into the barnyard, they saw men hauling charred boards from where the barn had stood yesterday morning and dumping them onto the bed of a decades-old two-ton truck.

"Let's take the food into the house," Kimberly said to Tara. "Then we'll find Chet and see how else we can help."

Anna was in the kitchen, preparing a pot of coffee, when they entered a couple of minutes later. The older woman didn't look quite as drained today as she had yesterday. Kimberly was thankful for that.

"We brought food for the volunteers." She held up the sacks in her hands.

Anna tried to smile, but she wasn't very successful. "Bless you, dear."

"Why don't you sit down and let me finish that?"

"No need. It's ready to go." As if in proof, she punched the Brew button on the front of the coffeemaker.

Kimberly set the food they'd brought on the counter, next to several casserole dishes covered with foil or cellophane. She hadn't been the only person to realize the volunteers and family would need to be fed.

Fingers jammed into the back pockets of her jeans, Tara asked, "How can we help, Ms. McKenna?"

"I really don't know, dear. You'll need to ask Chet or one of the boys."

Tara looked at her mom. "I'm gonna see if I can find Sam or Pete."

"Okay. Come get me if there's something I can do right now. Otherwise, I'll be out in a bit."

Her daughter nodded before leaving the kitchen.

Anna sank onto a chair and released a sigh.

Kimberly wished she had words of encouragement, but her mind was blank. She wondered if she should put the food into the refrigerator or if the men outside would want to eat soon. Indecision held her still.

Into the silence, Anna said, "The chief said he's convinced it wasn't arson that started the fire. No need for a lengthy investigation. That's good since Chet's determined to get up a new barn as quickly as possible. Bringing in a qualified investigator would surely take a lot of time."

"Arson?" Kimberly said. "I didn't know it was even suspected."

"It wasn't. But they have to consider everything at first."

Kimberly sat in a chair opposite Anna. "You look awfully tired. Why don't you go lie down? I can manage the food and coffee."

"No, dear. But thank you." Anna's smile was fleeting. "I don't think I could sleep even if I tried."

The kitchen door opened and Sam entered the house. "Tara said you brought fried chicken. Can I have some? I'm starved."

Perhaps Kimberly couldn't make Anna rest for a while, but she could make sure the elderly woman didn't have to feed the hungry. "Everyone must be starved by now." Kimberly stood, ready to take action. "Sam, we need a table set up in the yard in the shade. If you'll do that, I'll bring out the food and paper plates and cups and so forth. Then we can all eat."

MOST OF THE VOLUNTEERS WHO'D COME TO HELP with the cleanup didn't leave until suppertime. Amazing, the amount of work they'd accomplished.

Chet said a prayer of thanks for his friends and neighbors as he watched the last truck roll down the driveway to the highway, a cloud of dust rising behind the tires. As he started to turn toward the house, he noticed Kimberly's car still parked in the field. So the last of the volunteers hadn't left after all.

He rubbed the back of his neck with one hand, feeling the grit that had collected there during the day. He was sweaty and sooty and too tired to be hungry. All he wanted now was a shower and then to fall into bed. With any luck, he would be able to sleep.

He slowly climbed the steps to the porch, feeling like an old man. Inside, he found Anna seated at the kitchen table and Kimberly, wearing an apron, at the sink, washing a casserole dish. From the living room came the sounds of a video game.

"Pete and Tara are playing Mario something or other," Anna said. "Sam went up a bit ago to take a shower."

"That's where I'm headed."

Kimberly turned from the sink, drying her hands with a towel. "Tara and I should go home."

Chet wanted to ask her to stay. Wanted her there more than he cared to admit. To her or to anyone. Including himself. But now was not the time to add another complication to his life. And the attraction he felt for Kimberly Welch would be just that. A complication. She'd told him outright that she had no intention of remaining in Kings Meadow, and since he had no plans to ever leave here, nothing could come of his feelings anyway.

"Thanks, Kimberly," he finally said. "You've been a great help the last couple of days."

"Tara and I were glad to do what we could. We're so sorry this happened to you."

He nodded wordlessly, then headed for the stairs. Once inside the master bathroom, he shed his soot-covered clothes and got into the shower. Eyes closed, he stood beneath the pulsing water, turning it to the hottest temperature he could stand, and braced his hands against the tiles. The spray hit him on the top of the head. Water ran down the sides of his face.

Replacing the barn with one of equal size and quality would be expensive. Over a hundred thousand dollars, even with some volunteer help. He had insurance, but it wouldn't cover the entire cost of a new barn plus replacing everything else that was lost. He would need a loan for whatever the insurance didn't cover. Cash flow. It always came down to cash flow.

If we could just have one really great year where nothing went wrong. One without surprises. If I could just get a bit of breathing room . . .

He felt a sudden loneliness, a strong need to be able to pour out his concerns to someone who walked beside him, day in and day out. He couldn't do that with his sons. He couldn't do it with Anna McKenna either. He needed a partner, a life companion. He needed . . . He wanted . . .

Kimberly's image came to mind. He'd only known her a couple of months, and yet his thoughts were filled with her. As if he'd been collecting mental snapshots whenever he was with her.

She doesn't even like horses. She's afraid of them. I raise and sell horses. That's what I do! That's what I'll always do!

If Chet wanted to choose the most unlikely woman to fill his thoughts, Kimberly Welch was surely her. She didn't like small towns. Didn't want to live in Idaho. Didn't like horses. She would be all wrong for him. Any fool could see that.

He needed to nip this attraction in the bud. He *would* nip it in the bud. Now. Right now. His heart had been broken once before. Once was enough.

Nineteen

FOR CHET, THE NEXT TWO WEEKS WERE FILLED with insurance forms and bank loan documents and talking to contractors and suppliers. He hardly noted the end of the school year for the boys, although he was thankful for two extra pairs of hands on weekdays. He was also thankful that Anna didn't let him forget Sam's birthday, which he would have without her reminder. They marked the date with a cake and a few gifts, but nobody felt much like celebrating. The fire was too fresh in everyone's minds.

Tara came out to the ranch more frequently with the arrival of summer break, but Chet rarely saw Kimberly, other than at a comfortable distance at church. Tara told him her mother had a new job, thanks to the recommendation of Christopher Russell, the insurance broker. Kimberly was now working for the mayor of Kings Meadow as his personal assistant and, according to Tara, found her new position interesting.

Chet didn't doubt that. Mayor Oliver Abbott was as colorful

a character as he'd ever known. In his sixties, Ollie—as every-body called him—knew a thousand stories about the valley and its residents, and he loved to share them with anyone who would listen. He had a long, bushy beard and matching bushy eyebrows and crooked front teeth that showed when he smiled, which he did often. Ollie could have been the picture in the dictionary under the term *mountain man*. When he was in the office, he dressed up his boots and jeans with a plaid jacket he'd owned since the dawn of time—or at least since the '70s.

On the second Monday in June, Chet drove into town to sign a few more documents for his loan. When he was finished at the bank, he walked a block and a half east to Heather Books. He'd ordered a handbook on horsemanship to give to Tara for her birthday, which was a couple weeks after Sam's. Chet knew they didn't have to give the girl a gift, but he wanted to anyway. She'd been more help than bother over the past couple of months. A pleasant surprise.

Upon entering the narrow but deep bookshop located on the main drag through town, he greeted the owner, Heather Kilmer.

"I've got your order under the counter here," she said, reaching for it.

"I'm going to browse a bit first."

"Okay. Just let me know when you're ready."

He nodded before moving down the aisle on the right side of the store. Midway, he came to the history section—his favorite—and began to peruse the titles on the shelves. Not that he had much time to indulge in pleasure reading.

He pulled a large paperback volume on the Irish off the shelf and started to read the back cover.

"Hello, Chet."

He glanced left to find Kimberly standing nearby. He felt a strange catch in his chest. Did she always look this pretty? Her hair fell in dark curls over her shoulders. Her eyes looked a deeper green than usual. Probably the lighting in the store. No denying it. He'd missed seeing her, talking to her.

"Book shopping?" she asked.

"Just browsing." He shelved the book in his hand. "I hear you're working for the mayor now. How's it going?"

"Quite well, actually. It's never the same from one day to the next. Mayor Abbott is nice . . . and amusing." She smiled, her expression saying more about her new job than her words had. "Tara says it won't be long before the new barn starts going up."

"Not long. By the end of the week, maybe."

Kimberly glanced toward the shelves nearest her, then back to Chet. "And the guesthouse? Has Anna found any more antiques of interest?"

"Afraid I've been too preoccupied to ask her. I'm not even sure Anna's been going over there since the fire. If so, she hasn't mentioned it to me."

"But Tara's supposed to be helping her. She—"

"Don't worry, Kimberly. Tara's working hard around the ranch. She's more than paying for her lessons and Wind Dancer's keep."

Relief filled her eyes.

"You know," Chet said, "the Leonards owe you and Tara a dinner." He hadn't planned to say that. The words spilled from his mouth of their own accord.

"What?"

"The day of the fire. You were supposed to stay and eat with us that night. Something more than those sandwiches you helped make for the volunteers."

"Oh." A breathy sound, one that could mean anything. Then an expression he couldn't quite read flitted across her face and was gone. "You don't owe us, Chet."

"And the next day you brought chicken and potato salad and coleslaw to feed everybody who was helping with the mop up. We owe you two dinners."

She shook her head, which only made him all the more determined to make her accept his invitation.

"Come out to the ranch on Saturday with Tara. Anna's missed talking to you. I know that without asking. You can stay for supper. We'll have a cake for Tara's birthday. Bring Janet with you and it'll be a party."

"You know it's Tara's birthday?"

"Sure." He shrugged. "But if you have other plans . . ." He let the words trail into silence, wishing he hadn't given her an out.

Kimberly glanced at her wristwatch, as if it would provide an answer for her. "All right. We'll come. Now, I must get back to the office. My lunch hour is almost over." A fleeting smile. "It was good to run into you, Chet."

WHY DID YOU AGREE TO GO? WHY?

Kimberly quickened her pace as she headed toward the mayor's office.

Of course, she didn't have to look hard for an answer. She *wanted* to spend some time with Chet. She'd missed him. Which was silly. It wasn't as if they'd spent a lot of time together in the past. And yet, it had been enough that not seeing him left a vacuum in her life.

Okay, she would admit it. She found Chet Leonard charming in the extreme. Not to mention gorgeous to look at. But admitting it reminded her why it would be a mistake to give in to those feelings. He was completely unsuitable for her. Oh, there were attractive things about him and about his ranch, about the life he led there with his sons and Anna McKenna. Attractive . . . but not right for someone like her. She could admire the night sky without wanting to become an astronaut.

And besides, his invitation could be nothing more than neighborliness. It didn't have to mean he was attracted to her too. Folks were big on being neighborly in this town.

She opened the door to the city office building and walked to her desk where she opened a drawer and dropped her purse into the empty space.

"That you, Kimberly?" Ollie called from inside his office.

"Yes, it's me. Did you need something?"

"Nope." The mayor appeared in the doorway. "Don't need a thing." He pointed at her desktop. "You didn't find the novel you wanted?"

The novel! She'd forgotten the reason she'd gone into Heather Books on her lunch hour. Janet had talked her into joining the book club that met in the library each month, and she needed to buy and read this month's selection.

She settled onto her chair as she shook her head. "I'll have to check back later."

"That surprises me. Long as the club gives her enough

notice, Heather always has plenty of copies on hand for the women." The mayor knew just about everything that went on in his town—including, it seemed, what happened in the women's-only book club.

"It's my own fault. I ran into a friend and got to talking and forgot to ask for the book. It's almost time to start reading the next selection. Maybe I'll get that one instead."

Ollie closed his office door behind him. "I'm headed to a meeting with a couple councilmen. Then I've got a repairman due at the house. My wife wants me to be there. We may need a new furnace, and she doesn't want to make that decision on her own. Don't expect I'll be back to the office today. I'll see you in the morning."

"Okay. See you then."

"Don't forget. We lock up at three today."

As if his reminder was necessary. "I won't forget."

The place was quiet after the mayor left. The phone didn't ring even once. Tuesdays through Thursdays, there was a part-time employee in the office with Kimberly. Bonnie Clark was young, only two years out of Kings Meadow High. Her job was to answer the phone and to research any questions that came her way. On Mondays and Fridays, the two days they closed early, Kimberly was the only employee in the office. Last week, she hadn't minded. Today she did. Perhaps because her thoughts kept returning to Chet. She sighed. If only she could trust her heart to not get itself broken again.

Anna

1947

It was September before Miles—having finished the Leonard family portrait—began to paint the portrait of Shiloh's Star. Only the painting wasn't to be of the blood bay stallion by himself. Miles insisted Anna be in the portrait too. She couldn't refuse the request. Didn't want to refuse it. Agreeing meant spending more time with Miles, and she always wanted more time with him.

There was no doubt about it. Anna McKenna was in love. Thoroughly, completely, devastatingly in love. Did Miles have any idea how she felt about him? If he did, he didn't let on.

"That's perfect," he called to her from behind his easel. "Keep that expression. Try not to move."

It was much harder than it sounded, to hold any one particular expression, to stand like a statue. "Have you thought of asking Miss Carter to take a photograph and then paint from it? Everyone says her pictures are gorgeous. Then both me and Star would stand still for you and never change an

167

expression or swat at a fly." The idea appealed to Anna for more than one reason. If Miles was looking at a photograph while he painted, Anna would be free to move about and to gaze upon him with complete freedom.

"Hold still. And forget about a photograph. I could never capture the colors and the life I see before me now if I was looking at a black-and-white picture."

Anna forced herself to focus on the palette Miles held in his left hand, thumb stuck through the hole, board resting on his forearm. A kaleidoscope of oil colors covered the palette's surface. Miles twirled the tip of the brush in his right hand in one color, then another, then applied it to the canvas on the easel. It was pleasant to watch him work, even though she couldn't see what he was doing. He often pressed his lips together, one corner slightly higher than the other, and squinted his eyes. Whenever he glanced up, he seemed to see her but not see her. As if she were in his dreams.

She smiled at the thought. How grand it would be if Miles Stanley dreamed about her. It would only be fair. She dreamed about him. Often.

"Hey, Anna, I told you to hold your expression. Now you're smiling and your smile is too . . . happy. I want a look that's a little mysterious."

She laughed. "But I *am* happy."

"All right then. I'll paint the horse. *He* isn't smiling."

"You are."

"Am I?" He set aside palette and brush, then touched the corners of his mouth with his fingertips. "Well I'll be. You're right."

Any attempt to compose herself would be useless now. So

she didn't even try. Instead she pushed away from the fence and walked toward Miles. "I want to see what you've done."

Miles stepped around the easel, planting himself in her way. "No peeking."

"But—"

"No." He put his hands on her shoulders. "Not until it's finished."

"How long will that be?"

"A lot longer if you don't stand still."

She laughed again as she looked up into his eyes. Miles stood so close. It would be easy for him to lean in and kiss her. She wished he would do it. Whenever she dreamed of him, he always kissed her. If only he would do it for real.

Instead of kissing her, he turned her around and gave her a gentle push back toward the fence. "Go on. I need to work while the light's right."

Oh, the frustration! She wasn't a child. Young, yes, but not a child.

She arrived back at the fence and turned around.

"Move a little to your right. That's it."

You see so much, Miles, with those artist's eyes of yours. Why can't you see how much I love you?

He smiled as he picked up his paintbrush. "Perfect. Now stay put."

Somehow she would make him see more than the expression she wore. Somehow she would make him see into her heart.

Twenty

"Dad?"

Chet looked up from the computer screen.

"I need to talk to you." Sam's expression was grim as he entered the room.

Chet had always tried his best to be available to his sons. No matter when he was needed. No matter what they were interrupting. It had become even more important to him after they lost Rick. "Sure. What do you need?"

Sam sat on the chair at the corner of Chet's desk. "I think it was my fault."

"What was your fault?"

"The fire."

Chet leaned back in his chair, surprised into silence.

"It's been eating at me ever since it happened." Sam stared at a spot on the floor. "I was smoking a cigarette. In the barn. I heard something, thought somebody was coming. I didn't want to get caught so I put it out and left the barn quick." He looked up. "I . . . I'm sorry, Dad. I must not have put it out like I thought."

There was a lengthy silence, one Chet thought he should fill. Now wasn't the right time for a lecture on the dangers of smoking, but that seemed to be all he could think of.

"I thought I put it out, Dad."

"I'm sure you did." Chet cleared his throat. "How long have you been smoking, Sam?"

"Off and on for the past few months." The boy lowered his gaze again. "I don't do it much."

"Any is too much."

"Yes, sir. And I don't plan on doing it again. I promise."

Chet nodded. "I'm glad to hear it."

Possible causes of Sam's behavior—sneaking around, smoking on the sly, lying to his father by omission if not commission—raced through Chet's mind. But in the end, the reasons didn't seem to matter. Sam knew better.

"I'm going to have to think about this," he said after another silence. "There's going to have to be some kind of punishment, you know."

"Yeah. I know. But could we keep the reason between us?"

"Yeah, I suppose we can."

Sam stood. "I really am sorry, Dad."

"I know you are. And, Son?"

"Yeah."

"Thanks for owning up to it."

"Sure."

After Sam left the room, Chet got up and closed the door. Then he did some pacing, hands clasped behind his back. His office wasn't a large room, and pacing required frequent turns. To the window. To the bookcase. To the window. To the bookcase. It didn't take long to become almost dizzy with it. Or maybe what made him feel that way were the troubled turns of his thoughts.

How was he to handle this? As he'd said, there had to be some kind of punishment, whether or not a cigarette had been the cause of the fire—and they would never know for certain. So what did Sam's behavior warrant? He wasn't a grown man, but he wasn't a kid either. That made punishment a little trickier. There weren't a whole lot of options available to Chet. No cell phone to take away. No extra chores to be added when the kid already worked as hard as the hired hands.

Chet released a sigh. Looked like the truck would be off limits to Sam for a while.

LYING ON THE SOFA, KIMBERLY AWAKENED BY degrees. The book she'd been reading before drifting off was open on her chest, pages down. The television's audio had been turned low.

"Welcome back," Janet said from the easy chair.

"How long was I asleep?" She sat upright, lowering her legs over the side of the couch.

"Over an hour."

She pushed her hair back from her face. "Where's Tara? In her room?"

"No. She went over to Ned and Susan's. Helping out with Ned's colt, I think."

"You'd think after spending almost the whole day at the Leonard ranch she would get her fill of horses."

Janet laughed softly. "Only someone who was never horse-crazy herself would think that."

"You would know." Kimberly stifled a yawn, then said, "We're so different, Tara and me. How did that happen? I raised her. Shouldn't we appreciate the same things?"

"Not necessarily. We are all uniquely made. Besides, the two of you aren't all that different."

"You think not? It's like she was born and raised in Kings Meadow. She's happier in this small town than I've seen her in a long, long time. Maybe ever." She shook her head slowly. "What's going to happen when I find a job back in the city and we have to move?"

Janet tipped her head to one side and studied Kimberly. "Are you still looking? You haven't mentioned it in a while."

"Of course I'm still looking. Anytime I discover a position I'm remotely qualified for, I submit an application. So far, not even a nibble. It's depressing. That's why I don't mention it."

"Maybe you aren't supposed to go back to Seattle. Are you sure it's still what you want?"

"Of course I'm sure." Kimberly emphasized each word, as if to better convince her friend of its truth. Or maybe it was herself she needed to convince.

"You could do worse than settle down in Kings Meadow, you know." Janet turned off the TV as she rose from the chair. "I'm getting a Diet Coke. Want one?"

"No thanks." But she stood and followed her friend into the kitchen, where she leaned her backside against the counter. "I like working for the mayor, but it isn't a career. There's no way to advance or make more money."

"Are money and advancement so important?"

"You've never had to wonder how to feed your child, or you wouldn't ask that question."

"Sorry. I didn't mean to be insensitive. I know you have to earn a decent living. But maybe not in the way you think. Maybe God has something different in mind for you." Janet sipped her soda. "You've been happier these past few weeks. I'd like to see you stay that way."

"Being employed helps a lot."

"Oh, is that it? I thought it might have something to do with Chet Leonard."

Kimberly straightened away from the counter. "Why would you say that?"

"I don't know." Janet shrugged. "Just a gut feeling."

"Well, your gut is wrong. Chet's a nice guy, and he's been really good with Tara. Better than I could've dared hope that day I first went to talk to him about her and Wind Dancer. But I've got no interest in Chet other than as a horse trainer and riding instructor."

The words tasted like the lie they were. Her interest in Chet Leonard had become more than she was ready to admit. It had become . . . personal. Much too personal for comfort. She didn't want to walk into a doomed relationship on purpose. The best way to protect all concerned was for her to find a way out of Kings Meadow. The sooner, the better.

Twenty-one

DEVON PARRY, THE VET, PEELED OFF HIS LATEX gloves as he stepped out of the corral. "It doesn't look good, Chet. He's in a bad way."

"Are you saying you can't save him?" Chet looked through the rails at the ailing horse. Shiloh's Thunder had sired some of the best foals to come out of the Leonard ranch. It would be a huge loss if he died.

"I'll do my best, but I can't make any promises. We'll know what his chances look like if he makes it through until morning."

"He was fine yesterday."

The vet didn't answer. He didn't need to. Chet knew what Devon could have said. In his veterinary practice, Devon had lost horses to aneurisms, heart attacks, and toxins of one kind or another. An animal could be healthy in the morning and be dead by nightfall, and too often there wasn't anything a vet or the owner could do to save it. That was just how it was sometimes. Still, the prognosis felt like a sucker punch to the gut. First the barn. Now this.

The crunch of tires on gravel drew his head around. Kimberly and Tara. He wasn't in the mood for riding lessons or guests for dinner. But despite that, he felt a strange comfort at the sight of Kimberly through the car's window. And right now, he would take any comfort he could find.

Devon said, "I've given him something to ease the pain, but if you need me back before morning . . ." He let his words drift into silence.

Chet gave a curt nod, then moved away from the corral as Kimberly and Tara got out of their car. "Afternoon," he greeted them, trying to keep his concern out of his voice.

"Is something wrong with Thunder?" Tara asked. She knew the vet, of course. Chet had called Devon out to give her pinto a thorough physical examination soon after Wind Dancer had come to stay at the ranch.

Before Chet could answer her, he saw Pete exit the house and descend the steps three at a time. The kid still had it bad for Tara. If she returned his feelings, it wasn't obvious. At least not to Chet. The good news was the brothers weren't warring over her.

"What'd the vet say?" Pete asked as he came closer.

"Won't know anything for a while." Chet shook his head. "Listen, I don't have time to give a lesson right now. Why don't you and Tara saddle up and ride to Hazel Creek?"

"Sure thing, Dad. What horse do you want her to ride?"

Chet faced Tara. "Think you and Wind Dancer are ready to get away from the paddocks?"

Her eyes widened before she nodded.

"I think you're ready too. Both of you." He gave her a tight smile, letting her know that he meant his words. To Pete he added, "Keep it at a walk for today. Ride up to the creek and back. That'll give you several changes in terrain. Be cautious at the creek. I don't think it'll bother Wind Dancer but you need to be sure."

"Okay, Dad. We'll do fine."

The teens hurried away.

Kimberly said, "Shouldn't she have helped Anna for a while first?"

"Not today. This is for the best."

Her gaze went to the corral. "Is the horse dying?"

"Maybe. Probably. Doesn't look good."

She was silent awhile, then said, "I'm sorry, Chet."

He had a bad feeling that if he tried to answer her, he might choke on his own emotions. He didn't want to appear weak. Not to this woman. Thankfully, he didn't have to worry about it more than a few seconds before Anna's approach provided the much-needed diversion.

"Hello, Kimberly."

"Hi, Anna."

Anna embraced Kimberly, as if they hadn't seen each other in weeks instead of the previous Sunday at church. "Didn't Janet come?" she asked when she took a step back.

"She had some things to do this afternoon, but she'll be here for dinner."

"Oh, good. She's such a delight."

"Yes, she is." Kimberly glanced toward the cottage. "What are we doing today?"

"Today we're going to take photos and choose prices for

the items we want to sell on eBay. Sam's got his laptop up and running in the guesthouse for us, and I've got my little digital camera. So I think we're set."

"Well then. Let's get started."

Anna looked up at Chet. "You want to join us?"

"Maybe later."

"All right. But before we list everything online, you're going to have to give your okay."

"I trust you, Anna."

"I appreciate that, my boy. But I still want you to look things over."

He leaned down and kissed her on the temple. "Whatever you want. When you need me, just give a holler."

"KIMBERLY, I HAVE A GOOD MIND TO TAKE MY OWN sweet time with the work that's left." Anna tossed the words over her shoulder as she led the way into the cottage. "I'm going to miss having you spend these Saturday afternoons with me when we're done."

"I'll miss it too." Kimberly said it to be polite, then realized how very true it was. "I guess I'll have to come up with other excuses to visit you while I'm still in Kings Meadow."

Anna stopped midway across the small parlor and turned to face Kimberly. "You're leaving?"

She gave a slight shrug. "Not right away. But eventually. When I find a job that will support me and Tara . . . and a horse." Another shrug. "And that's a long shot as things stand right now."

Wearing a saddened expression, Anna sat at the small

writing desk. She clicked on one of the laptop keys, bringing the screen to life. Kimberly joined her there.

With another press of a finger, Anna opened a photo program. "Amazing, isn't it? Maybe you're too young to remember a world without computers, the Internet, e-mail, digital cameras, and smartphones." She clucked her tongue and shook her head. "So many of my friends in Florida refused to learn the latest technologies as they came along. They had no idea how much not knowing would cut them off from others. From children and grandchildren and great-grandchildren."

"You seem to know your way around the computer."

"I've always loved to learn new things. Still do." Anna tapped her temple with an index finger. "As long as the old brain stays sharp."

"I seem to be more interested in old things." Kimberly caressed the top and side of the writing desk. "Like this. It's at least a hundred years old. You can't find anything like it today. The craftsmanship is exquisite. Priceless, really."

"Well, we won't have to put a price on it. It's not for sale." Anna smiled. "I spent many years writing letters and keeping a journal on this very desk. It belonged to Violet, Chet's grandmother." Her expression turned wistful. "Violet gave the desk to me on my eighteenth birthday because she said it was made for a woman's use and the Leonard men admired horseflesh, not furniture." She laughed softly. "Still true."

"But you didn't take the desk with you when you moved to Florida. Why not?"

"Because it belonged here, on this ranch, more than it belonged to me. It's part of the history of this valley and of the Leonards." Her eyes seemed to look beyond Kimberly and into the past. "So much history."

"If only it could talk. It's a shame it got buried under all of the other things that were stored in this guesthouse. I'm glad you're going to use it again."

"Me too."

Anna

1947

ANNA AND MILES RODE THEIR HORSES TO THE FAR-
thest end of the Leonard land. On the hillside, framed by
trees of green and gold, was a small line shack, one of several
erected before the turn of the century to accommodate cow-
boys who needed to take shelter in foul weather. With the
grazing lands all fenced, the cabins hadn't been used in years.

"What's this?" Miles asked as they reined in their mounts.

Anna told him the history of the line shacks, then slipped
to the ground and reached into the saddlebag for the sandwiches she'd packed for them. "Come inside and we'll eat."
Her heart pounded in her ears as she opened the door.

Early that morning, she'd ridden to the shack by herself.
She'd swept it clean of dust and cobwebs. She'd placed a bouquet of colorful dried flowers in a jar in the center of the
rickety table. She'd put fresh linens and blankets on the old
tick mattress and built a fire in the stove to take away the
autumn chill from the dim interior. The room was still warm

all of these hours later. She moved inside and waited for Miles to follow.

Miles was leaving Kings Meadow next week. He was going to California to paint. He'd told her he would return in the spring. But would he? It was terrible to think she might never see him again. The ache in her heart was unbearable.

"Anna?"

She turned around. He stood framed in the doorway, the outside light a golden backdrop behind him. She wished she knew what he thought.

"Why are we here, Anna?"

"I love you, Miles," she whispered, unable to keep those words to herself another moment.

His gaze flicked to the small, inviting bed she'd made for them. Understanding dawned in his eyes. "Anna . . . we can't do this."

"I love you and you're going away."

"I'll be back in the spring. I told you."

She took a step toward him. "What if you don't return? What if you like California more than Idaho?" She took a quick breath. "What if you meet someone?"

"You're only seventeen."

"I'll be eighteen in the spring."

Miles closed the distance between them, took the bag that held their sandwiches from her hand and dropped it onto the small table. Then he gathered her into his arms, pulling her close, rubbing his chin against the top of her head. Tears slipped from beneath her closed eyelids and dampened his shirt. She didn't want him to ever let go.

Say you love me. Say you love me too. Please say it.

Softly, he said, "I'll only be gone six months, maybe seven. It isn't so very long."

It was an eternity.

"Anna, I can't break Abe's and Violet's trust." He leaned back, then tilted her head with his index finger beneath her chin so their eyes could meet. "I can't break your trust either."

"You wouldn't be break—"

"Maybe you wouldn't think so today, but one day you would. When you got married. It would matter to you then."

Tears welled up again, blinding her. What difference would it make once he was her husband? Didn't he want her?

"Anna . . . don't think that. You're wrong."

"Don't think what?"

"Believe me. I want you." His smile was gentle and loving. "But I care for you too much to take you to bed before we're married."

Her heart hiccupped. *Before? Not if?*

His hands moved up to cup the sides of her face. His fingers felt soft against her skin. "Listen to me, Anna. I'm not proposing. Not yet. You're young. After I'm gone, you might change your mind. You are the one who might meet someone else. I won't ask you to promise me anything today. We'll wait and see."

I won't change my mind. I won't.

He hadn't said he loved her. Not exactly. But the words were implied. He meant to propose to her when he returned. She could hold onto that while she waited for him, while she grew a little older.

Still cupping her face, he leaned down and kissed her for the first time. Her heart galloped in response. The room seemed to spin, and her legs were unwilling to keep her upright. It was more wonderful than she'd dreamed.

He drew back, although not far. When he spoke, his voice sounded gruff. "Come on. We'd better get you home."

Home for Anna would be wherever Miles was. Didn't he know that?

He turned, took hold of her by the hand, and drew her outside, into the soft light of the afternoon. When they reached her horse, he held her by the waist until she stepped up into the saddle. She missed the warmth of his hands at once.

"Anna."

She looked down at him.

"You'll be thankful for this one day."

Tears welled in her eyes, and all she could do was nod. There were no words left to be said.

Twenty-two

CHET AND SAM PREPARED THE DINNER THAT NIGHT, and no matter how often Kimberly—and Janet, who arrived around five o'clock—offered to help, they were turned down. "You're our guests," they were told.

Tara, the birthday girl, didn't get back from her ride with Pete until it was almost time to eat. Both of the teens dashed off to separate bathrooms to wash up and returned before all of the food had been set on the table. As Tara took her seat opposite her mother, Kimberly couldn't help seeing the sparkle of happiness in the girl's eyes. Would it still be there if they moved back to the city?

No. Not *if. When. When* they moved back to the city. It might take longer than Kimberly wished, but it would happen. She was gaining work experience. Her résumé wasn't as blank as it had been when they arrived in Kings Meadow. She didn't look as unemployable on paper as she had a year ago.

But Tara won't want to go.

Yes, she would. When the time came, Kimberly would be able to make her see why it was for the best.

With everyone seated at the table, Chet spoke a blessing, and then the passing of platters and serving bowls began. Baked glazed ham, one of Tara's favorite foods. Au gratin potatoes. Peas with baby onions. Homemade dinner rolls—one of Anna's specialties.

Kimberly's thoughts continued to wander, aware of the conversations taking place around the table but tuning them out until Tara spoke into a temporary lull. "Mr. Leonard, I was telling Pete that you oughta fix those little cabins up and rent them out. I mean the line shacks. You know. Fix them up for glamping."

"Glamping?" Chet raised an eyebrow. "What's that?"

"Glamorous camping. It started in Europe, I think. People are paying big money for the experience. It's camping without all of the inconveniences. Roughing it but with the same amenities as a nice hotel." Enthusiasm animated Tara's face. "You could give guests a dude ranch experience and provide all kinds of comfort. Nice beds. Fancy sheets and down comforters. Besides horseback riding, they could go white-water rafting too. That'd bring even more of 'em. And if you don't have enough cabins, you could do canvas tents on platforms."

Chet put down his fork. "How do you know so much about this . . . glamping?"

"One of my friends in Seattle. Patty's parents went glamping in Ireland this spring. They stayed in a yurt, and they rode bikes all around that part of Ireland. I saw some cool pictures of what they did over there, so I looked at glamping sites in the US. There's no reason you couldn't do it on your ranch. Who wouldn't want to come stay here? It's so pretty."

Patty. Patty Wainright. The girl's parents had been acquaintances of Kimberly's and Ellis's, although the Wainrights' wealth had given them entry into much higher circles of society. She hadn't known Tara was in touch with Patty again. Was that a good thing?

"I don't think I'm cut out to be an innkeeper," Chet said after a moment of silence.

"You wouldn't have to be anything like an innkeeper. Besides, Mom could run it for you. She and Dad used to take trips and stay in some fancy places. She'd know how to make it work, I'll bet, and she's good with people."

Kimberly felt her eyes widen. She knew plenty about what people desired in a luxury hotel. When Ellis was alive, they'd stayed in quite a few of them on their travels, both in the States and abroad. But in these mountains? In old shacks? Glamping? She was clueless. Why would anyone want to spend their vacations in a place like this?

For the peace and tranquility. For the beauty of nature. Because it's so pretty.

Fine. Tara was right. It *was* beautiful. But that didn't mean Kimberly wanted to be a part of this glamping nonsense.

Janet said, "Chet, I think Tara may have hit on a great idea. It could be a real moneymaker for you."

"Sounds like a lot of extra work and frustration," he answered.

Janet turned toward Anna. "Don't you have a bunch of things in the guesthouse you were planning to sell? Couldn't you use some of those items to fix up those cabins?"

"Yes. We could."

"I'll volunteer to help any way I can," Janet added.

"Me too," the three teenagers all said at once.

Anna looked at Chet at the head of the table. "It does sound rather exciting," the elderly woman said. "You could have guests from June through hunting season every year. You should at least look into it."

"I suppose I could do that," he said with obvious reluctance.

Kimberly felt sorry for Chet. With all the excitement generated around the table, nobody seemed to be listening to his hesitation. But she heard it. She heard it and sympathized. Because she didn't want to get caught up in it any more than he did.

IT WAS LIKE BEING SWEPT DOWNRIVER IN A STRONG current. To Chet, the idea of renting out the old line shacks sounded outrageous. Surely it would be a way to lose money, not make it. And yet there was a tug of anticipation in his chest as he listened to everyone tossing out ideas. Everyone except Kimberly. She looked as if she too thought the idea implausible. If he was crazy enough to try this glamping thing, would Kimberly consider helping with its operation? She already had a job with the mayor. But maybe she could help him out part-time. He liked the idea of seeing her at the ranch more often. He imagined the two of them sharing his office, using the computer. He imagined shared laughter. He imagined—

He brought the thought up short. Enough with his

imagination when it came to Kimberly. Better not to go in that direction.

"Nana Anna, where's my laptop?" Sam asked.

"Still in the guesthouse."

"Dad, can I go get it?" His son started to rise.

Chet shook his head. "Wait until after dinner."

"It would only take a—"

"After dinner."

Sam grumbled something as he settled back into his chair.

Chet heard the sound of a throat clearing even as he saw the gazes of those around the table shift to the doorway behind him. He knew, without looking, that it must be Blake. The ranch hand had volunteered to keep an eye on Shiloh's Thunder this evening. He wouldn't have interrupted Tara's birthday dinner unless the horse had taken a turn for the worse.

Chet set his napkin on the table and pushed back his chair. "You all finish eating. I'll be back as soon as I can."

Somber faces looked back at him. The excitement of moments before drained away. Like Chet, they all knew what must have brought Blake into the house.

Chet drew a quick breath as he turned around and followed his ranch hand through the kitchen and out the door. "Did you call the vet?" he asked as soon as they were outside.

"Yeah, I called him. He's tending another animal on the other side of the valley, but he said he'll come as soon as he can. I don't think it makes much difference now."

At the corral, Chet drew another breath, hoping to calm that sick sensation in his gut. Then he opened the gate and went in. The horse's breathing was shallow, his eyes closed.

He didn't even attempt to lift his head as Chet squatted and stroked his neck. Blake was right. It wouldn't matter if the vet got there or not. As if in answer to Chet's thought, Thunder made a soft sound, similar to a sigh, and then all was quiet. The stallion was gone.

Emotion tightened Chet's throat as he stood.

Blake said, "I'll see that he's buried first thing in the morning."

Chet nodded.

"I'm sorry, boss."

"Thanks."

Blake came to stand beside Chet. "He was a great horse."

"Yeah. One of the best."

"Want me to wait around until Devon gets here?"

"No, thanks." Chet turned his back toward the dead horse. "I'll call and tell him there's no need to come. See you in the morning."

Blake hesitated a moment longer, as if trying to find something more to say, then he left the corral. Chet stayed in the corral until the ranch hand had turned his truck onto the highway. Then he walked to the gate and pressed his forehead against the top rail.

God . . .

He wanted to pray but was unable to form the words.

God . . .

It wasn't just the potential loss of stud fees that made his heart heavy, although that mattered. No, it was more than that. The death felt . . . personal. As if he'd been abandoned. Again.

God . . .

190

Crazy. Made no sense. He was a practical man. Ranching needed a level head and a calm outlook. Animals took sick and died or they grew old and died. Dogs. Cats. Horses. They matured and were slaughtered for food. Cattle. Hogs. Sheep. He'd seen it countless times. He would see it many more times if he lived long enough.

A sound drew his head up from the railing. Kimberly walked toward him. Seeing her, the heaviness in his chest lightened a little. One more feeling that made no sense. He opened the gate and left the corral. Kimberly stopped and waited for him to reach her.

"Thunder?" she asked softly.

"He's gone." Chet glanced toward the house. "Did you have cake yet?"

She shook her head. "No. The spark kind of went out of the party after you left. I guess everyone knew what was happening out here."

"Sorry it spoiled Tara's birthday."

"She's more worried about you, I think."

From the look in her eyes he could see that the same was true of Kimberly. He wanted to hold her in his arms and draw strength from her slight frame. It was as if he'd held her before and knew how it would be. How holding her would make him feel. Alive again. He wanted to draw her close and bury his face in her long, dark hair. He wanted to breathe in the faint citrusy fragrance of her shampoo.

Uncertainty flashed in her eyes, as if she'd seen the direction of his thoughts. She moistened her lips with the tip of her tongue. Nerves, he thought. Or did she hope he would kiss her?

Perhaps he would have, were it not for the untimely arrival of Devon Parry. Made Chet wish he'd had enough time to call the vet and stop him from coming. Because now he would never know what might have happened if he and Kimberly had had a little more time, just the two of them.

Twenty-three

SUNDAY MORNING, PETE TOOK ANNA INTO TOWN. Sam stayed at the ranch with his dad for moral support. With a backhoe, it didn't take long to finish the unpleasant task of burying Shiloh's Thunder. Chet and Sam were back at the house before the rest of the family returned from church.

After washing up, Chet poured himself a cup of coffee while Sam made himself a ham sandwich. Then they both sat at the table. For a short while, there were no sounds in the kitchen other than the soft tick of the wall clock, the crunch of lettuce as Sam ate his sandwich, and an occasional slurp of coffee. Before long Chet's thoughts turned again to Kimberly and the increasing attraction he felt for her. Common sense fled. He wanted to be with her, and it no longer mattered to him that her intention was to leave Kings Meadow.

Suddenly, Sam said, "You need to ask her out, Dad."

"What?" He looked up, startled.

"You need to ask Mrs. Welch out on a date."

"Why would you say that?"

"Because you *like* her." Sam's tone implied his father was rowing a boat with only one oar in the water.

"Not sure liking her is enough, Son."

"Maybe not. But it's a good place to start."

Chet shook his head. "I tried dating again. Remember? It didn't work out."

"Come on, Dad. That wasn't the same thing. You were still hoping Mom would come back to us, even after the divorce was final. But she didn't come back and she's never going to. She's gone for good. Now you're ready to move on, to start over. It isn't wrong for you to want to find somebody to love you."

It was a bit strange, being lectured about dating and marriage and love by his son. Chet took another sip of coffee before replying, "Things are different at my age than yours."

"Yeah, you're right. They are different. You're smarter. You understand more 'cause you've lived longer."

If Chet was smarter, if he understood more, would his marriage have failed? Would Marsha still have abandoned him and their sons, turned her back on God, walked away and not even bothered to send birthday cards or make the occasional phone call?

"Pete and I talked about it last night, Dad. We think you oughta ask Mrs. Welch out. We like her too."

Oh, great! Not just a lecture. His teenage sons were plotting behind his back, as well. Pushing him in a direction he wasn't sure he wanted to go.

But that wasn't true. He *did* want to go in that direction. He'd admitted that to himself only moments ago.

"Ask her, Dad. The worst that can happen is she'll turn you down."

No, there was something worse than that. She could say yes. He could lose his heart to her. And then she could leave, go back to Seattle or some other big city, like she'd said she wanted. Could he recover if he fell in love with Kimberly and then she left Kings Meadow? If he was determined to date, wouldn't it be better to ask someone who *wanted* to stay in this valley?

Except he didn't want to try to find another woman. He wanted Kimberly in his life.

"I'll think about it," he said after a lengthy silence. "Now, let's drop it."

Sam grinned as he took his sandwich in both hands. "Sure thing, Dad."

"Hey, Kimmie," Janet called from the living room. "Come look at this."

Seated on a chaise longue in the shade of the patio, Kimberly set aside the book she'd been reading and rose to her feet. "Coming." She slid the screen door aside and entered the house.

"This is so cool."

"What is?"

"This glamping stuff." Janet looked up from her computer. "Your daughter is a genius to have thought of it."

Kimberly grabbed a chair and drew it up to the small desk next to Janet's chair. She leaned forward slightly as Janet pointed to different photographs on the screen. She remembered the excitement around the Leonards' dinner table last night. Then she remembered something else, something that had happened later, that moment when she'd seen something in Chet's eyes. Something she hadn't seen in a man's eyes for several years—desire. And her response? She remembered her response too. The flutter in her belly. The breathless anticipation. What would have happened if the vet hadn't arrived? Would Chet have kissed her? She'd wanted him to—and the wanting frightened her.

"Look at this adorable cabin," Janet said. "It makes me think of something you might see in the Swiss Alps."

Kimberly suddenly felt irritable. "And when were you last in the Swiss Alps?"

Her friend leaned back in the chair and turned her full attention in Kimberly's direction. "You're as prickly as a porcupine."

"Sorry. I don't know what's wrong with me."

Janet released a sound of disbelief, half laugh, half snort.

"What was that for?"

"Kimmie, you might not know what's wrong with you, but I do. You have feelings for a certain cowboy, and you're scared spitless. I get it. You loved Ellis, but he kept things from you and left you in a mess when he died. He hurt and disappointed you. But that doesn't mean you shouldn't let yourself fall in love again and be loved in return."

Kimberly felt her face flame as her annoyance grew. She shot up from the chair and stormed to the patio, the chaise longue, and her book. How could Janet have said that to her?

The trouble with living with a best friend was that said best friend didn't always respect a person's private space. Janet followed Kimberly outside and sat on the edge of a matching chaise longue. Her gaze was gentle, which Kimberly found even more irritating. "Stop running away from life."

"I do no such thing."

"Spare me, girlfriend. You do too. May I remind you that it was Ellis who died. Not you."

Kimberly sucked in a breath. "Janet!"

"Okay, that was harsh. But it's also the truth." Her friend pointed a finger at her. "Did it ever occur to you that maybe God sent you to Kings Meadow so you could meet Chet Leonard?"

"Well, if that's what God wanted, He could have found an easier way to do it than taking away everything I owned and leaving us alone and destitute. Couldn't He?"

"Maybe easy wasn't what you needed."

Kimberly hadn't been this angry in a long, long while. Or this hurt.

In one swift movement, her friend shifted from her chaise longue to the edge of Kimberly's. Janet's expression softened, as did her voice. "Kimmie, you're my dearest friend in all the world." She took hold of Kimberly's hand. "All I want is for you to be happy. You know that. But I feel like I need to shake some sense into you. Remember that line from *Auntie Mame* when Mame says, 'Live! Life's a banquet and most poor suckers are starving to death!' That's what I want to say to you. *Live!* Stop being so afraid of getting hurt again or being disappointed again. Take a chance. You might discover something wonderful."

Inside the house, the telephone rang.

"Think about it." Janet stood and went inside.

Think about it? The anger drained out of Kimberly, leaving an ache in her chest. Tears welled over and streaked her cheeks.

"The phone's for you, Kimmie," Janet said from the doorway.

Kimberly swiped at the tears and sniffed.

"It's Chet Leonard."

She felt her stomach flutter. *Most poor suckers are starving to death.*

"Shall I tell him to call back later?"

"No." Kimberly sniffed again. "No, I'll talk to him."

Anna

1948

LETTERS FROM MILES STANLEY STOPPED ARRIVING at the end of January. First Anna was concerned. Then she was angry. And finally came despair.

Whenever time and weather permitted, Anna rode to the line shack, far from the main house, far from Abe's and Violet's watching eyes. She rode to *their* line shack—hers and Miles's—where she had first confessed her love to him, where she had offered herself to him. Always, she built a fire in the stove and lay on the bed and wrapped herself in a blanket. Then she wept.

He hadn't said he loved her.

It was clear now that he didn't love her.

He'd never intended to come back to her.

Had he found someone new? Someone older? Someone prettier?

The pain in her heart was every bit as great as what she'd felt when her parents died. In some ways it was worse, because she knew how much her parents had loved her. They'd told her so often. But not Miles. Miles had kept those words to himself. They'd been implied but never spoken.

Her eighteenth birthday arrived in mid-March. The day mattered little to her. Growing up. Getting older. It didn't change anything. Miles had said it would but it didn't, now that he was gone. Now that he was silent.

Then a letter from California came in April, addressed to Anna McKenna. The writing on the envelope didn't belong to Miles. She knew his writing as well as her own. But her heart skipped at the sight of the address all the same. She opened it.

> *Dear Miss McKenna,*
>
> *My name is John Anderson. I'm an attorney. Miles Stanley hired me to put his legal affairs in order early this year. It is my sad duty to inform you of his passing after a lengthy illness and to advise you that you are the sole beneficiary of his last will and testament . . .*

There was more writing on the sheet of paper, but the ink blurred before her eyes. The letter fell from her hands and drifted like a feather to the floor.

Then she followed it, blackness swelling over her.

Twenty-four

IT WAS NO SMALL THING, SAM'S GIVING UP HIS TICK-
ets to see Josh Turner perform in Boise. Sam was every bit
as big a fan of the singer as his father, and he'd spent his own
hard-earned cash to buy the tickets when they'd gone on sale
months earlier. When Chet tried to refuse the offer, Sam had
said, "Take 'em, Dad. I'm the one who told you to ask Mrs.
Welch out. It's the least I can do. Don't want you falling on
your face by taking her someplace lame."

"Gee, thanks."

Feeling as nervous as any teenager, he arrived at Janet
Dunn's home a little after four o'clock that Friday afternoon.
Janet answered the ring of the doorbell.

"Come on in," she said, taking a step back. "Kimmie's
almost ready."

Chet ran the fingers of one hand through his hair as he
moved inside. True to Janet's word, Kimberly appeared out
of one of the bedrooms a moment later. She wore a little

black dress, and she looked stunning in it too. The dress had spaghetti straps and a full skirt that ended a couple of inches above her knees. On her feet she wore sky-high black heels. They made her shapely legs look like they were a million miles long. Her nails, both fingers and toes, sported apple-red polish that matched the small purse and sweater she carried.

"Wow," he said, sounding breathless.

A smile curved the corners of her rosy mouth. "Thanks."

Tara appeared behind her mother. "What time are you going to have her back, Mr. Leonard?" She sounded dead serious, but the twinkle in her eyes gave her away.

"Does she have a curfew?" he asked.

"One o'clock or she's gonna be grounded."

"Then I'll have her back before one. Don't want to get her grounded. If I do, she might not agree to go out with me again."

Kimberly turned and gave her daughter a quick kiss on the cheek. She said something softly. Too softly for Chet to hear—and he was sorry for that. Then she moved toward him. He stepped to one side and motioned her through the open door, following right after her, feeling more than a little out of place. What was he doing with this beautiful, sophisticated woman? She was completely out of his league.

All you have to do is get through the next few hours without making a fool of yourself.

He opened the passenger door, then with a hand on her right forearm, helped her into the cab of the pickup. When he started the engine a few moments later, he saw Janet and Tara on the stoop, waving and grinning. Were they the reason

Kimberly had accepted his invitation? He preferred to think she *wanted* to go out with him.

The drive down out of the mountains was mostly a silent one, Chet concentrating on the winding river road, Kimberly gazing out the window at the passing terrain. Pine trees gave way to sagebrush as they neared the valley floor.

Susan Lyle had told Chet of a nice restaurant near downtown. Warm and intimate but not too fancy or expensive. "The chef is marvelous," she'd promised. Chet found the place without any trouble and lucked into a nearby parking space. Inside, the restaurant had soft lighting. A maître d' escorted them to a table and, after they were seated, handed Chet a wine list.

"Do you care for something, Kimberly?"

She declined with a shake of her head.

"Thanks." Chet handed the wine list back to the maître d'. "Nothing for us."

When they were alone again, Kimberly asked, "Have you come here before?"

"No. Susan told me about it when she heard we were going to the concert."

Kimberly offered a hesitant smile. "I thought maybe you brought all your first dates here. It's very nice."

"There's only been one other first date since I got divorced." He shrugged. "It didn't go anywhere. I wasn't ready and neither was she. But she and her husband have become good friends."

"Her husband?"

"Allison and her ex remarried. I was glad to see it happen."

Kimberly's gaze wandered from Chet, taking in the room

and other diners. When she looked at him again, she said, "How do you know you're ready now? To start a relationship, I mean."

"Not sure how to answer that. Emotionally, I'm ready to move on. But I was comfortable being a husband, and I'm not so sure of myself as a date. Do they even call it that today? Dating. I think I've forgotten how a guy's supposed to get to know a girl. What's the best way to impress her?"

HE WANTS TO IMPRESS ME? KIMBERLY FELT A PLEAS-ant warmth in her chest. How flattering.

"Let's get the easy stuff out of the way first. Maybe that will help." He cleared his throat. "How long were you and your husband married?"

"Fifteen years. You?"

"Marsha and I were married for twenty-one years."

Kimberly took a sip from her water glass. "Did Marsha grow up in Kings Meadow too?"

Chet shook his head. "She was from Boise. We met at a rodeo and dated each other for a few years before we married. You and Ellis?"

"We met while I was in college and married right after I graduated."

"Mind me asking how he died? Was it an accident?"

Kimberly stiffened. Talking about Ellis made her uncomfortable—because thinking about him often made her angry, and her anger made her feel guilty. She hadn't shared the brutal truth of that anger with anyone. Not even Janet. "No, it wasn't an accident," she said at last. "He had a heart attack. There wasn't any warning. Just suddenly he was gone. He was only forty."

"Forty?" He shook his head again. "That's mighty young."

She lifted the water glass a second time and took a few more sips. "I believe it was the stress that killed him. Our finances had been unraveling for a long time, but he kept it a secret from me. Maybe if he'd shared the burden of all of—" She broke off suddenly, her throat tight.

"I'm sorry, Kimberly." Chet's words were as gentle as a caress.

She gave him a shaky smile. "Let's talk about something else."

"Okay. What about this? You aren't crazy about horses like your daughter." He put his forearms on the edge of the table and leaned toward her. "So, what are you crazy about? What's your passion, Kimberly Welch?"

"My passion?" Her gaze dropped to her hands, now folded in her lap.

She hadn't a clue how to answer. She'd been in survival mode for such a long while. And before that . . . before Ellis died? When she looked back, many of her activities seemed shallow and self-absorbed. Buying new clothes and jewelry. Visiting the spa regularly. Redecorating their home . . . again . . . and then again. Lavishly entertaining Ellis's business associates. Sending Tara to the best private school possible.

She drew a deep breath and looked at Chet again. "If I ever had something I was truly passionate about, I've forgotten it." She forced a smile. "Tell me yours."

"That's easy." He grinned. "I love the horses, of course. Always have. Love the ranch. Love living in Kings Meadow, knowing where my roots are. Above anything else, I love God and my family. That's what I'm most passionate about." He gave a slight shrug. "Doesn't sound very exciting to some, I suppose, but it's a great life."

He was wrong. There was something about the tone of his voice, about the look in his eyes, that made what he said sound most appealing. Simple. Homespun. Down to earth. It was exciting, only in a different way. Wasn't that odd?

"Penny for your thoughts," he said, his voice low.

"Hasn't the value for a thought gone up to at least a nickel?"

He chuckled, a sound so pleasant it caused her insides to twirl.

As if to rescue Kimberly from that feeling, the waitress arrived at their table to take their order. Neither of them had even glanced at the menu. Kimberly found the first thing that sounded good and pointed it out to the waitress. Chet ordered the same.

As soon as their server walked away, Kimberly turned the conversation to Tara and Wind Dancer, and Chet followed her lead.

JUDGING BY THE SMILE ON KIMBERLY'S LIPS WHEN the lights went up in the arena, she'd enjoyed the concert every bit as much as Chet had. Returning her smile, he took hold of her elbow and eased her out of their row and into the flow of people headed for the exits.

Night had arrived while they were inside the windowless arena. The air was cool enough for Kimberly to need the sweater she'd carried with her all evening. They stepped to one side of the departing throng and stopped. Chet took the red sweater from her hand and held it up so she could slip her arms into the sleeves. As he stood behind her, the breeze carried the now familiar citrus scent of her shampoo, teasing his nostrils.

Sam was right. Chet liked Kimberly. A lot. Far more than he'd been willing to admit up to now. Far more than he'd thought possible, given his past, given their differences. To be honest with himself, he could be falling in love with her. Which didn't seem like a smart thing to do. Unless, of course, he could convince her to stay in Idaho, in Kings Meadow, for good.

On the drive home, they talked about their favorite songs from the concert. Kimberly didn't know a lot about country music—that was obvious—but she'd become a fan of Josh Turner tonight. That pleased Chet.

After all, if she could change her taste in music, maybe he could change her mind about staying in Kings Meadow too.

Twenty-five

Kimberly awakened slowly the next morning. A dream tried to pull her back into sleep. A pleasant dream, though it hastened into foggy corners of her mind with the arrival of full consciousness. Stretching, she opened her eyes. Daylight seeped between slats in the blinds. She rolled onto her side and looked at the clock. It was already after eight. Despite the hour, she was in no hurry to get out of bed.

She closed her eyes again, remembering the previous evening. It had been close to midnight by the time Chet walked her to the door. They'd stood, facing each other, for the briefest of moments. Then Chet had leaned down and kissed her lightly on the mouth. Little more than a brush of lips against lips, but it had sent an unexpected jolt through Kimberly. The memory of it made her feel the same jolt all over again.

A groan escaped her. A cowboy. Really? *Really?* A horse-riding, horse-training, horse-loving cowboy whose family roots were over a century deep in this mountain community.

Chet Leonard was wrong for her for those and so many other reasons.

A soft rap sounded on her door, then her daughter's voice. "Mom?"

Kimberly rolled onto her back again. "I'm awake, honey. Come on in."

Tara entered the room, carrying a large mug of steaming coffee.

"Bless you." Kimberly pushed herself upright and leaned against the pillows and headboard, her arms outstretched to take the mug from her daughter.

Still in her pj's, Tara joined her mother on the bed, sitting cross-legged near the footboard. "How was it?"

"How was what?"

"Mom, you know what I mean." Tara rolled her eyes. "How was last night?"

Kimberly smiled, sipped her coffee, then answered. "If you'd stayed up, I could have told you when I got home. Are you sure you're interested?"

Tara reached out and lightly slapped her mother's shin beneath the covers.

"I had a very nice time, thank you very much. We both did. The concert was terrific."

"So did he kiss you?"

Kimberly cocked an eyebrow. "Not sure that is something you need to know, Miss Snoopy."

"Which means he *did* kiss you." Tara grinned, a look full of self-satisfaction. "I *knew* he would."

"Didn't you hear me, young lady? I don't want to have this conversation with my daughter."

"Oh, come on, Mom. I'm not some dumb kid. And you're not so old you don't like getting kissed by a handsome guy like Mr. Leonard."

"Not *so* old? Well, thanks for that." *And yes, Chet is definitely a handsome guy.*

"Pete kissed me on my birthday."

"*What?*" Kimberly nearly spilled her coffee as she straightened. She set the mug on the nightstand.

Tara nodded.

"But you never said a thing last week."

"When you were sixteen, did you tell *your* mom everything?"

Kimberly opened her mouth to reply, then pressed her lips together.

Tara grinned again. "Yeah, that's what I thought."

Kimberly grabbed a pillow and threw it. Tara dropped sideways onto the bed, laughing. Feeling young and silly—and happy—Kimberly pounced forward, wrestling with her daughter.

"CHET LEONARD, YOU HAVEN'T HEARD A WORD I'VE said."

Lost in a fog of pleasant thoughts—which was nice, for a change—Chet tried to blink his way back to full attention. "Sorry, Anna. Do you mind starting over? My thoughts were wandering."

"Oh, my dear boy." She smiled, understanding in her eyes. "I can see that. I'll bet I even know where your thoughts have gone."

"What do you mean?"

"You know what."

He shook his head, trying to deny the truth—that he'd been thinking about Kimberly and their evening together.

Anna laughed softly. "Have it your way. I said I want you to give some serious thought to this notion of glamping. I've looked at the Internet, and I believe Tara's idea has real merit. I have a little nest egg put away that I could contribute to getting things off the ground. It isn't a lot, but it could get us started on the right foot."

"I couldn't risk your savings, Anna."

"Why not? You've given me a home and family. Who else do I have to spend my money on if not you and your boys?"

Chet rose from the table and went to pour himself another cup of coffee. He should be outside, helping Sam and Pete with the morning chores, but he couldn't seem to get himself into gear.

Anna intruded before his thoughts could wander too far a second time. "If I can get some sort of business plan drawn up, will you look it over and see if it doesn't convince you to try? If we act quickly, we could be open for business by mid-July."

"Nana Anna, you're the limit." He leaned down and kissed the crown of the old woman's head. "I promise to look it over." He set his mug back on the counter, coffee untouched. "But right now I need to get to work. We can talk more at lunch."

A short while later, as he strode across the barnyard, he whistled a tune he'd heard the previous night. Which immediately made him think of Kimberly again. During the concert, he'd found himself looking at her instead of at the performers on the stage, her face bathed in the soft glow of colored lights. If not for the stage lighting, they would have been in complete darkness, lending a sense of intimacy to the evening. He'd had to stop himself more than once from putting his arm around her shoulders.

And, of course, there'd been that goodnight kiss at the door. He didn't know how he'd even dared to do it. Brief as it had been, the kiss had sealed something in his heart. He tried to deny it, still wanting to protect himself from hurt, but the attempt was pointless. He was a goner.

It surprised him, the depth of his feelings. He'd expected falling in love at forty-seven to feel different from falling in love in his twenties. Apparently he'd been wrong about that. The real difference now was that he had two teenage sons whose mother had abandoned them. She had a teenage daughter who had lost her father and home and everything familiar. He owned a ranch with cash flow issues. She had come to Kings Meadow out of desperation rather than out of choice. He was an Idaho cowboy, through and through. She was a city girl.

Lots of good reasons for him not to feel the way he felt.

Good reasons that didn't seem to matter at all.

Anna

1948

IT WAS A BLISTERING HOT DAY IN AUGUST WHEN Anna McKenna felt God reach into her heart and take away the pain of losing Miles, felt Him remove the regret for the life they would never share and the longing for the children they would never create. And into the place where the pain, regret, and longing had resided, God planted a new peace, a new understanding that she belonged to Him. She could trust Him with her future, in the valleys as well as on the mountaintops. He had been faithful thus far. He would be faithful from then on.

She rested her forearms atop a fence post and stared across the pasture. Princess, a two-year-old filly—Shiloh's Star's first offspring—grazed on the short grass that blanketed the paddock. Beyond her was Lucky, a yearling colt who favored his dam, and a five-year-old mare they called Snowball, Abe's purchase last spring. In the neighboring paddock, Golden Girl stood quietly while her four-month-old foal nursed.

Looking at the horses, Anna smiled. Four years ago, she'd been an orphan with nothing but the memory of her father's dream and the need to escape a cruel relative while holding onto her prized horse. But since then, she'd been made a member of the Leonard family, and Shiloh's Star had already sired three foals out of Golden Girl. This wasn't a notable Quarter Horse ranch yet—the sale of cattle still provided the main income for the Leonards—but it was a good start. Abe had caught Anna's vision. One day, horses would be everywhere on this land. She believed it with her whole heart.

"That is enough for now," she whispered.

Twenty-six

Chet looked up from the papers on his desk to meet Anna's anxious gaze. "Did you put this together?" He tapped the last page of the business plan with his index finger. "It's impressive."

"No." Her face broke into a smile. "Kimberly did most of it, with a little assistance from Janet and Tara."

"How'd she manage to gather all of this information so fast?"

Anna chuckled. "I told her it was urgent." Her head tipped to one side. "I may have led Kimberly to believe it was critical to the survival of the ranch that we get this new enterprise off the ground."

Chet felt his eyes widen. "You didn't?"

"Well . . . maybe. If I did, it wasn't on purpose."

Not good. He didn't want Kimberly believing he had major money problems. Her deceased husband had left her in a financial mess. The last thing she would want was to become serious about a guy who might do the same to her. And there was no denying he wanted her to become serious about him. Which was why he'd waited to ask her out on a second date. He wanted it to be perfect when the time came.

"Chet, have you asked Kimberly out again?"

He blinked. "Are you a mind reader?"

"Old age has some advantages. It can make a body more perceptive."

"No, I haven't asked her out again. Not yet. To tell you the truth, I don't know where to take her. It isn't like Kings Meadow has an abundance of choices."

"Take her up to McCall for a nice dinner. Or rent a movie and bring her here for dinner. The boys and I could make ourselves scarce."

Chet raked the fingers of both hands through his hair as he leaned back in his chair. "Are you playing matchmaker?"

"Do you need one?"

He pondered the question. "I think I can manage on my own."

"Good! Glad to hear it." She waggled her finger at the papers on his desk. "Now what about this. If you hire Kimberly, like Tara suggested, she'd have reason to spend a lot more time at the ranch."

He grinned. Of all the reasons he might want to try this glamping thing, spending more time with Kimberly was the best reason he'd heard yet. He'd like more time to woo and win the lovely widow. More time for her to fall in love. Not just in love with him—which he didn't think would be enough on its own—but also with Kings Meadow and the Leonard Quarter Horse Ranch.

That might take a miracle, Lord. Do You have one in mind?

His grin faded. "Do you think she'd want to take on another job? She's already working for the mayor."

"You leave Ollie Abbott to me." There was a glimmer of mischief in her eyes. "I'm sure the mayor can adjust Kimberly's hours to accommodate what will be needed out here."

"I can't offer her much in the way of compensation. Not at first."

"You leave that to me too."

"Anna . . ." He drew out her name in a warning tone.

She rose from her chair and folded her arms in front of her chest. "I mean to be an active partner in the Leonard ranch glamping enterprise. That means I will shoulder some of the cost as well as reap some of the reward. No arguments. Right now, I'm appointing myself the partner in charge of hiring personnel."

Chet was helpless before the whirlwind that was Anna McKenna. He knew it, and he was certain she knew it too.

Anna turned toward his office door. "I'm going into town. No point letting grass grow under my feet."

"As if that could happen," he called after her as laughter rose in his chest.

KIMBERLY LOOKED AT THE WALL CLOCK ON THE opposite side of the mayor's office. Two o'clock. The day was dragging by. In her first two weeks of employment with the city, she'd kept busy learning the ropes. But once she'd managed to get everything organized the way she liked it, it became obvious there wasn't enough work to keep her occupied for thirty-six hours a week. Especially not with Bonnie Clark answering the phones and doing research Tuesdays through Thursdays.

On her lunch hours the last couple of days and in the evenings, with Janet and Tara's help, Kimberly had worked on the business plan Anna asked her to research and write. It was hard to stop thinking about it now, especially when the hours crept by. The possibilities were both challenging and exciting. She wondered what Chet would think when he read the plan. Would he get excited too?

Thinking about Chet caused conflicting emotions to stir in her chest. The memory of their evening together, their conversation, the concert, the brief kiss . . . It was all surrounded by a warm glow. On the other hand, he still hadn't called to ask her out again, five days later. They'd spoken briefly at church last Sunday but had been interrupted by a neighbor who was having trouble with a horse. She hadn't seen him since. Had he had second thoughts? Maybe the kiss had meant nothing.

She wished . . .

Oh, she didn't know what she wished anymore.

A soft beep sounded as the glass door from the street swung open. A heartbeat later, Anna McKenna strolled into the office. She waved at Bonnie, then made a beeline to Kimberly's desk.

"Anna, what brings you here?"

"A proposition, my dear girl. Is Ollie in?"

Kimberly glanced toward the closed door to the mayor's inner office. "He's on the phone. Do you need to speak with him?"

"I do. But not yet. I want to talk to you first." She sank into the chair at the side of Kimberly's desk. "You did a wonderful job with that business plan. Why ever didn't you study business in college instead of the theater? You could've been a CFO of some corporation by now."

Kimberly didn't know how to respond to the generous praise, but it felt good to hear it.

"Chet was impressed with the plan and is willing to move forward. Only he is hoping you can help, as Tara suggested." Excitement made Anna's words come in a rush. "You have an eye for details and an eye for antiques and decoration. You obviously have a head for business and know how to use the Internet. You would be the perfect person for the position."

"Anna, I—"

"Chet can handle the physical labor and anything to do with the ranch and horses, but we need your help to get it off the ground this summer. Will you do it?"

It was difficult to keep from being swept away by the elderly woman's enthusiasm. But she had to say no. "Anna, I have a job."

"Oh, I know that." Anna waved away the response as if it were a pesky fly. "If you could work fewer hours here in the mayor's office, and if we could make up the difference in your salary, would you be willing to join us?"

"I suppose I—"

"Wonderful." Anna patted her chest with her fingertips. "I'm a partner, you know." Her grin caused the creases in her face to deepen and her eyes to twinkle. "Although I can't say a partner in what exactly. We are in desperate need of a name worthy of a page on a website. Something other than *Leonard Ranch Glamping*."

It was useless to resist. Anna's excitement was contagious. "I agree. That name doesn't work. I'll give it some thought."

"Good. Is Ollie off the phone?"

Kimberly glanced down. "He must be. The light went out."

"Don't get up." Anna stood. "I'll knock on his door myself." She did so, going into the mayor's office when he called for her to enter. The door closed behind her.

Kimberly felt a rush of affection for the elderly woman. Although *elderly* didn't seem an apt term for Anna McKenna. She might be eighty-four in real years, but she was decades younger in spirit. Chet and his boys were blessed to have her in their lives. But was anybody able to stop her when she set her mind on something?

Wait! Kimberly's gaze shot to Ollie's office door. Was Anna talking to the mayor about changing her hours? What would he think? She hadn't been working for him long enough to ask favors. What if he fired her? Panic tied her stomach in a knot and made it hard to breathe. The waiting was horrible. Minutes stretched by as if they were hours.

Finally, the door opened and Ollie stepped into view. "Kimberly, could you join us in my office?"

She swallowed hard as she rose. This was it. The proverbial second shoe was about to drop. She knew it. She just knew it.

But when Kimberly entered the mayor's office, Anna gave her a smile that assuaged her fears. In that moment, Kimberly knew that Mayor Oliver Abbot was no more resistant to Anna McKenna's charming determination than anyone else in this town.

Twenty-seven

THE GUESTHOUSE—WHICH ANNA HADN'T MOVED INTO AND probably never would—became the headquarters for *Leonard Ranch Ultimate Adventures: Luxury Mountain Glamping!* And if Chet had once thought he would have any real say in it, he was quickly disabused of the notion.

A desk and computer took up residence in the bedroom of the cottage, along with a separate phone line and answering machine. Allison Kavanagh, the woman who had designed the website for the Leonard Quarter Horse Ranch, was hired to create a separate but linked site for the guest ranch. Kimberly's work schedule for the mayor had been modified to allow her to spend four afternoons a week with Anna. Tara was involved most of the time as well, and Sam, Pete, and the hired men got into the act. Even Janet came out when she wasn't at work. In fact, everybody seemed eager to finish their normal duties so that they could help Nana Anna launch *Ultimate Adventures*.

Chet did what he was told, and he couldn't quite decide

if that irritated or amused him. Both, actually. Often at the same time.

The plan was to begin with remodeling the line shack within the shortest distance of the ranch complex. Spruce up the cabin's rustic look while making it tight against inclement weather. Of course, the glamping experience came more from the lush beds and fancy linens and the meals that would be prepared for them than from the setting.

The men cleared a trail that led a short distance up the mountainside behind the cabin to a secluded place where time and weather had carved a bowl out of the rocks. Just enough water from an underground hot spring mixed with cold water from the creek to make it the perfect temperature. A nature-made hot tub that wouldn't need any upkeep from the Leonards. All the better.

Chet was alone, pounding an instructional sign into the ground near the hot springs pool, when Kimberly appeared at the top of the path. The day was hot, and she wore khaki shorts and a sky-blue sleeveless blouse. Her dark hair was captured in a ponytail, her head covered with a baseball cap the same color as her top. Her hat sparkled with sequins. When he saw her, he straightened and with the back of an arm wiped away the sweat on his forehead.

"Wow," she said. "This is incredible. I didn't even know about it until today."

"It's really something at night. Sit in the hot springs and stare up at the stars, steam rising all around you. Makes all your cares drift away."

Kimberly took a couple of steps closer to the pool. "Sounds like I should try it out before the guests make it theirs."

Chet's mouth went dry as he imagined Kimberly in the hot springs pool—and him with her.

"Seriously. Would that be all right one evening?" she said.

"You bet." He cleared his throat. "Maybe sometime soon. The two of us."

Her eyebrows rose. Surprise filled her eyes.

Chet cleared his throat again. "I've been wracking my brain, trying to think of someplace I could take you that would beat the concert we saw. I kept coming up empty. Maybe I've been trying too hard."

"Yes." A small smile replaced the surprise. "Maybe you have been."

"How about tomorrow night? You could stay for dinner and then we could ride up here together."

"Ride?" Her smile faltered.

"In the truck."

She released a breath. "Okay. I'll bring my suit with me."

"You know, if you'd give it a chance, I think I could help you get over your nervousness around horses."

"I doubt it."

"The woman I see before me is courageous. Not afraid to try something new."

"Courageous. Me?"

"Yes. You." He schooled his expression, wanting her to know he was serious. "Anna couldn't have done any of this without you. You've been amazing."

"Everybody's done their part." A pretty blush pinkened her cheeks. She turned away, as if suddenly interested in the surrounding trees and the sky above and the water cascading over rocks and spilling into the pool.

Chet was tempted to step up behind her and kiss her nape beneath the swing of her ponytail. But his feet stayed planted where they were.

She turned to look at him again. "Do you think it can succeed? Really and truly?"

"I think it might. Maybe not this summer, although if we can get the word out, August could be a good month."

"I . . . I hope I'm around to get to see it."

He understood the meaning behind those words. She was still looking for employment that would take her away from Kings Meadow. *If I have anything to say about it, Mrs. Welch, you'll still be here.*

KIMBERLY COULDN'T SLEEP THAT NIGHT. SHE KEPT thinking about Chet and the hot springs. She kept thinking of all the reasons why letting her attraction for him go any further would be a bad, bad, bad mistake. But even so, she knew when she drove out to the ranch the next day, she would have her swimming suit with her, and she would go with him to the hot springs. It was inevitable—she had to.

"*You know,*" his voice whispered in her memory, "*if you'd give it a chance, I think I could help you get over your nervousness around horses.*"

Could he? Really? Tara would be surprised if Kimberly learned to ride. But it was silly to even consider it. She didn't have time to take lessons and Chet didn't have time to give them. They needed all hands on deck to make the *Leonard Ranch Ultimate Adventures* a success.

Sometimes she wondered if Chet took his cash flow issues

seriously enough. Not that she had the details, but Anna had implied that bringing guests to the ranch this summer was critical for its survival. Was it? Kimberly knew all too well that blithely continuing on as if nothing were wrong could be dangerous for all concerned.

With a sigh, she sat up in bed and turned on the lamp on her nightstand. Then she reached for the notebook she'd started carrying with her everywhere. The first fifteen or so pages were filled with ideas and questions and calculations. Using a black gel pen, she wrote: *How much must Chet make before the summer is over in order to improve his bottom line?* She couldn't come right out and ask him that question, but maybe she could get Anna to tell her more.

Only it wasn't Kimberly's business.

Or was it? Chet had asked her out. He'd kissed her. He'd asked her out again. Was that enough to make his finances any of her business?

No. It wasn't enough. Still . . .

Chet wasn't the type to spend time with a woman just for the sake of spending time with her. He would want a relationship to go somewhere. He would want it to lead to marriage. He didn't have to spell that out to her. She knew it about him instinctively. It was who he was at his core. A Christian cowboy. A very good-looking, extremely appealing Christian cowboy.

Groaning softly, she pushed the notebook off her lap. Her gaze went to the clock. One o'clock and still awake. But she had to try to sleep or she would be worthless tomorrow. She turned off the light and slid down on the mattress, pulling the covers over her shoulders.

"You know, if you'd give it a chance, I think I could help you get over your nervousness around horses."

It might be fun to try. It would please Tara. Maybe that alone would be reason enough to try.

Kimberly rolled onto her side and tucked an arm under the pillow. She had a lot to be thankful for, but more than anything she was thankful that the past three years hadn't sent her daughter into a downward spiral. That could have happened so easily. Tara could have gotten into drugs or gangs. She could have run away from home. Or she could have done her best to make her mother's life a living hell. That happened in many families, with or without some traumatic event shaking the foundation. But none of that had happened to them. Kimberly and Tara had a close relationship—most of the time. All things considered, that was no small miracle.

"Thank You, Lord," she whispered as exhaustion tugged her toward slumber. "Please help me figure out . . . what You want . . . me to . . . do."

Anna

1950

FIVE-YEAR-OLD RICHIE SLAMMED HIS BOOT HEELS into the pony's sides but got little results for his efforts. The Shetland had a will as stubborn as his master's.

Anna clucked to her gelding and rode up beside the boy. "Richie, honey, try to relax a little. This is supposed to be fun."

"But he won't go faster!" His voice rose in a whine. "I wanna go faster!"

The boy's petulance had more to do with the somber mood in the ranch house the last few days than his pony's lack of obedience. Violet had learned from the doctors, following a recent miscarriage, that it was unlikely she would be able to conceive again. The news had left Richie's parents heartbroken.

"Tell you what," Anna said. "You can ride with me on Champ. He likes to run."

"Can I? Really?"

"Yes. This once." She knew Abe wanted the boy to learn to ride his own pony rather than doubling up with adults, the way he'd been doing since he was six months old. But if it would keep Richie out from under foot in the house for a while, she thought Abe would approve. "Come on. Let's put your pony up."

A quarter of an hour later, Champ cantered away from the barn, Anna in the saddle, Richie right behind her, arms tight around her waist.

At the beginning of June, the grass in the fields was belly high in some places and a lush shade of green. Wildflowers were in abundance, too, splashing the valley floor and hill-sides with yellow and pink, lavender and blue. White-faced cattle grazed in clusters, their calves cavorting nearby.

Eventually Anna slowed the gelding to a walk and guided him along a deer track into the forest. They climbed steadily up the mountainside, going higher and higher. "Think we can go high enough to touch the sky, Richie?"

"Nah. Can't never touch the sky, Anna."

"Are you sure? Well, that's too bad." She patted his hands with one of her own. "It would be fun to try. Guess we'll do that another time."

They rode in silence for another half an hour before the trail they followed burst through the trees and rose up to a rocky plateau. From there they could see the entire valley. They weren't touching the sky, true enough, but they were gazing upon something beautiful all the same.

She wished she could paint like Miles. Perhaps then she

could capture on canvas the splendor of this country. Perhaps she could show others how deep her love of this land had burrowed into her heart.

She wished she had some talent with words, but she wasn't a writer. How did one go about describing all she could see with her eyes? What was that shade of blue overhead? What exactly was that scent on the breeze? Were there words adequate enough for any of it? Perhaps not.

Anna twisted around and took Richie by his upper arms, then lowered him to the ground. As the young boy stepped away from the horse, Anna dismounted and followed after him. They stopped a few steps back from the edge of the rocky outcropping. Richie reached up and slipped his small right hand into her left. She closed her fingers around his and squeezed tight.

In that moment the future blossomed in her heart. Her tomorrows spilled before her imagination. Life and death. Joy and sorrow. Laughter and tears. A life lived to the fullest.

"I promise, Lord," she whispered, lifting her gaze. "I promise to live life abundantly."

Twenty-eight

THE NEXT DAY, ON THE THIRD OF JULY, KIMBERLY gave her approval for the new website to go live. *Leonard Ranch Ultimate Adventures* was officially launched and ready to start booking guests for the months of August and September. It was nothing short of a miracle. So much had been accomplished in such a short period of time.

As she closed out of her e-mail program, the sound of laughter drew her up from the chair and out to the barnyard. The men who were constructing the new barn had left about an hour ago, she supposed to begin the three-day weekend a bit early. The voices she'd heard belonged to Tara and Pete. They were seated on the top rail of the corral, watching Sam and a young horse in what appeared to be a battle of wills. The horse arched his back and crow-hopped along the far side of the pen.

Crow-hopped? When had Kimberly learned that term? It made her smile, realizing she also knew what it meant. Not only that, but she could state with confidence the horse Sam rode was a buckskin, which meant the animal had a golden-brown coat with black mane, tail, and stockings.

When she was almost to the corral, she spied Anna seated on a bench in the shade of a nearby shed. She shifted her direction and went to join the older woman. As she sat beside Anna, she asked, "What's so funny?"

Anna chuckled. "Nothing really. We're giving Sam a hard time right along with that little horse there."

As if in response to Anna's words, the horse began to buck. Kimberly knew what that word meant too. It meant danger. It meant someone could get hurt. But the glimpses she caught of Sam's face told her he wasn't afraid. Just determined. As for Pete and Tara, they were having a grand old time. They whooped and laughed and shouted encouragement to Sam.

Anna patted Kimberly's knee. "See how Sam stays relaxed and goes with the horse. He's not going to fall. You can be sure of that. Watch. He's going to give up the fight now."

"Sam?"

"No, the horse."

And just like that, the buckskin came to an abrupt halt in the center of the corral. His dark tail switched a few times. He twisted his head around, as if to give Sam a hard look. The boy said something to the horse in a low soothing tone.

"Did Wind Dancer ever buck like that with Tara?" Kimberly asked softly.

"You know, I couldn't say for sure." Anna gave Kimberly's knee one more pat. "I guess you'd have to ask her."

"I don't think I want to know."

"My dear, it would do you a world of good to get over this fear of yours. There is nothing more wonderful than riding a horse through this valley and up the trails in those mountains. Nothing like it." Anna frowned. "Did something happen that made you nervous around horses? Did you get thrown or kicked?"

Kimberly shook her head. "No, nothing like that. I don't know why I'm so nervous around them, really. It's always been that way. Janet had to coax me onto her pony every single time when we were kids." She looked toward her daughter, still seated on the fence. "Tara was born loving horses. It was simply always there. I think . . ." She looked at Anna again. "It would be fun if we could go riding together one day."

A smile brightened Anna's face. "Then let's make that happen."

"Could we . . . could we keep it a secret for a while? In case I fail miserably."

"You won't fail. Chet and I will see to that."

CHET WAS HOT, GRIMY, AND SWEATY WHEN HE AND Blake rode into the barnyard. There wasn't a whole lot of time before dinner would be on the table. He said good-bye to his hired hand and wished him a good holiday. Then he tossed the reins to Tara—all alone in the barnyard at the moment—and asked the girl to cool down the horse for him.

"Sure thing, Mr. Leonard."

Chet headed for the house. Anna and Kimberly turned in unison when he entered the kitchen. Kimberly stirred something on the stove top. Anna was setting the table.

He spoke before either of them could. "I need a quick shower. Can dinner wait about fifteen minutes?"

"Sure." Anna waved him toward the stairs. "You go on. We won't eat without you."

He glanced at Kimberly. "I won't be long."

She gave him a quick smile before turning back to the stove.

Chet didn't have the words to describe what her smile did to his insides. Would giddy apply? No. He wasn't the giddy sort. Never had been. Still . . .

In his bedroom, he yanked off his boots and dropped his dirty clothes into the hamper. He got into the shower, not minding that the water was cold at first. Not such a bad thing on a hot day like today. He lathered and rinsed faster than he'd ever done before.

Why all the rush? The family wouldn't eat without him, like Anna had said. But hunger wasn't the reason he hurried. He was eager to sit down with Kimberly. Across the dinner table. In his pickup. At the hot springs. All day he'd been filled with anticipation for the evening to come. And at some point during this long day, he'd realized he felt hopeful. Really hopeful. About everything. He was through trying to protect his heart. Time to toss any remaining caution to the wind. Nothing risked, nothing gained.

When he reentered the kitchen, his hair still damp from the shower, the three teens had joined Anna and Kimberly. They looked like a family, everyone helping, everyone knowing their places. Chet paused to study them, so perfect with each other. The brothers were getting along, and as of late, Pete and Tara had been acting more like best buddies than potential boyfriend and girlfriend. Was there a chance the six of them could become a real family?

The conversation during dinner was lively, especially the retelling of Sam's training session with one of the two-year-olds. While Kimberly looked at Sam, Chet looked at her. Something had changed about her, he thought. What was it? He couldn't put his finger on it, but something was definitely different.

When the meal was over, Anna volunteered Pete and Tara to do the dishes while Sam took care of the evening chores. Looking at Chet and Kimberly, Anna added, "You two scoot." She flicked her hands toward the door. "Go on and enjoy your evening. The kids and I have a couple of movies to watch, so no need to hurry back."

Chet resisted the urge to hug her, but he said thanks with his eyes.

Half an hour later, wearing swimming suits beneath their shorts and shirts—with towels and a blanket in the back, along with a dessert and a jug of pink lemonade in a picnic basket—Chet drove the truck away from the ranch complex. June had been dryer than usual, and a huge sand-colored cloud rose behind them as they headed north.

"You'll never guess what I agreed to today," Kimberly said, breaking the silence that had filled the cab.

Chet glanced over at her. "What's that?"

"I agreed to learn to ride. Or at least to learn to be less afraid."

His eyes widened as he returned his gaze to the dirt road, delight erupting in his chest.

"I'm as surprised as you are." She laughed softly.

"What changed your mind?"

"I really don't know. Perhaps because it will please Tara if I at least try." She reached over and touched his right forearm, drawing his eyes back to her for a moment. "But don't tell her. I want it to be a surprise."

"That's not going to be easy. Your daughter is here whenever you are."

"You're right. I hadn't thought of that. Maybe Anna will have some ideas."

"I guess we can send her off riding with one of the boys while we give you a lesson."

"Mmm." Kimberly was silent for a short time, then said, "Pete kissed Tara on her birthday."

"He did?" Maybe he'd been wrong about those two.

"I don't think we have to worry about them. They act more like siblings."

Chet hid a smile, but there was no denying he was pleased by her choice of words. Siblings meant family, and family was what he was hoping for.

Is THIS WISE? KIMBERLY WONDERED WHEN THEY were nearly to their destination. *Should I let myself care for him? We want such different things.*

Only, was that true? What *did* she want? She used to know with certainty. A few short months ago she knew. Even a few weeks ago. Now it all seemed muddled.

Chet parked his pickup by the renovated line shack, grabbed the basket, blanket, and towels, and then he and

Kimberly walked up the mountainside to the hot springs. She felt a shiver of nerves.

What do I want? What?

When they arrived at the small pool, Chet spread the large blanket on a level piece of ground and set the picnic basket nearby. Sunset was still an hour away, but the sun had fallen far enough beyond the mountains to lengthen shadows and cool the air on this eastern slope. The sounds of the rushing creek were soothing to the ears.

Kimberly turned her back to the water and looked through the trees to the valley below. Everything she could see from this spot was part of the Leonard ranch.

She'd read somewhere that the average American moved eleven times in a lifetime. And job-hopping was the new normal. Few stuck with their first or second or even third careers for the rest of their work lives. And yet, for a hundred and fifty years, the Leonard men had stayed in this valley and managed this ranch. Six generations of them, counting Chet's sons. What was it like, to have that kind of stability? It sounded wonderful.

"Want some lemonade?" Chet asked, intruding on her thoughts.

She faced him. "Not yet."

"A little music." He lifted a small cloth bag from inside the basket. Out of it came an iPod and a pair of small speakers. A few moments more and music mixed with the sounds of nature.

She didn't recognize the song, but the tune was catchy.

"Shall we soak a bit?" Even as he spoke, he removed his shirt and tossed it onto the blanket.

There were those nerves again. She turned away before he could catch her staring at his bare, muscular chest and toned abs. Oh, mercy! It had been a long, long time since she'd noticed a man's physique. Any man's other than her husband's. Ages. Forever. Chet's muscles were sculpted by hard work, not hours in the gym, and she liked knowing it.

She steadied herself with a deep breath. Then stripped to her one-piece swimming suit and joined Chet at the pool. He stood in the middle of the naturally shaped bowl, the water up to his waist, and held out his hand to help her descend. Heart slamming against the wall of her chest, she took hold and stepped where he indicated. Moments later, both of them were seated on a submerged ledge, steam rising around them as they faced one another from opposite sides.

"The temperature's perfect." She was desperate for something to take her mind off of how wonderful he looked, his black hair curling slightly in the moist air.

"It would be too hot—enough to take your skin off—without the creek water to cool it down." He raked wet fingers through his hair. "Has kind of a sulfur smell that I'm not crazy about, but it sure feels good to soak in when your muscles are sore and tired."

"Do you come up here often?"

He shook his head. "Not often. Never seems to be time to fit it in." He shrugged. "Or maybe I don't ever have a good enough reason to take the time."

His eyes told her she was all the reason he'd needed. It pleased and frightened her in equal measure.

Chet closed his eyes and leaned his head back against

the rocks. "So you said the website is up and running. What's next?"

Bless him. This was much safer territory. "Advertising. Getting the word out every way we can. Including social media marketing."

"And you know how to do all of that?"

"No." She shrugged, even though he wasn't looking at her. "But I can learn." As she spoke those words, she realized how true they were and how good it felt to be confident about something.

"Never doubted you for a moment, Kimberly."

Strange, it felt even better to know that Chet had confidence in her.

Without rising from the water, he moved across the pool until his face was mere inches from hers. "Kimberly," he said, his voice low and husky, "you've become important to me. Do you know that?"

Throat dry, eyes misting, she nodded.

"All I want is a chance." He drew closer.

Her pulse quickened in expectation.

"And now I think it's time I kissed you again."

Her lungs forgot how to breathe on their own. She had to think about it, force herself to draw air. Then his mouth was on hers. Gentle, yet demanding. Tentative, yet assertive. The kiss—very different from the one on the night of the concert—made her insides twirl and then melt. Beneath the surface of the water, their bodies remained apart. Only their lips touched. Which for some reason made it all the more wonderful and exciting. She wouldn't have minded if it had gone on for hours.

But it didn't.

Chet drew back, and his eyes met hers once again. "You really know how to steam things up, Mrs. Welch."

"We're in a hot spring, Mr. Leonard," she whispered back. "It's always steamy."

They smiled in unison, as if knowing they had created a special memory, one that would make them smile when they spoke of it in the future.

Twenty-nine

Janet's laughter preceded her into the kitchen the next morning. "That must have been some hot tub."

Kimberly turned, coffee mug in hand. "Why do you say that?"

"Because you were humming."

"I was not. Was I?"

Janet laughed again. "Yes, m'dear, you were. And if I'm not mistaken, it was an old George Strait hit. 'Love Without End, Amen.'"

A slow smile curved Kimberly's mouth. She remembered the song playing on the iPod last night. "You're right. I *was* humming. Guess I remembered the tune but not the words."

"So? Spill. How was your date?"

"Very nice." She felt her smile broaden.

"And?" Janet wiggled her fingers, as if trying to pull more words out of Kimberly.

"And none of your business." Kimberly tried to look stern but she failed.

Janet clapped her hands. "I *knew* it! You two are perfect for each other."

"Hardly perfect."

"Why?"

Her smile slipped. "Nobody is perfect." She moved away from the coffeemaker and stood at the sliding glass door, staring up the sloping ground toward the home of Ned and Susan Lyle.

"I didn't say *he* was perfect. I said the two of you are perfect together."

Kimberly released a sigh, her good humor drained away. "I wish you'd attend to your own love life."

"I have no love life, Kimmie. That's why I need to meddle with yours."

"Thanks a lot." She turned around. "Look, I don't know where this attraction is going. Let's not make it more than it is. It may go nowhere."

"And it may go somewhere," Janet countered.

"You don't give up, do you?"

"Nope."

Kimberly shook her head slowly, her smile returning. "You're hopeless."

"Hopeful, my friend. Not hopeless."

THE FOURTH OF JULY FUN BEGAN IN KINGS MEADOW in the afternoon with a parade along the meandering main street of town. Afterward there was a public barbecue in the city park, followed by games, music, dancing, and fireworks. The celebration of Independence Day had been much the same when Chet was a boy. Then the recession of the eighties had come, and the town had been forced to cut back in countless ways. The Fourth of July had been one of the victims. But when Oliver Abbott was elected mayor, he put the old traditions of parade, food, and fireworks back onto the township's calendar. It felt good for the community to come together again. Mighty good.

This year, Chet took a place at one of the many propane grills lined up on the west side of the park, flipping burgers and hot dogs for the people of Kings Meadow. One grill over from him was Tom Butler. The Methodist minister had been one of the first responders when Chet's barn caught fire, and not long after, he'd bought one of the Leonard horses. A friendship had formed between them over the past weeks, based upon mutual respect and a similar sense of humor.

Kimberly and Janet were the first customers at Chet's grill. He felt a quickening in his chest when he saw Kimberly, and he couldn't help noticing that when he smiled, she blushed.

Janet held a plate out toward Chet so he could drop a burger onto the bun. "So you'll know, Anna has your blanket and chairs right next to ours." She pointed with her free hand.

He didn't bother to look to see what she meant. His eyes remained on Kimberly. Her blush deepened.

Man, she's pretty. What he wouldn't give to kiss her again, right here, right now.

After Kimberly got her hamburger and the two women walked away, Tom said, "How are things going with you and the lovely widow?"

Chet figured by now there wasn't anybody in Kings Meadow who didn't know he'd taken Kimberly to a concert in Boise. More than a few might know about their visit to the hot springs last night too. Gossip rode a fast horse.

"Don't care to tell me?" Tom prodded.

"Sorry." He looked at his friend. "What did you say?"

Tom chuckled in reply.

Chet turned his attention to the grill, flipping hamburgers and hot dogs before they burned. A good thing too. A rush of hungry citizens, fresh from three-legged races and other games, ended their conversation. It seemed the men at the grills barely had time to breathe for the next forty-five minutes.

The afternoon was a hot one. The first thing Chet wanted when he turned off the propane and closed the cover on the grill was something cold to drink. Tom wanted the same thing, so they headed for a booth where high school kids were selling lemonade, bottled water, and Diet Cokes. Both of them ordered the latter with lots of ice. When they got their beverages, they wandered toward the creek and some available shade. A fallen tree provided a bench.

"So," Tom said after he'd downed about half of his Diet Coke. "You were going to tell me how things are going with you and Kimberly Welch."

"Was I?"

"Yes, you were."

Maybe it would be good to talk to a third party about his feelings, Chet realized. Anna and his boys weren't exactly impartial. And he needed an outsider's view to know if he was being a romantic fool or if this was something God could be behind.

"I am a good listener," Tom added.

"For a Methodist." Chet grinned. His comment was already a well-used joke between them. No matter what they were talking about, if it had to do with Tom, one of them added, "For a Methodist."

Tom shook his head, as if exasperated.

Chet took a few more swallows of his drink. Then he looked toward the park. He couldn't see Kimberly or the rest of the family in the crowd. "I think I might be falling in love with her," he said at last. With a shrug, he added, "Maybe I already *am* in love with her."

"Then I suppose that means things are going well."

Again, he shrugged. "I'm not sure she plans to stay in Idaho. When I first met her, she seemed eager to get away from Kings Meadow as soon as possible. Last I knew, she was still hoping to find employment elsewhere."

"And she hasn't changed her mind?"

"Maybe." He thought of the two of them at the hot springs. "I can't say for certain."

"Perhaps you should ask her outright."

Chet turned toward Tom. "I'm afraid to ask. What if she's unsure right now, but by asking, I force her to make a choice?"

"And she makes the wrong one. Is that what you mean?"

"Exactly." Again Chet looked toward the park, searching the crowd for a dark ponytail poking through the back of a pink baseball cap. He didn't see her. Nor did he see Janet, Tara, either of his sons, or Nana Anna.

"Chet, is something else troubling you?"

He turned toward Tom once again. "I guess there is." He drew a deep breath. "I don't want to date Kimberly just to have a female friend. I want it to go somewhere."

"Of course."

"But that's when I get nervous. My wife walked out, Tom. One day she packed up and disappeared. Sure, some of it had to do with Rick's death, but there's got to be other reasons she threw away marriage and sons and even denied her faith the way she did. She said she no longer believed in God. She divorced me so fast I hardly knew what hit me. Maybe I'm not meant to be a husband. Maybe I'm no good at it." He finished the last of the beverage in the plastic cup. "Is it even right, in God's eyes, for me to want to marry again?"

"Whoa. You had a lot more on your heart than I guessed."

To be honest, Chet hadn't known all of that had been worrying him until he said it. "Sorry. I shouldn't've—"

"No, don't be sorry. You need to work this through. But I doubt we've got enough time now to give it the study it deserves. Could we get together in the next couple of days? Somewhere quiet, just the two of us."

"Sure. That'd be good." Chet stood, suddenly eager to get back to the hubbub of the Independence Day crowd.

Tom got up from the log. "Before you go, let me say this. There are biblical reasons for divorce, and there are allowances for new marriages. First Corinthians 7 says, 'Yet if the unbelieving one leaves, let him leave; the brother or the sister is not under bondage in such cases, but God has called us to peace.' It would be good for you to remember that. You are not under bondage, and God wants you to have peace. Perhaps knowing that will calm your troubled thoughts."

Tom's words were a balm to Chet. Not that he had everything worked out yet, in his head or his heart, but it was a beginning.

Anna

1960

Anna sat in the stands of the small rodeo grounds with Abe and Violet, waiting for Richie's turn at calf roping. Correction, *Richard's* turn. At fifteen, he'd made it clear he detested his old nickname. Anna tried to comply, but it wasn't easy. He'd always been Richie to her. Almost from the first moment he drew breath.

"Look, Abe." Violet pointed at the program in her hand. "Emma Carter's taking photographs of all of the events. We'll have to buy some of the ones she takes of Richard."

Abe nodded but said, "We'll see. Might not be able to afford them. You forget how famous Miss Carter is these days."

"No, look. She's giving a special rate for photographs from the rodeo. We can actually have some framed Emma Carter's on our walls of our son and his horse."

Anna touched Violet's wrist. "Richard's up next."

The boy sat astride a tall bay gelding named Rocket.

Richard had started training the horse—the last foal out of Goldie before the brood mare had passed away—for roping events a couple of years ago, and both horse and rider were shaping up to be winners. Championships would bring more notice to the Quarter Horses of the Leonard ranch. That would be a good thing. Despite all of the mares he'd added over the years and all of the yearlings and two-year-olds they'd sold in the past decade, Abe still considered the horses a side business. Anna dreamed they would become much more to him. The way they were to his son.

A calf bolted from the chute, bringing Anna's attention back to the rodeo. Rocket—as good as his name—shot out of the box at a gallop. The lariat sailed through the air, the loop falling over the calf's head. Before the horse could slide to a full stop, Richard vaulted from the saddle. He hit the ground running, one gloved hand sliding along the rope. In what seemed a heartbeat, Richard grabbed the calf, flipped it onto its side. With Rocket keeping a steady tension on the rope, Richard used the piggin' string he'd carried in his mouth to tie three of the calf's legs together. Tie complete, he put his arms into the air to stop the clock. Then he returned to Rocket, stepped into the saddle, and urged the gelding a few steps forward to relax the tension.

Anna held her breath as they waited the six seconds required. The calf struggled but didn't get loose.

Applause went up from the spectators, and it grew louder when the announcer called out his time. Nine point eight seconds. It was the best time so far. Professional calf ropers could get the job done in seven seconds, so this was an amazing time for an amateur, especially one as young as Richard.

It showed the boy's dedication. All those hours of practice were paying off.

Before Richard left the arena, he looked into the stands and waved at Anna and his parents, grinning from ear to ear.

"I think I'll go down and see him," Anna said as she stood. "Waiting until the event is over to see if his time will hold up is going to drive me crazy."

She hurried down the steps and walked around the corrals and pens at the far end of the arena. Trucks and trailers were parked all over a field on the north side of the rodeo grounds. Horses were tied to quite a few of the trailers. Some were munching on hay. Others were being groomed by their owners. Others stood snoozing, eyes closed, tails swishing.

The Leonard truck and trailer came into view. Anna saw Rocket tied near the back of the trailer, the left stirrup tossed over the seat of the saddle. A few steps more and she saw Richard. Only he wasn't alone—and he was too busy kissing a girl to see Anna's approach.

When she was only a few steps away from them, she cleared her throat. "Excuse me."

Richard hopped back from the girl, flushing crimson as he spun toward Anna.

"That was a fine run, Richard. I see you're celebrating even before you win."

"Uh . . . yeah . . . uh . . . Anna, this is Claudia. Claudia Durst."

"Hello, Claudia. I'm Anna McKenna."

The girl—who looked to be Richard's age or a little younger—tilted her chin. Defiance lit her blue eyes. "Nice to meet you, ma'am."

How could a word like *ma'am* make Anna feel so much older than her thirty years?

"And you." Anna's gaze returned to Richard. "Calf roping's about over. You'd better get back to see if anybody beat your time. I'll finish unsaddling Rocket."

"Okay. Thanks, Anna." His gaze shot to the girl. "I'll see you later." Then he strode away. Long strides. A man's strides.

"I'm gonna marry him someday," Claudia announced, sounding sure, as only one her age could sound.

In her heart, Anna felt a little boy's hand slip from her grasp.

Thirty

A TEMPORARY FLOOR HAD BEEN CONSTRUCTED NEAR the raised gazebo where the musicians played. Kimberly watched the dancers, moving in time to the melody. She'd never seen so many cowboy hats in one place in her life. Immediately she thought of Chet and the Stetsons he wore much of the time. He had a brown one for work—battered and always a bit dusty—and a crisp, clean black one for church.

And he looks just as good in one as the other.

She wondered where he'd gone when the barbecuing ended. She'd expected him to join her and the others, but he'd never shown up. Not that she missed him or anything.

Liar.

Kimberly caught a glimpse of Tara and Pete spinning by. A new song was playing, something up-tempo featuring a fabulous fiddle player. When had her daughter learned to dance like that? All that turning and dipping and slipping under arched arms and changing directions. The sound of boot heels stomping on the wooden floor filled the air, almost as if it were part of the music itself.

"I take it you like that song," Chet said from behind her.

His words flowed over her, as smooth as warm honey. "Why do you say that?" She glanced up as he stepped around to face her.

"Because you were tapping your toes."

"I was?"

"Yep." He jerked his head toward the dance floor. "Care to give it a try?"

She shook her head. "I've never danced like that. I'd make a fool of myself."

"With the right partner, it's easier than it looks."

She doubted that was true.

Chet looked toward the raised gazebo where the band played. As if on cue, the music stopped. There was silence, long enough for the musicians to turn a page. Then they started up again. Something slow and romantic sounding. "Who doesn't like to dance to a classic Anne Murray song?" He looked back at her and held out his hand. "Could I have this dance?"

She seemed unable to resist taking it and letting him pull her up from her lawn chair. He led her to a corner of the dance floor, then drew her into position. Her right hand disappeared into his left. His right hand settled into the small of her back, his touch sending a very pleasant shiver up her spine.

"Follow my lead." His voice was husky, and a crooked smile curved his mouth.

She swallowed as he turned her around and guided her right into the circle of other dancers. She stumbled a little, but that firm hand in the small of her back steered her as surely as a bit turned a horse. The rest of the dancers faded into the distance. There were just the two of them, moving smoothly around the floor. The singer said something about having this dance for the rest of her life, and the look in Chet's eyes said he was asking that very same question of her.

It was unfair of him to be so wonderful. She hadn't come to Idaho to stay in Idaho, and Chet Leonard would never leave Kings Meadow. What future could they have?

But that question was beginning to sound hollow. An excuse, not a reason.

WAS IT POSSIBLE GOD HAD FASHIONED KIMBERLY SO she would fit this perfectly in his arms?

If Chet could have his way, the song would have gone on until darkness fell and the fireworks began. But he didn't get his way. The music ended. Couples moved off the floor. Others moved onto it, ready for the next song. Chet hoped for another slow song. He wasn't that lucky. It was going to be a hand-clapping, boot-stomping, line-dancing tune instead.

"Come on." He offered his elbow. "We'll let the pros have this one."

The look of relief in her eyes made him grin.

"Would you like something to drink? They've got Coke and lemonade at the high school stand over there."

She shook her head, at the same time letting go of his arm. The warmth of her touch lingered on his skin.

"Want to stroll around the park or go back to your chair?" he asked.

Her smile was tentative. "Let's walk. I haven't looked around much. I've been chatting with Anna most of the time."

He hoped she would take his arm again as they moved away from the dancers and musicians. She didn't. Still, as they walked, looking at the various booths, greeting friends and neighbors, he liked that others were seeing them as a couple. The worries he'd voiced to Tom had already ceased to eat at him.

I love her, Lord. I know it's fast, but I also know it's true. If it's Your will, I'd sure like her to stay in Kings Meadow and become my wife.

A future together. A future with Kimberly at his side. He wanted it more than he should. He wished he could tell her right now how he felt, but it was better to wait. Not because he was unsure. He wasn't. Not any longer. But he wanted to do everything possible to make her sure as well.

"How about a shaved ice?" He pointed to Aloha Shaved Ice, a tropical hut on wheels complete with a thatched roof, fake palm tree, and servers in grass skirts. "The profit goes to help the food bank."

"Okay."

"What flavor?"

She read the sign and chose raspberry. He ordered two of the same. *That way our lips will be the same color when we're done.* The thought made him feel like a teenager on his first date. He grinned.

"What?" Her eyes narrowed in suspicion as he handed her the first paper cone filled with ice and syrup.

"Nothing. I'm feeling good tonight." He leaned closer. "I think it's the company I keep."

The suspicion left her eyes, replaced by something Chet couldn't define. Uncertainty, perhaps. *Fine, Mrs. Welch. I'll just have to make you certain.*

They moved away from the shaved ice stand and through the milling crowd.

"I didn't know this many people lived in Kings Meadow," Kimberly said after a period of silence.

Chet glanced around. "They come from all through these mountains. Quite the personalities, some of them. You know, the ones who live in school buses parked on old logging roads. Some real storytellers among them. Like Ollie Abbott. Like Anna. The history of this area is kept alive in their stories."

"You're a true romantic. Aren't you, Mr. Leonard? And not only in matters of the heart."

He pondered her statement before answering, "Do you think so, Mrs. Welch?"

"Yes, and it suits you."

"Thanks." He wished he could stop, take her in his arms, and kiss her.

From the gazebo came a tapping on a microphone, followed by an announcement that the fireworks would begin in fifteen minutes. That surprised Chet. He hadn't realized how deep the dusk had become. Maybe because wherever Kimberly was there seemed to be an abundance of light.

She was right. He *was* a romantic.

Thirty-one

THE FIRST RESERVATION FOR *LEONARD RANCH Ultimate Adventures* came in from the website the week following the Fourth of July. Kimberly recognized the names on the reservation immediately. Jeffrey and Irena Wainright. Parents of Tara's friend Patty. The reservation was for Cabin #1 for two adults plus a canvas tent for two teenagers. That meant Patty and her little sister were coming too. The family would arrive on the first of August and depart on the eighth.

Kimberly wasn't sure how she felt about her old acquaintances spending a full week in Kings Meadow. She'd changed so much from the woman she'd once been. She was a far cry from the wife and mother the Wainrights had known years ago. What would they think of her now?

But at this precise moment, Kimberly didn't care much about *Leonard Ranch Ultimate Adventures* or the Wainrights. At this moment, all she cared about was surviving the next half hour in this round pen.

Chet stood in the center of the enclosure, holding a lead rope that was attached to a tall, dark-colored mare. "Come on, Kimberly. She won't hurt you. Come on over and meet her."

Why did I agree to do this? It's so big. Doesn't he have a shorter horse I could use?

"Kimberly?"

She looked down at her boots. "I can't seem to make my feet move." She hated the tremble in her voice. She wanted to be brave around the horses like everybody else. Like Tara. Like Anna.

"Maybe I tried to put you in the saddle too soon." Chet led the horse to the fence and looped the rope around a post. "Back in a bit, girl." He patted the mare's neck. Then he took hold of Kimberly's elbow and steered her out of the round pen and into the new barn, straight to a stall holding a sorrel colt.

She was proud of herself for knowing the little fellow was a sorrel. A few months ago she would have called him a light reddish-brown. Learning various terms was progress too. Right?

Chet opened the gate and the two of them went inside. He knelt on the stall floor near the colt's head. "Come here, Kimberly," he said softly.

She moved to his side.

"Now run your hand along his neck and back and over his rump. Get the feel of him."

She did as he asked, noting the softness of the colt's coat, feeling the quiver of muscles underneath his skin.

"Now kneel down beside me."

Again, she obeyed.

"Look in his eyes. See the intelligence? Rub his muzzle. It's like velvet."

Chet was right. The colt's muzzle was smooth. Pleasant to the touch.

"Now look at me, Kimberly."

She turned her head toward Chet. He was so close she could see the shadow of a beard beneath his skin. So close she could smell the musky aftershave he wore.

"I will never ask you to do anything I don't believe you can do," he said, his tone and expression solemn. "That's my promise. I'll never put you in a dangerous situation. I'll be right there with you every step of the way. I won't rush you. I'll encourage you."

Her heart rat-a-tat-tatted in her chest, as much in response to his nearness as to what he'd said. It had been over a week since he'd kissed her in the hot springs pool, and suddenly all she could think about were his lips and—

The colt nudged her with his muzzle, pushing her sideways. Chet caught her before she could topple over in the straw. The tension broken, she laughed.

"Ready to try again?" he asked, smiling again. "Just sit in the saddle. We don't have to let the horse move until you say it's time."

She drew a deep breath and nodded. "Yes. I'm ready to try again."

FEAR OF HORSES—OR ANYTHING ELSE—DIDN'T HAVE to make sense. Chet knew that. Some people were afraid of riding a horse because they'd had a bad accident on one or they'd seen a bad accident somebody else had. But others were afraid because of the what-ifs that took place in their minds. They could create a thousand possible bad outcomes without any help at all: What if the horse throws me? What if I fall off and can't get back on? What if the horse doesn't like me? What if . . . He was convinced, from everything he'd been told, that Kimberly's fears were of the latter variety.

Chet knew something else besides. God didn't want her to carry fear around with her. So he prayed for her. Not entirely for altruistic reasons. He knew that his own happiness might depend on Kimberly overcoming her fear.

When the two of them returned to the round pen, Anna waited nearby, seated on her own horse. "Wondered where you got off to." The old woman looked relaxed and natural up in the saddle. No fear of falling and breaking a hip. It was good for Kimberly to see that.

"Where have you been?" Chet asked Anna as he opened the gate.

"Trying to clear a few cobwebs from my head. That happens best when I'm on horseback."

He knew the feeling. "Kimberly's going to sit on Sunset for a bit. Mind keeping your eyes peeled for Tara and Pete? We'd hate to spoil the surprise."

"Don't mind at all. But I heard Pete say he was taking Tara up to see the old McHenry sluice box. If that's where they went, they won't be back for at least a couple more hours."

"Sluice box?" Kimberly glanced from Anna to Chet and back again. "What's that?"

Chet answered, "Gold miners used them all over the Boise Basin. Zeb McHenry mined these mountains around the same time my great-great-great grandfather came to this valley. But McHenry's sluice was just a rough wooden trough. Nothing fancy like the kind miners use today."

Kimberly looked toward the nearest mountain. "And it's still up there after all this time?"

"Parts of it."

"Amazing."

He held the stirrup for her and watched as she put her foot in it, grabbed the horn, and pulled herself into the saddle. It wasn't exactly graceful but neither was it tentative. Apparently her mind was on Tara, Pete, and Zeb McHenry's sluice box.

"Maybe you and I can ride up there sometime," he said.

She looked down at him, and he knew the instant she realized where she was, what she'd done. Surprise flashed in her eyes, and then the corners of her mouth tipped upward in the smallest of smiles. Proud of her, he grinned while patting the mare's neck. Kimberly leaned forward and did the same.

Chet wondered if that small step into the saddle represented a much bigger step toward their future.

Anna

1970

EARLY IN THE MORNING OF HER FORTIETH BIRTH-
day, Anna lay in bed in the cottage that had been built for
her, staring at the ceiling and mulling over the events of her
life. Later today, she knew there would be cake and presents
in the main house, along with lots of hugs and laughter. But
for now she was alone. Well, not completely alone. Max the
cat was curled up against her hip, purring.

And the Lord was with her, His presence sweet. His
presence was always sweet. Forty years had taught her that.

Forty years. She pictured herself at twenty, less wrinkled
but also less wise. Some would think she was old. An old
maid. Maybe she was.

She thought of Miles Stanley, the only man she'd ever
loved. He'd been gone twenty-two years already, yet it seemed
only a blink of time. She didn't mourn him anymore, but
she did remember him with great fondness. Sometimes she

wondered how different her life would have been had they married and had children.

Thinking of children brought a different image to mind—little Chet, Richard and Claudia Leonard's son. Chet was two and a half already and always on the go. A bundle of energy if ever there was one. Running both his mother and his Nana Anna—as he called Anna—to a frazzle most days. Oh, that child was the apple of Anna's eye, to be sure. It saddened her that Abe hadn't lived to meet his grandson and that Violet had known Chet only while he was still a tiny infant.

No one had been thrilled when Richard announced he was foregoing college to marry Claudia as soon as she graduated from high school. There'd been many a late-night row between Richard and his parents over that decision. Neither Abe nor Violet had thought Claudia was the right girl for their son. But in the end, they'd relented. It turned out they were wrong about the girl. All wrong.

Last December, during the televised lottery drawing for the draft, Anna had been more than a little glad that Richard had both a wife and child to keep him out of the army and away from Vietnam. Remembering it now, she said another prayer of thanks to God for his safety.

She reached down to scratch Max under his chin. The cat's purring revved like a boat motor, making Anna chuckle.

Sounds from outside told her the ranch was coming awake. Claudia would be gathering eggs and feeding the chickens soon. Richard would be tending the livestock in the barn and corrals. She should rise and go help, and yet she stayed in bed, continuing to ruminate.

What would Abe think of the ranch now? In the last five years, all but a small herd of cattle had been sold off. Richard was fully committed to making the Leonard ranch one of the finest Quarter Horse ranches in the country. More brood mares had been purchased whenever there were funds to spare. A couple of studs with fine pedigrees had been added too. Of course, in her mind, none of those horses would ever be as fine as Shiloh's Star had been or as good as his offspring were today, but she couldn't argue with the wisdom of adding new bloodlines to the mix.

From outside her bedroom window, voices raised in song burst forth. "Happy birthday to you . . ." Perhaps calling it a *song* was a bit generous. The performance was decidedly off-key, more shouting than melody.

She reached for her robe and pulled it on as she left the bed and walked to the window. She brushed the curtains aside. There stood Claudia and Richard, Chet in his father's arms, along with their one and only ranch hand, all of them bundled up against the chilly March morning.

Anna's heart welled with thankfulness for the family God had given her. She might have been orphaned as a child. She might never have married or given birth. But she'd been given surrogate parents who'd loved her. She'd helped raise Richard, and now she was Nana Anna to that adorable child in his daddy's arms. Life was sweet.

Even for an old maid at forty.

Thirty-two

THE LAST TWO WEEKS OF JULY PASSED IN A BLUR.
Kimberly and Tara spent every spare moment at the ranch,
and with each passing day, Chet's love for Kimberly deepened. He came up with lots of errands for Tara and one or
both of the boys to run, giving Kimberly at least a little time
each day on the quiet mare Chet had selected as her horse.
And the lessons, brief though they sometimes were, were
working. Kimberly had a growing confidence around and on
the mare.

It was time to give Tara her surprise. Chet and Kimberly
decided it would be the day before their first guests arrived at
Ultimate Adventures. After that, no one would have time for
themselves for a good long spell.

Chet stood in the doorway to the guesthouse office, his
shoulder leaning against the jamb. Kimberly sat at the desk
and read to him off the computer screen. "That means we'll
have guests at the ranch at least twenty days in August." She

looked up and met his gaze. "Do you think we should close reservations for the month?"

It was difficult to care about business when she looked so pretty in that green blouse. It was the same shade of green as her eyes. Her time in the sun with the horse had brought out a smattering of freckles across her nose too. Adorable.

"Chet."

"Sorry. What did you ask?"

"Come over here and look at the budget and this balance sheet, boss man. If my calculations are right, the Leonard ranch is going to turn a nice profit. And this is even with the great discounts you're giving during the first month in business *and* after you pay the chef's salary."

Okay, that managed to get his full attention. He pushed off the doorjamb and went to stand beside her chair. He looked at the printouts on the desk, then picked up one sheet of paper to look at it more closely. "Really?" He glanced at Kimberly. "Are you sure?"

"I've been over it a half-dozen times. I'm as sure as I can be."

"Just from renting out that old line shack and pampering folks with a few well-cooked meals and some super comfortable beds?"

She grinned at him. "Yes. Just from that. And it looks like the glamping website has brought additional traffic to the Leonard Quarter Horse website too. A noticeable increase. That's what Allison Kavanagh said in an e-mail I got earlier today. That's got to be a good sign, don't you think?"

One more reason he loved Kimberly. Because she cared about what happened on this ranch. Maybe he should—

The sound of a truck engine starting up in the barnyard interrupted the direction of his thoughts. A good thing for now. He wanted to give Tara her surprise first. Then he wanted to ride with Kimberly up to the plateau that overlooked the valley. He wanted her to see this land he loved, though not as much as he loved her.

"Let's see what Tara's up to," he said, offering his hand.

Kimberly's smile faltered a little. Then she drew herself up with resolve. She placed her fingers in the palm of his hand, a look of trust in her eyes. It made Chet feel like he could do anything.

KIMBERLY'S HEART THUMPED HARD AS SHE RODE Sunset toward the barn door. From outside, she heard Tara and the boys laughing over something, but the laughter stopped abruptly as Kimberly emerged into the light on horseback. The look of surprise on Tara's face was priceless.

"Mom?"

Kimberly grinned. "Hard to believe, isn't it?" She reined in, stopping the mare.

"When? How?"

"Sam and Pete kept you busy while Chet and Anna worked with me." She stepped down from the saddle, pleased that she did so without clinging to the saddle horn as if her life depended upon it. "We wanted to surprise you."

Tara hurried over and gave her mom a big hug. "I never had a clue. I never would've thought you'd even try. This is so cool. It's so cool. We'll be able to go riding together. It's gonna be so much fun. What made you decide to try?"

"You, silly." She brushed Tara's nose with the pad of her thumb. "I wouldn't have succeeded without all the encouragement I got."

Tara almost hurled herself at Chet, giving him the same bear hug she'd given her mother. "Thanks, Mr. Leonard. Thanks so much."

Chet's expression was comical. He didn't know what to do with this overt display of affection. Anna got a hug next. Thankfully Tara didn't knock the older woman off her feet with her enthusiasm.

The ring of the telephone intruded.

"I'll get it, Dad," Sam said, then jogged toward the house.

"You knew about this and didn't say a word?" Tara said to Pete.

He grinned, and she punched him in the arm.

Chet moved to stand beside Kimberly. Her heart quickened at his nearness. "Thank you," she whispered.

"You're welcome. Listen, I was hoping maybe the two of us could—"

"Hey, Mrs. Welch!" Sam called from the house. "The phone's for you. It's on the Adventures line."

"I'll get it in the guesthouse." Kimberly handed the mare's reins to Chet. "Did you decide to take more reservations in August or not?"

"Whatever you think best. I trust you to make the right decision."

Those words meant more to her than she could express. She touched his forearm and smiled. Then she hurried toward the cottage. When she reached the office, she sank onto the chair and forced herself to take a few deep, slow breaths. She didn't want to sound winded when she answered the call. Finally she picked up the handset. "Mrs. Welch speaking."

"Kimberly!"

She didn't recognize the woman's voice, didn't know how the person had known her first name.

"It's Irena Wainright."

Dread filled Kimberly. Was Irena calling to cancel their reservation? *Please don't let that be the reason.*

"I know I'm going to see you tomorrow, but I couldn't wait to tell you something."

Her pulse began to regulate itself again. "Oh? What's that, Irena?"

Kimberly and Irena had been friendly acquaintances, years ago. Not close, like their daughters, but casual friends whose lives were similar in many ways. Occasionally their social circles had crossed. They'd worked on a few of the same charities. They'd shopped in some of the same upscale boutiques. But after Kimberly's life had begun to unravel, she hadn't seen anything of Irena. Why would she? Their worlds had suddenly moved far apart.

"Kimberly, I'm sure you remember that Jeffrey sits on a number of nonprofit boards. Including the board of directors of the Wildwood Center. Well, today they had to dismiss the managing director, and I thought of you the instant he told me. You have a degree in the performing arts as I recall. Isn't that right?"

"Yes, but that was a long time ago. I never actually used it. I got married and then Tara came along. I'm afraid my degree is pretty worthless." She'd learned that after Ellis died and she started submitting applications anywhere and everywhere.

"Listen, there's no point having a husband on the board of directors if I can't use his influence to help a friend. Jeffrey knows you, and he thinks you'd do great at this job. He says it's yours if you want it. I know you could do it."

"I don't know, Irena. Managing director? I've never—"

"Don't say you aren't capable. You created the *Leonard Ranch Ultimate Adventures* from scratch from what Tara told Patty. It's obvious you have a head for business, and you have the degree the Wildwood Center requires, whether you've ever used it or not."

Kimberly felt dizzy.

"Promise to think about it. The salary is good. High five figures to start. I know you'd love the work. So think about it."

"Yes. I'll think about it. Of course."

"I'll bring along all of the details when we come tomorrow. See you then."

"Thanks, Irena." She swallowed to relieve the sudden dryness in her throat. "See you tomorrow." Kimberly ended the call and put the handset in its cradle. As she withdrew her hand, she noticed it was shaking.

A chance to go back to Seattle. A real chance. It was what she'd wanted and hoped for all these months. She should be excited, joyous, ready to go pack her bags.

Only she wasn't, and she had to wonder, *What do I want and hope for now?*

CHET KNEW SOMETHING HAD CHANGED THE MOMENT he saw Kimberly's face. She looked stunned . . . uncertain . . .

perhaps lost. He strode over to where she stood outside the cottage's front door. "Is something wrong?"

She shook her head.

"Who was on the phone?"

"Mrs. Wainright." Her eyes widened. "She called to tell me about a management position with a prestigious theater company in Seattle. A job her husband says is mine if I want it."

Chet's stomach dropped. "You studied theater in college, didn't you?"

"Yes, but I never did anything with my degree. I've submitted I don't know how many résumés over the last few years for positions like this one and never even got an interview."

"What did you tell her?"

"I promised to think about it." She brushed some stray wisps of hair off her face. "She'll bring all of the information with her when they come tomorrow."

He'd lost his heart to Kimberly, and now she was going to leave, go home to Seattle where she'd always wanted to be. How could she not? This was what she'd told him she wanted from almost the first time they'd met.

And Kimberly had seen enough of his financial information to know ranching had more lows than highs, plenty of times when the future would seem unsure. She'd seen that everyone had to pitch in to help with chores, that there was always more to be done than hours in the day to do it. She'd seen enough to know this way of life was a day-to-day commitment to the land and the livestock as well as to one another. It wasn't glamorous. It was dirty boots and dusty jeans and sick animals and early mornings and late nights. It was a valuable horse dying unexpectedly. It was a barn burning to the ground. It was hard winters and summers plagued by drought. How could he ask her to embrace that kind of life when she'd made it clear from the beginning she wanted something different?

"That's great," he finally said. "Really." He looked away, back toward his family and her daughter and the mare Kimberly had been riding such a short time ago.

"It is, isn't it?" she replied softly.

"Yeah. Really great." He glanced at her again. "Listen, I remembered something I need to do in town. I . . . I'll see you tomorrow afternoon."

He didn't wait for her to answer. He strode to his pickup, hopped into the cab, started the engine, and drove away. He may as well have been driving away from his future.

Thirty-three

KIMBERLY DIDN'T SLEEP THAT NIGHT. EVERY TIME she closed her eyes, she saw Chet walking away from her with that long stride she'd come to love. It had hurt, his leaving like that, but it wasn't as if she couldn't guess why. He figured she was leaving Kings Meadow, and he wasn't about to ask her to stay. And that's what hurt the most.

Please, God. Make him ask me to stay.

Chet had never actually said the words, "I love you," but he'd seemed to say it without words in a dozen different ways. The concert. The hot springs. The riding lessons. The kisses. The dancing on the Fourth. The work they'd done together on *Ultimate Adventures*. All of it had brought them closer to each other.

Around six o'clock in the morning, still unable to sleep, she arrived at another conclusion: She didn't want to leave Kings Meadow. Not for any job. Not for a big salary. Not for a return to the big city. Not because she'd fallen in love with Chet—and she most definitely loved him, despite all her attempts not to. No, it was because she'd found a new kind of life here. A good life. A contented life. She'd found a new family, too, although she couldn't claim them as hers. Not yet. But she wanted to claim them. If only Chet would ask her to.

Several hours later, Kimberly and Tara arrived at the ranch. Wearing jeans, boots, cotton top, and a cowboy hat, Kimberly hoped she didn't look as tired and frayed as she felt. Anna was alone when they got there. Chet and the boys were all up at Cabin #1, putting fresh linens on the beds, checking supplies, and making sure the large canvas tent was secure should a strong wind blow through. The ranch hands had separated the "dude stock" into a paddock and were now busy cleaning saddles and tack. Two used golf carts, purchased the previous week, sat in readiness for the use of the guests.

"What can we do, Anna?" Kimberly asked.

"Not a blessed thing. Everything for tonight's barbecue is ready and in the coolers. The grill's in the back of one of the pickups. Chet took brochures for all the different excursions that are available up with him to the cabin. You know the Wainrights already signed up for white-water rafting on Tuesday and gold panning on Wednesday. That leaves them several days still to fill, if they choose."

"They might want to relax in the hammock or go riding."

"That's what I'd do," Anna said with a smile.

Kimberly glanced in the direction of Cabin #1. Should she go up there to see Chet or should she wait until he returned?

"Mom," Tara said, "I think I'll brush the horses so they'll look their best when Patty gets here."

"Okay."

Tara hurried toward the barn.

Kimberly drew a quick breath. "I guess I'll see to a few things in the office."

Before Kimberly could head for the guesthouse, Anna asked, "Did you and Chet have a quarrel?"

"No." It was the truth—they hadn't quarreled—but still it seemed a lie.

"Something happened." Anna's eyes narrowed as she studied Kimberly. "He's been in a strange mood ever since yesterday, and you look like you've been dragged through a knothole."

Kimberly would have loved to bare her soul, but it didn't feel right to talk about her feelings with anyone before she talked about them with Chet. Only, what if he didn't feel the same way? What if he never meant to propose as she'd begun to believe he might? Maybe she'd been wrong about him. Maybe he'd wanted a girlfriend and not a wife. Once burned, twice shy. And if he didn't love her, if he couldn't love her, wouldn't it be better if she relocated to Seattle, far from the memories of another broken heart?

"My dear," Anna said. "Would you do me a favor while you're in the office?"

"Of course. What is it?"

"Pray about whatever is troubling you."

Sudden emotion overcame her. Before she could burst into tears, Kimberly nodded and hurried away.

"Pray about whatever is troubling you."

She hadn't prayed about her feelings for Chet, had she? She hadn't asked for God's will to be done when it came to where she should live or what work she should do. She rarely prayed much beyond those arrow prayers of "Help me, Lord!" or "Please, God." That wasn't the kind of praying Anna meant, and Kimberly knew it.

In the office, she closed the door behind her. Instead of going to the desk, she went to the single bed that stood in one corner of the former bedroom. She knelt on the rug and folded her hands atop the bedspread. The position felt awkward. But it shouldn't, and it shamed her. Kneeling in prayer should be the most natural of positions for someone who professed to be a Christian.

She closed her eyes and tried to think of the right words to say. But eventually she realized she didn't need to censor her words. She didn't need to sound intelligent or righteous. She needed to be honest, to pour out her heart. And so that was what she did. Talked things over with the Father who loved her. No pretense. No shaving of the truth. Frank. Honest. And more than a little broken.

CHET DIDN'T HAVE ANY CHOICE BUT TO BE AT THE house to welcome their guests. If he could have avoided it, he would have. He wasn't ready to face Kimberly again. Not yet. There was an ache in his gut that wouldn't go away, and he knew seeing her would only make it worse. As it was, he managed not to run into Kimberly until after the Wainrights came up the drive in their rental minivan, a big dust cloud trailing behind them.

Anna, Tara, and the boys joined Chet, and they walked as a group toward the vehicle that had parked in a recently designated parking area. "Where's Kimberly?" he asked Anna in a low voice.

"In the office."

He glanced back at the cottage, wondering if she'd heard the sounds in the barnyard. She must be eager to see her friends.

The front doors of the vehicle swung open at the same time the side doors slid toward the back. Their guests' feet had barely touched the ground before Tara raced over to one of the girls, and the two of them embraced. They laughed and hugged and laughed again. They talked rapidly at the same time. Chet hadn't a clue what either of them said, but they understood each other.

Once Jeffrey Wainright joined his wife on the passenger side of the van, Chet stepped forward, offering his hand. "Welcome to the Leonard ranch."

"Thank you. We're glad to be here." They shook hands. "Beautiful country."

Chet heard Kimberly's approach a moment before Irena Wainright smiled and called out her name. The women didn't embrace as their daughters had, but they clasped hands and greeted each other with warmth.

Irena took one step back and gave Kimberly a thorough study. "Look at you. You've gone native."

Chet hadn't noticed what Kimberly wore. He'd just been glad to see her and wondered why he'd been so desperate to avoid her. But now he noticed. From the top of her white hat to the tip of her boots, she looked one hundred percent Idaho cowgirl.

And it broke his heart that it might not be true.

Anna

1984

HIS NAME WAS WALTER CUNNINGHAM, A SUCCESS-
ful real estate developer. He was six feet four inches tall,
blond-haired and blue-eyed, and was about the prettiest man
Anna had ever laid eyes on. She'd met him for the first time
when snow still blanketed the ground on the Leonard ranch.
She'd fallen in love with Walter by the time the first wildflowers appeared. He'd asked her to marry him on a warm
August night as falling stars glittered across the heavens.

And today, the first day of autumn, was her wedding day.

Fifty-four years old and a bride at last. Who would have
thought it? Not her. She'd long ago given up on falling in
love again or ever getting married. She hadn't minded. Not
really. She'd had sweet memories of Miles. She'd had the
joy of watching Richard grow up and then again the joy of
watching Chet grow up. She'd had work she loved in a place
she loved. She had many good friends. Her life had been full.
So very full. And it was about to get more so.

It surprised her that she'd had the courage to say yes to Walter. Not only to marriage but to leaving the Leonard ranch, leaving Kings Meadow, leaving Idaho. A new adventure.

She smiled at her reflection in the mirror.

Life itself was an adventure. With God lighting the way ahead, she could walk bravely into the future, wherever it took her. The Lord had sustained and blessed her through the last fifty-four years. He would sustain and bless her through however many years were yet to come.

Thirty-four

THE FIRST DAY OF THE LEONARDS' NEW GLAMPING enterprise passed in a blur of activity. There'd scarcely been a moment to breathe, let alone think. But now their guests had been fed and were settling in at Cabin #1. Chet heard Irena invite Kimberly to stay and talk awhile. More about the job, he assumed. So he rode back with Sam, leaving his truck for Kimberly and Tara.

Restless and feeling the need to be alone, he saddled his horse and rode up the mountainside, headed to the plateau where he'd intended to propose to Kimberly.

Too late now.

Not everybody was cut out to live in a place like Kings Meadow. Not everybody was meant to be a rancher, either. Or a rancher's wife. He'd always known that. And yet, he'd hoped. Maybe he'd been wrong to hope.

At the plateau, he didn't dismount. He stayed in the saddle, staring across the valley. The evening shadows were growing long, but he could still make out the location of Cabin #1 in the distance. The pale canvas tent made it easier to find.

Was Kimberly still there with her friends? Were they telling stories and making her long for Seattle and the life she'd once had? Maybe she'd never stopped longing for that life. Maybe he'd fooled himself into thinking she had or ever could.

When his marriage had come apart, he'd tried for a long time to hold onto the wife who didn't love him, the woman who didn't want him or the life he could give her. Marsha had hated the ranch, hated him, in the end. He couldn't allow himself to make that same mistake with Kimberly. He wouldn't try to make her want to be here, to be with him. She had to want it on her own.

God, You're going to have to get me through this. Right now, it doesn't feel like I'll know how.

Sounds from the forest intruded. He twisted in the saddle in time to see Kimberly ride her mare out of the trees. She was gripping the saddle horn hard, nervous but determined. He could see that from where he was.

"Kimberly?"

She gave him a weak smile.

"What are you doing here?"

"I need to talk to you."

Did he want to hear what she had to say? Not likely. All the same, he felt proud of her for riding her horse all this way. She'd never ridden this far before.

"How did you find me?" He dismounted and stepped toward her.

"Sam came with me most of the way. He said this is where you come to sort things out when you don't know what to do."

"He said that, did he?" Chet took hold of the mare's reins near the bit and waited for Kimberly to slip down from the saddle. "He knows his dad."

"I've come to know you rather well myself."

Why was she here? To torture him?

"Chet, you've done your best to avoid or ignore me all day."

"No, I—" he started, then closed his mouth on the lie.

She took his hand and led him toward the edge of the plateau, her gaze taking in the stunning view of the valley below. "I can see why you come up here to think. It's beautiful."

You're beautiful.

She turned and faced him, her nearness forcing her to look up and him to look down. "Do you know what I was doing before the Wainrights got here? I was praying. Really praying. About everything. But especially about you."

His heart seemed to stop.

"Especially about us."

It started up again.

"Chet, I've been a fool not to say this to you before. I have to say it now, before it's too late." She inhaled deeply, then met his gaze again. "I love you. Surely you must know that."

"But that job in Seattle. It's the life you wanted to go back to."

"I'm not interested in a job that would take me away from you." Her smile warmed him. "Did you hear me say I love you?"

"I heard." He took hold of her upper arms, staring hard into her eyes. "But are you sure you want to stay?"

WAS SHE SURE? WHAT A QUESTION. KIMBERLY HAD never been more certain of anything in her life. Couldn't he see that?

She grinned at him. "I rode all the way up here. On a *horse*, for pity's sake. Of course I'm sure." Then she rose up on tiptoe while drawing his head toward her and let her kiss tell him what words could not.

When the kiss ended, Chet didn't let her pull away. Instead, he drew her close, her cheek resting against his chest, his chin pressing lightly on the top of her head. She listened to the beating of his heart, in perfect time with her own, and suddenly she felt like crying for joy. This was almost more happiness than one person could stand.

"I love you, Kimberly. Marry me."

Okay, *now* it was more happiness than one person could stand.

"Will you?" he whispered.

"Yes," she whispered in return. "Yes, yes, yes."

He kissed her again, long and sweet and tender, and she let the happy tears fall. The end of the kiss was made salty by them.

"I love you." He cradled her head between his hands. "It's a love without end, Kimberly." His eyes were full of the promise.

She smiled, hearing the melody of the song that had suddenly become theirs, and whispered, "Amen."

Reading Group Guide

1. Kimberly sometimes feels angry at her deceased husband for keeping her in the dark about their finances. Is she justified? Does she deserve some of the blame?
2. Violet tells Anna that God doesn't need her to pretend how she feels about losing her parents. Do you sometimes pretend when you go to God in prayer? How can you be more open and honest before Him?
3. Janet Dunn opens her home to her childhood friend and daughter. How have you exercised the gift of hospitality lately to friends and/or strangers?
4. Do you think the unexpected death of a spouse or the desertion by a spouse would be more difficult to overcome? Why?
5. Both Chet and Kimberly have trusted friends/mentors who speak truth into their lives. Do you have someone

who speaks the truth in love to you? How do you
cultivate and protect those special relationships?

6. Kimberly believes God could have found an easier way to
bring her to Kings Meadow. Janet responds that "easy"
may not have been what Kimberly needed. Has God
used difficult circumstances to bring you to a new place
of understanding? Are you able to be grateful for it?

An Excerpt from
Whenever You Come Around

chapter 1

CHARITY ANDERSON PULLED INTO THE DRIVEWAY
of her parents' home early on a Friday morning. The wood
shutters were closed over all the main floor windows. Her
parents might as well have put up a sign: *Owners Away! Help
yourselves!* Then again, this was Kings Meadow. Neighbors
looked out for neighbors and their property. It wasn't like in
the city where you could live next door to people for a decade
and not even know their names.

The lawn had been allowed to go wild. Her dad had said
he wasn't going to pay for anybody to mow the lawn when he
wasn't there to see it. But Charity, admittedly a bit of a neat
freak, would either hire someone to mow or buy a couple of
goats to graze on it. She couldn't bear to leave it the way it
was now.

She exited her automobile. Cocoa, her brindle-colored
dog—a Heinz 57 mixed breed with a stocky body and short
coat—jumped out right behind her. Cocoa immediately began
to sniff around.

"Your nose must think it's in heaven, Cocoa." Charity headed for the front door. "Come on, girl. Let's check things out."

The calendar said June, but the cold, dreary interior of the darkened house felt more like February. The first thing Charity did was to turn up the thermostat to get some heat pumping into the rooms. The next was to open all the shutters to let in the light. That helped. Not quite so desolate.

Charity had never stayed in her girlhood home when no one else was there. It would feel strange without either her parents or her sister, Terri, for company. Charity's parents were on a three-month tour of Europe and the Mediterranean. The trip of a lifetime, they called it. One they'd scrimped and saved for the last thirty-five years. As for Terri, she lived with her husband and daughter near Sun Valley, close to a three-hour drive from Kings Meadow. Too far for frequent visits.

But solitude was the reason Charity had come to Kings Meadow. She needed a respite from all distractions in her everyday life, and this was the perfect place to escape the hubbub. There was only a small area of this valley in the high country where a person could get cellular service—kids up here didn't spend their lives texting their friends—and while there was Internet service available through the cable provider, it was far from the high speed she was used to.

The second-floor bedroom Charity had shared with her sister up until Terri got married hadn't changed much. It still bore many of the traces of teenage girls. There were some possessions Terri and Charity hadn't wanted to take with them when they moved out, things their mother had been unable to get rid of. Even after giving the room a fresh coat of paint, some of the pop star posters had gone back on the walls. The memories those posters stirred to life made Charity smile as she unpacked her suitcases, placing clothes in the old chest of drawers and hanging other items in the closet. A closet that had been too small for two clothes-conscious girls.

As she stowed her now empty suitcases under the bed, she looked out the window and saw Buck Malone exit the house next door and stride to his battered, old pickup truck. Her heart did a crazy—and unexpected—flutter at the sight of him. A remnant from when she was fifteen and suffering unrequited love for the drop-dead gorgeous high school senior who didn't even know she was alive.

The truck engine started, and in moments, he was gone from view.

Buck Malone. She hadn't seen him in years—surprising given the small population of Kings Meadow, but somehow they'd managed to miss each other when she came to visit her folks. Or maybe it wasn't surprising. Most of her trips home happened during the summer when he was guiding people on trail rides and camping trips.

She gave her head a shake. Her teenage crush for Buck Malone was ancient history. It didn't much matter now.

Turning from the window, she saw Cocoa seated in the bedroom doorway, watching her with a patient gaze. "Guess we'd better think about stocking the refrigerator so we don't go hungry. Let's go to the store."

Her dog knew what "Let's go" meant. She raced down the stairs and danced around impatiently until Charity caught up with her, purse slung over her shoulder. When Charity opened the door, the dog dashed outside and sniffed around the yard a bit before meeting her mistress at the car.

Charity loved Cocoa. She'd rescued her from the shelter when the dog was an awkward-looking pup of about eight months old. Charity had been told the puppy was to be destroyed in three more days if no one adopted her first. Maybe the girl at the shelter had seen Charity coming or maybe she'd spoken the truth. Whatever. Charity had left the shelter with Cocoa on a leash. She'd never been sorry for it either. The dog might not be beautiful in dog show terms—she was definitely not a purebred anything, and part of her right ear had been torn off in a fight at the shelter— but she was smart as a whip and loved Charity as much as she loved her.

Charity opened the car door and Cocoa jumped into the driver's seat, hopped over the console, and sat on the passenger seat. The dog didn't care where they were going. She just liked to go. Charity laughed as she got in and started the engine.

The drive to the grocery store in Kings Meadow didn't take more than ten minutes, even with a couple of Stop signs between the Anderson home and the market. There was plenty of parking available in the small lot at this time of day. She chose a spot farthest from the store entrance.

"You stay, Cocoa."

The dog looked at her as if to say *Okay*, and then poked her head out the open passenger side window.

Charity was glad she didn't have to worry about Cocoa jumping out of the car to chase after a cat or another dog. Or for that matter, a horse or a coyote or a deer, any of which could also wander down the main drag at any hour. Cocoa would stay where she'd told her to stay. She was that kind of a dog.

Inside the market, Charity was greeted by name by the lady at the checkout stand. Not unexpected. Most residents had been in Kings Meadow for decades, some families for several generations, and everybody knew everybody. While many young folk left this small mountain community right after high school, a surprising number—surprising to Charity anyway—never left, or they returned after a few years away.

"Hi, Mrs. Cook," Charity said.

"I hear you've come to stay for the summer."

"That's my plan." She could have added that she had a book due in September. In truth, the book was already many months past due, but her new make-or-break deadline was September first.

"We're all so proud of you, dear. You're a shining success story."

"Thanks, Mrs. Cook."

Feeling like a total fraud, Charity yanked a shopping cart free from the others and started down the first aisle.

BUCK'S BROTHER, KEN, RAN HIS HAND OVER THE saddle Buck had finished making the day before. "Nice. Who's it for?"

"Kimberly Leonard. A gift from her husband."

"There's a city girl I never expected to stick around for long."

Buck glanced down at the leather bridle on his workbench.

"I guess love'll do that to you. But I wouldn't know for sure. You're the one who's lucky when it comes to love."

"No argument from me." Ken chuckled.

Buck meant what he'd said. Ken was definitely lucky in the love department. Ken and his wife, Sara, had fallen in love in high school, married while Ken was still in college, had three kids in quick succession, and now, ten years later, they were expecting their fourth. Buck on the other hand had never found a woman who made him want to settle down to the life of a family man. Not yet anyway. Maybe someday. He hadn't given up hope for it to happen. But it would take someone special.

"You getting ready for a trip?" Ken asked, intruding on Buck's thoughts.

"Yeah. I leave next week. A dozen boys and two leaders from their church are packing in for a week to clear some trails. All but one are bringing their own horses. I'm told the boys and leaders are all skilled riders."

"That'll be nice for a change."

"You've got that right."

Buck loved his work as a wilderness guide. What wasn't to love? Spending most of the summer and early fall on horseback, riding through the beautiful Idaho backcountry, sleeping under the stars. Oh, it wasn't perfect. Some of his clients weren't ready for the trips they went on, whether that was their riding skills or their ability to rough it or—worse yet—both. When that happened, a trip could be challenging. But even then, he loved what he did. It was a simple life. He made enough money to feed his horses and pay his mortgage. And in the winter, he had the saddle shop work to keep him occupied and bring in a little money every now and then.

Changing the subject, he asked, "How's Sara?"

"Tired." His brother's expression turned grim. "This pregnancy's been a lot harder on her than the others. I'm worried, to tell you the truth. She might have to go on bed rest until the baby's born, and that's not easy with three kids to look after."

"If there's anything I can do, all you gotta do is ask."

"Thanks, Buck. I appreciate it." Ken turned on his heel. "I'd best be moving on. Sara gave me a list of things I need to do before I go home."

"Tell her I'm praying for her."

"I'll do it."

After Ken left the small saddle shop in the center of town, Buck bid the owner a good day, then drove to The Merc. He parked his truck a couple of spaces over from a silver Lexus. He'd seen the luxury SUV parked in the Anderson family's driveway when he'd left his house this morning. Had to be the same one. There weren't a whole lot of cars like that one in these mountains. A whole lot meaning none.

Only one person he knew would have a car like that and be at the Anderson house—Charity Anderson herself. He hadn't seen her in person in a long time. Years. But he'd seen her picture in the newspaper a couple of times and heard about her plenty. Not many Kings Meadow High graduates went on to publish a series of bestselling novels for young adults before they turned thirty. Which made folks around here proud of her success.

As if summoned by his thoughts, Charity came out of the market, pushing a cart full of bags. At least, he thought it was her. Only he didn't remember Charity Anderson being such a knockout. The photos in the newspaper hadn't done her justice. She wore skinny jeans and a sky-blue fitted top and high heels that didn't belong anywhere in these mountains. When she glanced up and saw him, she stopped still, a strange expression crossing her face before it was replaced with a smile.

"Hi, Buck."

"Hey, Charity. Is that really you? Our paths haven't crossed in a month of Sundays. How are you?"

"I'm fine." She used the remote to open the back of her vehicle. "How about you?"

He strode over to help load the canvas bags full of groceries into the car. "Here. Let me get those for you."

"It's okay. You don't have to—"

"My mom would tan my hide if I didn't help a lady."

Charity took a step back, leaving him more room to work.

He had all the bags loaded into the vehicle in a matter of moments. After closing the rear door, he turned toward her again. "How's the trip for your folks so far? Are they having a great time?"

"Yes. I had an e-mail from them last night. They're still getting over the jet lag but are enjoying the sights of London before they head to Paris."

"Glad to hear it. Are you up here for long?"

She didn't answer at once. "For the summer, actually." The words seemed to be forced out of her, as if she didn't want him to know.

"The summer? I guess that means I'll see more of you then, now that we're neighbors. You knew I bought the place next door to your parents, right?"

"Yes, I knew. But I don't plan to be out and about much. I'll be writing most of the time. And listen, I really must get back to the house. There's still much to do before I can get to work."

It wasn't often that Buck got the brush-off, but that was what this felt like. Had he offended Charity sometime in the past? He didn't think so. What could he have done? He hadn't known her well, back when she lived in Kings Meadow. As he recalled, she'd been a quiet, bookish sort. A little on the plain side, really. Nobody that stood out in any special way. Definitely different from the woman before him. "Sure," he said at last. "Don't let me keep you."

Buck took a step back and started to turn around. Something solid struck him with force against the back of his knees, knocking him off balance. He heard Charity make an alarmed cry as his feet flew out from under him. He tried to break his fall with his hand. Despite it, he hit the ground hard. There were a few moments when he felt nothing but surprise. Then the pain shot through him. A white hot haze of pain. So bad he couldn't be sure where in his body it came from. He closed his eyes against it.

"Cocoa. Bad dog." Charity's voice seemed far away. "Get in the car. Get in the car now."

Buck groaned and tried to push himself up from the blacktop. The pain became more specific as his right arm crumpled beneath him.

"Buck." Charity knelt beside him. "Oh, Buck. I'm so sorry. Cocoa never jumps out of the car unless I release her. Never. I don't know why—"

Someone called Charity's name.

"We need the EMTs, Mrs. Cook," she shouted back, looking toward the store entrance.

At least, Buck thought the store was in that direction. The world felt upside down and inside out right now, so he couldn't be sure of anything.

"I think you've broken your wrist. Try to hold still."

"I must've twisted my ankle too." He spoke through clenched teeth, the pain focusing in that new part of his body. "It's like it's on fire."

"The EMTs will be here soon." She took his left hand in hers and held on firmly.

Buck squeezed his eyes shut again. He didn't doubt something was broken. A couple of somethings more than likely. He'd been busted up before. Both arms. Several of his ribs. A concussion. But never at the start of the tourist season. If he had a broken bone or two, as suspected, he would be in a world of trouble. He'd have to find another guide to fill in for him on the trips he had booked in the next few weeks. Finding somebody good on such short notice wouldn't be easy, and nothing about this accident was going to help his bottom line.

Oh, man. He hoped he was wrong. He hoped nothing was broken.

Hoped . . . but knew better.

The story continues in Robin Lee Hatcher's
Whenever You Come Around.

An Excerpt from
A Promise Kept

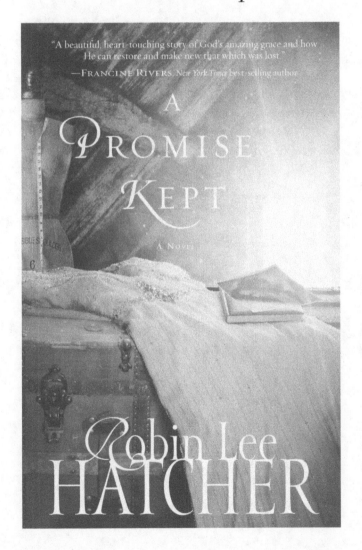

"A beautiful, heart-touching story of God's amazing grace and how He can restore and make new that which was lost."
—FRANCINE RIVERS, *New York Times* best-selling author

A
PROMISE
KEPT

A NOVEL

Robin Lee
HATCHER

Allison

May 2011

THIS WASN'T THE LIFE ALLISON KAVANAGH HAD imagined for herself, but it was what her life had become. Like it or not, she had to get on with it.

She turned the key in the lock.

Hidden away in the mountains north of Boise, the two-story log house—built many decades before but completely remodeled on the inside—was open and airy with a state-of-the-art kitchen, modern efficiencies throughout, and spectacular views of the rugged Idaho mountains from every window. The place had been left to Allison four years earlier in her great-aunt's will. Never in her wildest dreams had Allison imagined she would end up living in it one day. Perhaps Aunt Emma had seen the future a little more clearly than she had.

Welcome to your new home.

A lump formed in her throat, but she fought back the tears. She was weary of crying—it was all she'd done for months and months. Sometimes it felt like years and years.

Setting her mouth, she dropped her purse onto the small table inside the front door.

Some of her own furniture filled the living room. She was glad of it. Made the place feel a little less foreign to her. Not that it *was* foreign to her. She'd visited her aunt's home many times throughout her life, and after it had come into Allison's possession, it had served as an occasional getaway, a place of peace when life's storms became too much to handle.

Dear Aunt Emma. The sister of Allison's maternal grandmother, Emma Carter had been considered somewhat of a "rebel" in the family. Never married and financially independent because of her success as a nature photographer, added to sound investments and careful spending, she'd lived as she pleased. Oh, the stories Aunt Emma used to tell about World Wars I and II, the Roaring Twenties, the Great Depression. If ever a woman was born with the gift of storytelling, it had been Emma Carter. No wonder Allison had adored her.

"How do I get on with my life, Aunt Emma?" she whispered.

If Aunt Emma were still alive, she would have answered honestly and directly. No mincing words. Emma Carter had never sugarcoated anything for anybody. Not even for her favorite—as she'd always called Allison—and only—as Allison had pointed out in return—great niece. But Aunt Emma was gone. Allison would have to find the answers on her own or muddle along as best she could without them.

She passed through the living room and walked down the short hallway to the master bedroom. The new queen-sized four-poster she'd purchased sat against the opposite wall, bare of bedclothes other than a quilted mattress cover.

Staring at the bed, she felt her aloneness afresh. It burned through her like salt in an open wound.

She looked away.

In a corner of the bedroom sat her large desk and credenza. It too was naked. Allison hadn't entrusted her MacBook, large external display, or printer to the movers. Those important items were still in her car in the driveway.

A design deadline loomed closer. She'd best get her office set up and make certain the Internet was turned on as promised by the cable provider. Her to-do list was too long to ignore, even for a few days. And besides, keeping busy took her mind off many less pleasant realities. Immersing herself in work had been her salvation. For years, really, but especially over the past eleven months. Ever since the day she'd uttered her ultimatum.

The lump in her throat returned. She swallowed again.

"Tough love" some would have called her take-it-or-leave-it demand, and she'd been certain tough love was required in the situation. But she'd believed what she said would be that last straw, that illusive bottom, those words that would change everything.

They *had* changed everything. Just not the way she'd hoped they would. Not the way she'd wanted. Not for the better. Not as promised.

Why didn't You keep Your promise?

It was the most she'd said to God in a while. The ability to pray seemed to have shriveled inside of her. One more loss added to so many others.

With a shake of her head, Allison retraced her footsteps to the living room, went out onto the wide redwood deck that circled three sides of the house, and descended the steps to her pale gold SUV parked in the driveway. From behind the driver's seat she released her dog from his crate and set him on the ground. Gizmo sniffed at his new surroundings.

"You stay close. I don't want an eagle or a bear having you for lunch." The tricolored papillon perked up his ears, and she couldn't keep from smiling. "You're such a good boy."

She'd bought Gizmo from a local breeder to help fill the vast emptiness that had surrounded her after her husband walked out the door, leaving her and her ultimatum in the dust. Having an active puppy around had helped ease the emptiness too. There was always something she needed to do for the little guy—feed him, take him for a walk, give him a bath, let him out to do his business.

She'd read somewhere that owning a papillon meant never going to the bathroom alone, and it was true. Gizmo followed her everywhere. He slept on the unused right side of the bed. He sat near her feet when she ate, a hopeful expression on his face even though she never let him eat table scraps. He curled up beside her on the sofa while she watched television. He lay in his dog bed under her desk when she was on the computer. He was her constant and best companion, and she loved him for making her feel less alone.

Perhaps she would become that crazy old lady who lived in a log cabin in the mountains, talking only to her dog. Or dogs. She could get Gizmo a friend or two. Or maybe she should acquire a half-dozen cats. She could give herself a funky haircut and let it go all frizzy and kinky. She could dress in bright, baggy clothes. But then, who would know if she was crazy or not? Who would see her? A dense forest separated her from her nearest neighbors, and she was miles up a winding high-way to the nearest town. Not to mention that her only child, Meredith, lived halfway across the country.

A crazy old lady. She closed her eyes and released a sigh. Forty-five wasn't old, but some days it seemed like it. Some days forty-five felt like ninety.

She went to the back of the Tribeca and opened the rear door. Her LED computer display was in its original box with a handle. She grabbed it along with her laptop case and headed into the house. And for the next several hours, while she hooked up electronics in the bedroom and the living room and otherwise settled in, she managed to keep her thoughts from returning to the sad place they too often traveled to.

That was no small victory.

The story continues in Robin Lee Hatcher's
A Promise Kept.

About the Author

Photo by J. L. Whitt Photography

BESTSELLING NOVELIST ROBIN LEE HATCHER IS known for her heartwarming and emotionally charged stories of faith, courage, and love. The winner of the Christy Award for Excellence in Christian Fiction, the RITA Award for Best Inspirational Romance, two RT Career Achievement Awards, and the RWA Lifetime Achievement Award, Robin is the author of over sixty novels.

Allison believes God promised
to save her marriage. So why did
He allow it to end in divorce?

It all started with an ad in a mail-order bride catalogue . . .

This charming bouquet of novellas introduces you to four Hitching Post Mail-Order Bride Catalogue prospects in the year 1870, all eager for second chances . . . and hungry for happiness. Year in, year out, they'll learn that love often comes in unexpected packages.

AVAILABLE IN PRINT, E-BOOK, AND E-SINGLES

In 1885 five western preachers sit around a campfire talking about unlikely couples they've seen God bring together.

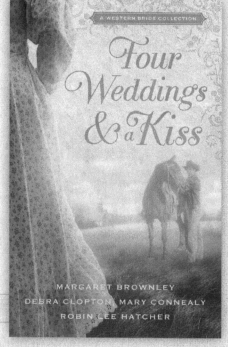

AVAILABLE IN PRINT AND E-BOOK

9780310259275-A